Ravens & Roses

A Women's Gothic Anbthology

Edited by Cassandra L. Thompson

Ravens & Roses

A Women's Gothic Anthology

Edited by

Cassandra L. Thompson

Quill & Crow Publishing House

Ravens & Roses: A Women's Gothic Anthology
Edited by Cassandra L. Thompson
Published by Quill & Crow Publishing House

While some of the stories included in this anthology are based on historical fact, the stories in this novel are works of fiction. All incidents, dialogue, and characters, except for some well-known historical and public figures, are either products of the author's imagination or used in a fictitious manner. Any resemblance to actual persons, living or dead, or actual events is purely coincidental. Although real-life historical or public figures do appear throughout the story, these situations, incidents, and dialogues concerning them are fictional and are not intended to depict actual events nor change the fictional nature of the work.

Cover Design by Liliana Marie Creative
Interior Formatting by Marie Casey

Printed in the United States of America

ISBN 978-1-7371049-1-9
ISBN (ebook) 978-1-7371049-3-3

Publisher's Website: www.quillandcrowpublishinghouse.com

Table of Contents

Untitled, Sophie Brookes....10
Introduction, Cassandra L. Thompson....11
Untitled, Danielle Edwards....14
I. Daughter of Salt & Sea, Kristin Cleaveland....15
Untitled, Melanie Whitlock....36
II. The Devil's Servant, Judith Crow....37
Fiery Valentine, JayLynn Watkins....56
III. The Wig Maker, Catherine McCarthy....57
Weeping Willow, Ayshen Irfan....72
IV. It Will Come, Olivia Claire Louise Newman....73
Untitled, Sheena Shah....90
V. The Fruits of Wartime, Rebecca Jones-Howe....91
Rotten Love, Ginger Lee....116
VI. Vera, Helen Whistberry....117
Burning, K.R. Wieland....134
VII. Lucia & Tatiana, Alexa Rose....135
Garden to Goddess, Erin Quill....152
VIII. Death Cry of the Magpie, Carla Eliot....153
Untitled, A.L. Garcia....166
IX. Lolita, A.L. Garcia....167
Untitled, Marie Casey....187
X. Red Eyes, Liz M. Kamp....189
Untitled, by Fizzy Twizler....201
XI. The Vigilante Witch of East End, Tara Jazdzwewski....203
Author Biographies....213

Come forth her dark power
Hiding amongst the macabre
Her ghastly treasures of torment

Silk of a raven's wing
Black petals on a rose
And the sting of its thorn

Concoction combined
The swirl of smoke and blood
Reflecting in her eyes

Deathly rise of the goddess
Bring the world to its knees.

Sophie Brookes

Introduction

Even as a writer, I struggle to express how much this project means to me. The words just fall short. I will simply say: it is one that is near and dear to my heart.

Studying Gothic literature was one of my favorite aspects of higher learning and I still relish opportunities to study different pieces of art under its lens. Operating Quill & Crow Publishing House, an independent Gothic press, gives me the opportunity to do so in brilliant ways.

Our first call for submissions was an anthology called *Anomalies & Curiosities: An Anthology of Gothic Medical Horror*, and my hope was to gather stories that brought a Mary Shelley feel. What I discovered instead were different takes on what medical gothic horror should be. I follow my intuition on all things bookish, so I formulated a new direction to go in. The stories included in that anthology were all amazing, but I had about a dozen more that dripped Gothic horror but didn't quite fit with the rest. But I just couldn't give them up. Interestingly enough, all these authors were women.

After a bit of discussion with my associates, it was decided that a woman's anthology was the only logical solution. I invited a few more friends of mine to contribute and the result is now in your hands. And I couldn't be prouder.

Like all publications, this one is the result of many different talented people.

I would like to express my sincere gratitude to associate editor and Quill & Crow poet, Jordan Alyssa Duncan. She was a huge part of the success of this anthology. I would also like to thank William Bartlett for his editing contribution and for giving my eyes a break. I'd like to thank Spyder Collins for casually mentioning that I should do a women's anthology at the same time I realized we needed to do a women's anthology – when two minds think alike, it's good to listen.

I would also like to thank the brilliant authors who offered us such wonderful stories. Kristin Cleaveland, Judith Crow, Carla Eliot, A.L. Garcia, Tara Jazdzewski, Rebecca Jones-Howe, Liz M. Kamp, Catherine McCarthy, Olivia Claire Louise Newman, Alexa Rose, and Helen Whistberry created Gothic tales unique in their own way, which I believe makes for a fulfilling collection.

Included in this are the lovely Dark Poet Society poetesses who donated their poetry to head each tale. You ladies are amazing, and I am consistently humbled to write alongside all of you. This includes the heart of Quill & Crow, Marie Casey, for her constant support, and most recently, for her formatting assistance.

And last, but definitely not least, there would be no Quill & Crow without Lauren Hellekson, who was so excited to learn I was putting together a women's anthology, she created the perfect cover in under an hour. I am blown away with every cover she puts together for our house. This one is no exception.

It is my sincere hope that you will enjoy these stories and poems as much as we have. Because when it comes to horror, primarily Gothic horror, we ladies got this.

Dreadfully Yours,

Cassandra L. Thompson

lost in a blue grey reverie
ocean depths of his forlorn eyes
my heart drowning in the aching
salty waves crash in memories
moonlight inspired trysts birthed dreams
in fullness of devastation
hopes setting sail in harsh storm winds
now I stand by troubled waters
sands of time burn against my feet
your ghost haunts sweetly in her smile
lo, I am anchored in this place
two small hands holding me from you.

Danielle Edwards

I

Daughter of Salt & Sea

Kristin Cleaveland

There was to be no wedding. Miss Marina Danforth would be traveling from Boston by ship, first class on the *Sea Maiden*. Upon her arrival, she and Lord Joseph Henry would be privately married on his estate, Harrowhold Manor, by the local vicar.

Mrs. Alice Clarke, the housekeeper of Harrowhold, was weary of answering the maid's questions about the matter. Bridget Reilly, the young maid, continued to register her disappointment. "I just don't understand why the master wouldn't be wanting a wedding for his new bride. Do you suppose she's very ugly?"

"Don't be ridiculous," Mrs. Clarke said brusquely. "I'm sure she's perfectly lovely. The master has informed me—not that it's any of your business, mind you—that Miss Danforth is still mourning the death of her mother, who died of consumption only a few months ago. She's hardly in the state for a large wedding. Mind the silver," the housekeeper said pointedly.

"But why get married so soon, then?" asked Bridget, picking up a fork and polishing cloth. "Surely she's not ready to leave home now?"

"Miss Danforth has no more living relatives. I heard that she comes from a very old New England family, but she is the only one left. They say," Mrs. Clarke continued in a hushed tone, "that her mother left her with almost nothing. They also say"—here the housekeeper lowered her voice further— "that something is…unusual about the family. They had a reputation for madness on her mother's side. Some even say they were cursed."

Mrs. Clarke stood up straighter and pointed out another spot on the silver. "But you know all that servants' gossip is nonsense. You didn't hear it from me, and you won't speak a word of it," she commanded. "Now hurry up and finish. The linen needs airing."

The staff at Harrowhold worked feverishly to ready the house for Miss Danforth. Never one to overlook a detail, Mrs. Clarke asked Lord Henry if he knew his bride's favorite colors. The master of the house had only seen Miss Danforth once; they'd been introduced at a society function when he was in Boston on business. She was tall and slender, with wide-set green eyes that gave her an almost otherworldly appearance. Her skin was pale as white marble, fair enough that he could see blue veins beneath the skin of her neck and collarbone. Piled atop of her head in loose curls was glossy hair so black it shone almost blue in the light. Miss Danforth had worn a shimmering cerulean silk. Lord Henry thought back to this moment and responded, "Blue, I think. Blue and green."

Thus inspired, the industrious housekeeper used her considerable influence with local merchants to procure yards of fine silk in deepest blue, shot through with iridescent tones of silver and green. She ordered a crushed velvet brocade in the same marine color, with intricate designs woven in silver thread. Five seamstresses worked at a feverish pace to create silk bed linens and a velvet spread with matching hangings, which were then draped over an enormous four-poster wooden bed in what was to be Miss Danforth's chamber. After she and Bridget finished making up the bed, Mrs. Clarke surveyed her work with satisfaction. When Miss Danforth brought a candle to her bedside, her linens would sparkle like the sea in the flickering light.

On the day of Miss Danforth's scheduled arrival, her quarters were ready and waiting. She had a beautiful porcelain basin and pitcher, with stacks of soft, fluffy towels and face cloths bleached to blinding white. Despite Lord Henry's wealth, he had not yet installed indoor plumbing at Harrowhold, seeing fit to bathe in a large metal tub when necessary. For the time being, Miss Danforth would have to do the same.

For Miss Danforth's sitting room, Mrs. Clarke had selected a deep blue velvet sofa and matching chaise that complemented the newly made canopy bedding. She had also purchased a beautifully carved wooden dressing table with a mirror and an embroidered stool, and a silver brush set that Bridget polished to a shine. There were creams in tiny pots, fragrances in ornate bottles, and combs of silver, tortoiseshell, and ivory for Miss Danforth's hair. "Do you think she will be happy here?" Bridget asked Mrs. Clarke, marveling at the luxury. "I can't imagine not being happy, in a room like this."

"I am sure Mrs. Danforth will be pleased," Mrs. Clarke replied confidently. "We have chosen the very best of everything."

"I hope she won't find it too dreary here. It can be very dull sometimes."

"If you are finding it dull here, I can easily find more work for you to do," said Mrs. Clarke. "I suggest you be grateful for your position and set your mind on your obligations."

"I suppose she might be having a little one before too long." Bridget brightened. "That would be a pleasure, a child at Harrowhold!"

"That's certainly none of your business to speculate," Mrs. Clarke sniffed. But her face softened, and she added, "Yes, it would be a fine thing.

There was a persistent drizzle of rain when Miss Marina Danforth disembarked the *Sea Maiden*. After such a long voyage, her legs were unsteady on solid ground. Marina sat down on her trunk to get her bearings. Not long after, a young man approached her, tipping his cap.

"Pardon me, miss, but would you happen to be Miss Marina Danforth? My name is Samuel Hardy, sent from Lord Henry at Harrowhold. I've brought your carriage." His eyes were kind and turned up at the corners when he smiled. "Lord Henry sends his apologies; he has obligations in London today, but will be returning to Harrowhold tomorrow evening."

Seeing such a friendly face brought Marina a feeling of relief. Samuel extended his hand and helped her up from her trunk, then looked around. "Where is the rest of your luggage, Miss Danforth?"

Marina shook her head. "I haven't any other pieces," she said quietly. "I've only got the one."

Samuel hefted the steamer trunk. "Well, that's easy enough." He smiled again. "This way to the carriage, Miss."

As Marina and Samuel approached the carriage, she saw that it was drawn by two black horses, their coats dark as midnight and brushed to a glossy shine. The carriage was black as well, with silk curtains drawn over the windows. Marina took Samuel's hand and tried not to let him see her tremble as he helped her into the carriage. After she had tucked in her skirts, Samuel closed the door behind her, and she settled into the plush velvet seat. She told herself not to be foolish, but she couldn't help feeling it was a bad omen—the black horses looked just like the ones that had drawn her mother's coffin to her grave a few short months ago.

From the small purse she carried, Marina withdrew a handkerchief she had dabbed with her mother's favorite perfume. It smelled of sea breeze and moonlit waves; Marina could almost taste the salt on her lips. She held the handkerchief to her face and took a deep breath. "Mother, watch over me," she whispered. Then Samuel shook the reins and urged the horses forward, and Marina was drawn away from the Sea Maiden and the crashing waves, every hoofbeat pulling her farther from home, bringing her inexorably toward the unknown fate that awaited her at Harrowhold.

Bridget had a feeling Mrs. Clarke was growing impatient and hoped she wouldn't be too angry with Sam Hardy. The housekeeper always said the boy was stingy with the whip, apt to daydream instead of hurrying the horses along. Bridget knew the table was laid and waiting for Miss Danforth's arrival, and Mrs. Clarke hated to serve a cold dish.

Finally, the maid and the housekeeper heard the sound of horseshoes on cobblestone. Mrs. Clarke approached the door and Bridget followed, wiping her sweaty palms on her apron. "Stop fidgeting," Mrs. Clarke demanded. "She'll think you're still a child." After what seemed like an eternity, the door swung open, and Samuel stood at the threshold with a smile on his face and a beautiful young woman at his side. "Mrs. Clarke. Bridget," he said, tipping his cap. "Allow me to present Miss Marina Danforth. Miss Danforth, this is your housekeeper, Mrs. Clarke, and your new maid, Bridget. You won't find their equal in all of England, if I dare say so." He beamed at Bridget, who flushed brilliant red.

"Welcome to Harrowhold, my lady," Mrs. Clarke said with a curtsey.

Bridget followed suit, adding, "We're ever so happy to meet you."

"The pleasure is mine, I'm sure," Marina responded. The entryway of Harrowhold was vast, tiled in white and black marble, with a grand staircase on each side leading to the floor above. A silver chandelier hung from the ceiling, gleaming with hundreds of crystal pieces. Bridget saw Marina looking up and said, "Polished every one of them myself, if you please, miss."

"Really, Bridget," Mrs. Clarke admonished at the same time Marina said, "Oh, it's lovely."

Mrs. Clarke turned to Samuel. "Better get those horses to the stable. I'm sure Miss Danforth is hungry and tired from her journey."

Samuel nodded and turned to go. "It's been a pleasure, Miss Danforth," he said kindly. "I hope you will be very happy here."

As Mrs. Clarke led Marina toward the dining room, Bridget stopped for a moment. "I'll save you a nice chop," she said to Samuel. "And some of that good chocolate cake Mrs. Clarke bought in town."

At a table set with silver, china, and crystal, Marina marveled at the luxury. She and her mother had dined simply.

"It's just a small dinner," Mrs. Clarke said, apologetically. "Since the master is away. But we have some lovely lamb chops with mint, new peas, and there are roasted potatoes. We have bread and cheese, some plums, and there is a chicken consommé for your starter."

"And chocolate cake for dessert," Bridget added.

Marina smiled gratefully. She hadn't realized how hungry she was. She would have liked company at dinner, but only one place had been set at the long table, and she was clearly expected to dine alone. As she ate, with Bridget bringing and clearing each course, humming cheerfully, she felt her strength return.

When she had finished her generous slice of chocolate cake—and declined an offer of another—Mrs. Clarke appeared at the foot of the table. "I'll show you to your room, Miss Danforth, if you are ready."

Marina followed the housekeeper from the dining room and up the grand staircase, where she was shown into a room at the end of a long hall. "This will be your bedchamber," Mrs. Clarke explained. "Lord Henry has the rooms on the opposite side."

Mrs. Clarke couldn't hide her satisfied smile as Marina admired all the carefully selected appointments of her bedroom. "It's beautiful," she said, her voice catching in her throat as she looked at the bed with its linen of silver and blue. "My very favorite."

The housekeeper nodded. "We hoped you would like it. Samuel's brought up your trunk, and Bridget has laid a fire in the grate. We'll bring you some hot water so you can freshen up. If you need us, just ring." She gestured to a long bell pull that hung near the bed.

"Thank you, you've been so lovely. Everything is just perfect." Marina tried not to let her voice tremble.

Mrs. Clarke took her leave with a curtsy. "I wish you a good evening and restful sleep, Miss Danforth. A bride should look her very best on the day she is married."

Marina's heart flipped at the housekeeper's words. "Yes, of course," she said. "Thank you again."

When Mrs. Clarke left the room, Marina's legs felt weak under her. The bed had been turned down, and Marina hurriedly took off her shoes and stockings, then loosened the buttons of her dress. She climbed into bed without undressing, falling asleep so quickly that she did not even hear Bridget come in with water for her washbasin. "Good night, miss," Bridget whispered, as she filled the pitcher.

Marina slept deeply that night, lulled as if rocked by waves. As she slowly drifted towards morning, she dreamt she was swimming upward from the bottom of the ocean but couldn't break through the surface. Finally, she opened her eyes. The sky was gray and dull, and rain spattered the diamond-leaded glass windowpanes. It was her wedding day.

There was a flurry of activity at Harrowhold that morning. Lord Henry was scheduled to return from London that afternoon, and the marriage would take place that evening. Lord Henry had informed the servants he expected the day to proceed like any other. He despised fuss and pomp of any kind, and only attended society functions when required for business. He planned to be back at work the day after the wedding and assumed his bride would be able to entertain herself.

"What a pity, no honeymoon for Miss Danforth," Bridget said as she laid the breakfast table.

Mrs. Clarke hesitated a moment, but sternly replied, "That's none of our business, Bridget."

When Marina came into the dining room for breakfast, Mrs. Clarke and Bridget endeavored to be as cheerful as possible. Bridget, who had left her family behind in Ireland, knew what it was like to be a young girl without a mother. The ladies bustled around, putting flowers in vases, pouring tea, and talking enthusiastically about the day's events.

"I'll help you dress, of course," Bridget said. "I can arrange your hair, too, if you like."

"Thank you," said Marina softly. She ate sparingly, which came as no surprise to Bridget; she assumed Marina's nerves would not allow her to eat much. After only a little tea and toast, Marina excused herself and went to her rooms to wait for Lord Henry's arrival.

After helping Mrs. Clarke clear the breakfast dishes, air the beds, and straighten the parlor, Bridget knocked on Marina's door. "I've come to help you dress, miss."

Marina's voice was quiet on the other side. "Come in, Bridget."

As she opened the door, Bridget could hardly contain her excitement. "Which gown will you wear, Miss Danforth? Did you have a new one made?"

Marina shook her head. "Everything happened so quickly, I didn't have time to think about a dress. I've been wearing black these last few months—for my mother. But of course, that won't do. I'll have to wear my blue silk, although Lord Henry has already seen it."

The maid helped Marina into her gown, then led her to the dressing table and picked up the silver brush she had polished so carefully. "I used to do my sisters' hair, back home," she said, pulling the brush gently through Marina's curls. "But we never had anything like this. Do you want the silver combs? Or the ivory? I'm not sure the tortoiseshell will suit the blue silk."

"Whatever you think is best," Marina answered, as Bridget brushed, twisted, and pinned. Her face looked unfamiliar in the glass, like she was seeing herself for the first time. The reflection in the mirror gazed back at her as if it knew something Marina didn't.

"Oh, you look lovely," Bridget said, her eyes shining. "Still so pale, though. Here." She picked up a tiny pot and handed it to Marina. "Just a bit of rouge on your cheeks, and a touch on your lips. A bride should be blushing. Lord Henry won't know," she assured her.

When her preparations were complete, Bridget helped Marina to her feet. "You look perfectly lovely. Lord Henry will be so pleased, I'm sure."

"Thank you, Bridget," Marina replied. "Is it—is it time now?"

"I believe so, Miss," Bridget answered, checking the watch that hung on a chain from her apron. "I'll take you down to the parlor. The vicar should be arriving soon."

Marina nodded, pale despite the rouge. Bridget led her to the parlor. Marina sat on a brocade sofa and watched the rain on the windows.

As Bridget left the parlor, Mrs. Clarke rushed up to her, looking unusually perturbed.

"I reminded Lord Henry to buy flowers for Miss Danforth in London, but he's come home without them. He said he didn't think it necessary."

"Not necessary!" exclaimed Bridget. "But a bride must have a bouquet!"

"We'll have to use some we have here already," Mrs. Clarke declared.

"But we haven't the right ones! It will look strange."

"We have some of those yellow roses, and some ivy," said Mrs. Clarke. "Those are for friendship, and that's important in marriage."

"I suppose you're right," Bridget agreed. "It will have to do. And—well, we are her friends, too. She has no one else."

Mrs. Clarke nodded briskly, and a bouquet of yellow roses was quickly arranged from the vase in the dining room.

Bridget found a length of ribbon and tied it around the stems. "Something blue, for luck."

The ladies were interrupted by the ringing of the front doorbell. "The vicar!" exclaimed Bridget.

"I'll go to the door. You give her the bouquet." Mrs. Clarke dashed from the room.

Bridget knocked on the door of the parlor and heard Marina call, "Come in." She looked relieved to see it was Bridget.

"Here, Miss Danforth. From Mrs. Clarke and myself, I mean—from Lord Henry." Bridget flushed red and looked at the ground, holding out the bouquet.

A shy smile brightened Marina's face. "For friendship," she said quietly.

Bridget nodded, feeling her throat tighten. The next thing she knew, Lord Henry and the vicar were standing in the hall behind her. "Good luck!" Bridget whispered, before bowing to Lord Henry and the vicar, then darting away.

Lord Henry entered the room, his eyes widening as he looked at Marina. "Miss Danforth," he said. "It's a pleasure to see you again. I hope you have felt very welcome here at Harrowhold." He extended a hand to her; she took it and stood.

"Thank you, Lord Henry. I am very pleased to be here."

The vicar smiled kindly at Marina, then looked at Lord Henry. "Shall we begin?"

In only a few moments, the ceremony was over. Miss Marina Danforth was now Lady Henry of Harrowhold.

The dinner after the wedding passed in a blur. Marina tasted everything Mrs. Clarke had to offer. Lord Henry, despite not wanting a fuss, had two slices of the sponge cake with cream. Marina's wedding bouquet sat in a vase in the middle of the dining room table, and Bridget promised to dry the flowers for her to keep. Lord Henry was not much for conversation, but he told Marina that his business in London had gone well and asked about her journey to Harrowhold. Finally, Lord Henry adjourned to his study to enjoy a brandy and cigar. "May I visit your chambers later?" he asked Marina.

She nodded, not meeting Lord Henry's eyes. After he had left the room, Marina sat at the table by herself for a few moments. She was young and inexperienced, but she knew what happened between husband and wife. Lord Henry had never been married, but Marina knew nothing of his life before her. He might have had many mistresses—might still, as far as she knew. She felt anxious, but also curious about the events to come.

When Lord Henry came to Marina's room that night, smelling strongly of smoke, she was sitting on the chaise in her dressing gown, gazing out the window as rain continued to fall.

"I am sorry it wasn't a finer day," Lord Henry said. "It often rains at Harrowhold."

"I don't mind it," Marina said softly. She had taken the combs out of her hair—Bridget had chosen the silver—unpinned her curls, then brushed her hair until it fell around her shoulders, black and glossy as ink. Her face, usually pale, was flushed, not just from rouge. Candlelight reflected in her green eyes like moonlight on the sea.

Lord Henry took Marina's hand. "In all my life, I never felt the need to marry," he said. "I am so often away, and my work occupies much of my thoughts. But now that I am older, I have begun thinking about the future of this estate. I want a son to inherit my name, and my land. When I saw you in Boston . . . something drew me, like the tide to the shore. I couldn't help wanting to bring you here, to make you my own. Your eyes are so beautiful, yet so strange. I have never seen your equal." He shook his head. "Forgive me. I am foolish."

Marina rose from the chaise and stood before Lord Henry. He reached for her, touched her hair. Marina untied the belt of her dressing gown, thinking Lord Henry would undress her. Instead, he leaned forward and kissed her cheek. Marina stood still, unsure of how to respond. Lord Henry took her hand and led her to the bed, so Marina took off her dressing gown and got under the covers in her nightdress. Lord Henry extinguished all the lamps and candles before coming to Marina's bedside and—she assumed—undressing in the dark.

Without another word, Lord Henry reached for Marina. He pulled up her nightdress, positioning himself on top of her. Marina expected him to kiss her, but he did not. As he pushed her legs open, Marina felt a moment of panic. She had not thought it would happen like this. Wasn't there supposed to be more? But he was pressing against her now, hard and insistent, and she felt a sharp pain as something opened inside her and stifled a cry as he twined his fingers in her hair, breathing fast.

Then, as quickly as it had begun, it was over, and Lord Henry was lying beside her on the bed. Marina said nothing, tears leaking from the corners of her eyes. Her loins ached, slick with her blood and his leavings. Her husband sat up, stood, and pulled on his dressing gown. "I may not see you at breakfast tomorrow. I must be at my office early." Marina couldn't see his face in the dark. "Good night. I hope you sleep well."

"Good night," Marina managed.

The door closed behind him, and Marina was alone.

As the next days and weeks passed, Mrs. Clarke and Bridget spoke to each other often about their concern for Marina. She was always kind to them, but rarely smiled, and passed most of her time alone in her room, staring out the window. Lord Henry was the same as ever, leaving early and coming home late, sometimes off on business for days at a time.

"Do you think he's terribly cruel to her?" Bridget asked Mrs. Clarke one day after Marina had looked especially despondent at breakfast.

Instead of telling Bridget it was none of her business, Mrs. Clarke looked worried. "I have never thought him to be a cruel man, only indifferent. But perhaps that is its own kind of cruelty."

"I'm worried for her health," Bridget said. "Do you see those dark circles under her eyes? I know some nights she walks the halls. I saw her once, but she didn't see me. Frightened me half to death."

Mrs. Clarke nodded. "I've seen her too. I think she walks in her sleep. One night, I followed her around for an hour, afraid she would fall down the stairs. They say never to wake a sleepwalker, you know."

The color drained from Bridget's face. "You don't think—the curse..." Her voice trailed off.

Mrs. Clarke sniffed. "That's ridiculous, just a rumor." But she looked far less confident than she usually did.

It was only a few nights later that the entire household woke to bloodcurdling shrieks. Bridget and Mrs. Clarke ran downstairs from their quarters, straight to Marina's door. "Lady Henry, are you all right?" Mrs. Clarke called, knocking loudly. The ladies opened the door to find Marina sitting straight upright in bed, eyes wide and staring.

"My lady, wake up! You're having a nightmare!" Bridget cried, shaking her.

Mrs. Clarke dashed to the stand that held the basin and pitcher. "Stand back!" she told Bridget. Then she tossed the water in Marina's face.

The screaming stopped. Marina's eyes gradually refocused, and she came back to herself. "What happened?" she asked.

Bridget lit a candle with shaking fingers. "You were dreaming, Lady Tyler. You had a terrible nightmare."

Mrs. Clarke handed Marina a towel. "What has upset you, my lady? It seems that you have been unwell, if you don't mind my saying so."

Marina wiped her face. Water dripped from her black hair, making her look as if she had crawled from the sea. "I dream that I am looking for my mother, but she is lost to me. Sometimes I am wandering labyrinthine mazes—like a city, abandoned, or catacombs—but I can't feel my legs. It's as if I am floating, somehow."

"My lady, perhaps we should call a doctor. He could give you some laudanum to help you sleep," Mrs. Clarke suggested.

"No! No doctors. I have a horror of them. I saw enough of them when my mother was ill. She told me never to trust them."

Mrs. Clarke and Bridget exchanged looks.

"Of course. Whatever you wish, my lady," Mrs. Clarke said. "Would you like me to stay with you tonight? I will sit up by your bed, if you wish."

Marina grasped her hand. "Oh, thank you, please. The nights are so dreadfully long."

Mrs. Clarke fetched a chair and set it by Marina's bedside. She gently urged Marina to lie down, drawing the bedclothes over her. She rubbed Marina's wet hair with the towel and arranged it on her pillow. "You rest now, my lady. I will stay with you until morning."

"Thank you," Marina murmured, her eyes closing. Mrs. Clarke tentatively reached out a hand and stroked Marina's hair. "Go back to bed, Bridget," she said. "We will sort this out in the morning."

Despite Mrs. Clarke's best efforts, Marina's nightmares only worsened as the weeks went on. Bridget tried to soothe her nerves with chamomile tea and lavender, or warm milk before bed, but nothing could alleviate her night terrors. Lord Henry no longer visited her bedchamber and was growing even more distant. One day, he confronted her over breakfast.

"Marina, I must insist that you see a doctor. I don't know what is troubling you so, but I can no longer tolerate your wailing in the night. It's disturbing my rest and affecting my work."

Marina went pale. "Joseph, please. I don't need a doctor. I can sleep on the upper floor with Bridget and Mrs. Clarke. Then, perhaps, you will not be disturbed."

Lord Henry scoffed. "I won't have my wife sleeping with the servants. I'll send for Doctor Collins today so he can examine you. We will say no more on the matter," Lord Henry declared, picking up his newspaper. Marina choked back the panic rising in her throat.

When the doctor arrived later that afternoon, Marina had dressed well, arranged her hair, and added rouge to her cheeks. Doctor Collins was not easily convinced. "Your husband tells me you are having nightmares," he said.

"Yes—a bit. It's really no trouble to me, though. Just a minor inconvenience."

The doctor raised an eyebrow. "It's more than a minor inconvenience to your husband," he said. "He says it's affecting his sleep. And I assume that it is affecting your marital relations, as well."

Marina flushed, more with anger than embarrassment. "I will not discuss that with anyone other than my husband."

The doctor was undeterred. "It sounds to me that you are suffering from typical feminine hysteria. Unfortunately, this is common among the weaker sex. I imagine that you have too much time on your hands, and too much emotion overwhelming your nerves. If you were to bear a child, I expect it would calm you and resolve your issues."

Marina felt her temper rising. "I can assure you, I am not hysterical. I simply suffer from nightmares, a condition that afflicted my mother as well. It is harmless."

Doctor Collins shook his head. "I don't expect you to understand. But heightened emotions are a clear indicator of hysteria. In order to calm your nerves—and, perhaps, to make you more amenable to your husband—I prescribe a course of hydrotherapy. I will send assistants from the hospital to set up the apparatus at your home. Unless, of course, you would like to be admitted."

"Hydrotherapy?"

"It's a treatment that involves the patient being submerged in ice-cold water for periods of time to make her less excitable. There is a variant known as thalassotherapy, which uses sea or salt water for the beneficial effects of minerals. I believe this would be the best course of treatment for you."

When Marina began to protest, the doctor continued, "Your husband has instructed me to solve this problem by any means necessary. I assume you have no desire to be taken to the asylum—nor would you like to have your uterus removed, I presume. I suggest you comply with the prescribed treatment, or things will be much harder for you."

That night, Marina cried herself to sleep. Not long after, her wailing began.

The next morning, Mrs. Clarke answered a banging on the door to find Dr. Collins, flanked by four large men dressed in hospital uniforms. "I've brought the hydrotherapy tub for Lady Henry," he announced. "Please show my men where to install it."

Mrs. Clarke's mouth was a thin, tight line. "Lady Henry's chamber is upstairs," she said, "although I do not believe she wishes to participate."

"That is no matter," Dr. Collins replied. "Lord Henry has given me explicit instructions that she be treated."

Mrs. Clarke derived some satisfaction at the difficulty Dr. Collins and his men had in getting the heavy tub up to the second floor. After they had placed it in Marina's chambers, they then lugged the large tanks of salt water to her room to fill the tub. "This water should be kept as cold as possible," Dr. Collins instructed Mrs. Clarke. "Add ice before she bathes, if you can."

When the tub had been installed, Dr. Collins ordered Bridget to fetch Marina from the parlor. "Lord Henry has instructed me to make sure she begins therapy," he said. "She will need to go upstairs and undress. I will observe her treatment."

Mrs. Clarke was horrified. "She will do no such thing," she exclaimed. "That is highly inappropriate."

"I am a professional, Mrs. Clarke," said Dr. Collins. "I can assure you Lady Henry's body is nothing I have not seen before."

Despite Mrs. Clarke and Bridget's stringent objections, Dr. Collins was firm. "If she will not bathe here, I am authorized to take her to the asylum for treatment."

"I will do it," Marina said, marching upstairs to her bedchamber. "I will not be taken to the asylum." Her voice was thick with angry tears.

She entered her bedchamber, followed closely by Dr. Collins and Mrs. Clarke, who refused to let Marina face the doctor alone. "Disrobe, please," he demanded.

Marina removed her garments. Her cheeks were flushed, but to Mrs. Clarke's admiration, Marina looked Dr. Collins directly in the eyes.

"Go ahead, get in the tub. We are equipped with straps and restraints to keep you submerged, if necessary."

Marina did not acknowledge the doctor but walked past him and tentatively dipped her fingers in the icy salt water. She slowly climbed in and sank into the water, closing her eyes.

Dr. Collins nodded in approval. "See? You are calmer already. I prescribe a course of treatment every day for two weeks. We will see if your nightmares resolve."

Marina kept her eyes closed and did not acknowledge the doctor's presence any further. Dr. Collins was finally satisfied with her acquiescence and released her into the care of Mrs. Clarke. After some time, Bridget tentatively entered the room. "Mrs. Clarke? Lady Henry? Do you require assistance?"

Bridget approached the tub and gasped to see Marina sleeping peacefully in the frigid water as Mrs. Clarke watched over her. "Maybe that doctor was right," Bridget whispered.

The housekeeper was not convinced. "If she gets better, it's nothing to do with that charlatan. But we will see what happens."

Much to the surprise of everyone at Harrowhold, including Marina herself, the hydrotherapy seemed to improve Marina's health. Lord Henry's sleep was no longer disturbed, and he was much more cheerful at breakfast. Marina took to spending her days in the tub, even asking for extra ice in the water. She put her head under and practiced holding her breath for longer and longer periods. She could stay submerged for minutes at a time and fell almost into a trance as she sank into the water. Visions filled her mind once again of a sunken city, a civilization deep beneath the waves. This time, she was not frightened. She welcomed the dreams.

One evening, after Marina had soaked for several hours, a strange mood overcame her. Her heart beat faster and blood tingled throughout her limbs. She felt as if everything in her was crying out, but she didn't know why. She toweled herself off lightly, then draped her dressing gown over her body without even a nightdress underneath. Slowly, she walked down the hall, leaving wet footprints on the plush carpet. She knocked quietly at Lord Henry's door.

"What is it?" he called.

"It's Marina," she said softly.

Lord Henry opened the door to his wife, who stood in the hall dripping and shivering in the thin gown that clung to her body. "What are you doing here?"

"I'm not sure," Marina said. "I wanted—I wanted to see you."

She took her husband's hand and led him toward his bed, then pushed him into the mattress with a strength that surprised even herself. When she slipped off her gown, her flesh was covered with goosebumps, her long hair clinging to her body like seaweed on driftwood. She climbed onto the bed and crawled toward him, trailing drops of freezing water. She reached to undo his dressing gown.

"Marina!" Lord Henry exclaimed, but he made no move to stop her. She did not respond, nor bend to kiss him. Instead, she straddled him and guided him inside her.

Lord Henry gasped. "So cold!" But he said nothing more as Marina rocked her hips on top of him. In only a few shuddering moments, it was over, and he lay on the bed, soaking wet and freezing. Marina slid off her husband, left her dressing gown on his floor, and walked back to her room naked, without a word. That night, she slept better than ever before.

It was not long after that Marina announced to the staff of Harrowhold that she was with child. Bridget cried out in delight, and Mrs. Clarke even shed a tear. "I never had a child, since my husband died so young," she told her. "I am so very glad for you." Then they were urging her to sit down and put her feet up, talking about all the baby clothes that would need to be made and the furniture to be ordered.

Lord Henry said he was pleased to hear about the child, but that a man had little place in matters of childbirth and child-raising, so he left Marina to her own devices. For the first time since she arrived at Harrowhold, Marina passed her days happily.

Then one night, when the baby's time was drawing near, Marina was jolted from her sleep by sharp, sudden pain. She sat up with a start and reached for the bell pull that hung by the bed, giving it several sharp tugs before she sank back into her pillows.

"I had another nightmare," Marina said when Mrs. Clarke and Bridget rushed to her side. "I saw my mother on the shore, and I tried to reach her, but the sea was carrying her away. She told me the baby was in danger. I asked her what to do, and she said I would know when the time came. Then she disappeared beneath the waves." Marina's breath came shallowly, and her features contorted in fear. "The baby's coming," she said. "I can feel it. There isn't much time."

Bridget ran for the door. "I'll send Sam for the doctor."

"No!" Marina exclaimed. "No doctor." She grasped the ladies' hands. "Promise me that no matter what happens, you will take care of my baby. I fear that something terrible may happen."

Mrs. Clarke nodded. "I will protect your child like my own," she said. "Bridget, bring hot water and towels." She arranged the pillows and helped Marina prop herself up. She stripped the blankets from the bed and pushed Marina's nightdress up around her waist. The contractions started almost immediately and remained steady. "The baby is coming, soon," Marina gasped. Bridget screamed as blood soaked the silk sheets.

Marina felt faint.

"You need to push now. The baby can't wait," Mrs. Clarke said sternly.

Gripping Bridget's hand, Marina pushed as pain tore through her body. It took all her effort to stay conscious, when suddenly, there was a great rush of blood, and she fell into oblivion as she heard Bridget and Mrs. Clarke scream.

When Marina opened her eyes again, Mrs. Clarke was holding a wrapped bundle in her arms, an expression of wonder on her face. "My lady," she whispered. "You have a baby girl."

Bridget stood next to her, eyes wide. "My lady," she stammered. "The baby—she is different."

"What do you mean?" Marina tried to push herself up, but fell back, exhausted.

Mrs. Clarke said, "She is a fine baby with a good, strong cry. She may be a little unusual…but she is a beautiful child."

Mrs. Clarke handed the baby to Marina. The little girl had dark black hair and ruddy cheeks. Her eyes were the same sea green as her mother's. "She's beautiful," Marina gasped, and loosened the blankets to see more of her daughter. Mrs. Clarke and Bridget held their breath.

When Marina saw her daughter's body, she was stunned into silence, her eyes wide. She pulled her baby close. "I understand now," she said.

As Marina labored, Lord Henry sent Sam Hardy to fetch Dr. Collins. Bridget and Mrs. Clarke stalled him as long as they could, but eventually he demanded to see his wife and newborn child. Mrs. Clarke swaddled the baby tightly and placed the tiny bundle in Marina's arms. "You just stay calm," she whispered. "Everything will be all right."

Lord Henry came into the room where Marina lay exhausted, clutching her baby to her breast. He looked pointedly at Mrs. Clarke, and she took her leave with one last glance at Marina.

"So," Lord Henry asked, a slight smile forming on his lips, "is it a boy?"

"No," Marina said. "A girl. Cordelia, after my mother."

"A girl." Lord Henry's voice was flat. "Well, I suppose it can't be helped. We'll try again. Let me see her, then."

"No," Marina protested. "I need to feed her. You can see her in the morning."

"Nonsense. Let me hold her." Lord Henry reached for the baby in Marina's arms.

Marina felt the situation slipping out of her control. "Be gentle," was all she could say as Lord Henry picked up their daughter. "A fine baby girl, at least," he said, smiling. "Ten fingers and toes, yes? Let's count to make sure."

Before Marina had time to object, Lord Henry loosened the blankets swaddling baby Cordelia. Marina held her breath as she watched him observe the two tiny fists, with ten pink fingers each. Her heart sank as he opened the blankets further, where there would be no toes for him to find. She watched her husband's face contort in horror as he saw four thick, silver-green tentacles, writhing and squirming, covered in suckers and scales. Lord Henry gasped. "What is this thing? Marina, what have you done?" He held the baby away from him. The blankets fell to the ground.

"I know she's different, Joseph," Marina pleaded. "I realize now what runs in my family. She's still our daughter. We can still love her."

"Love her? You're out of your mind. I should have sent you to the madhouse when I had the chance. This thing is an abomination. Smother it, drown it, dash its brains out on the hearth! This is no child of mine."

"No!" Marina screamed and grabbed for Cordelia, but she had lost too much blood to stand.

"Shut up!" Lord Henry hissed. "We haven't much time. The doctor will be here soon. We'll tell him it was born dead."

His eyes landed on the hydrotherapy tub, still filled with salt water. While Marina screamed, he ran to the tub and held Cordelia over it. "You'll thank me, eventually," he said. "You cannot be a mother to a monster." With that, he let Cordelia go. Marina heard the sickening splash and felt something break inside her. When Lord Henry turned back from the tub, wiping salt water from his hands, he could not process what he saw.

The creature on the bed was no longer his wife. Her wide-set eyes, once green like the sea, were now completely black. They bulged from the side of her head as if threatening to burst. Her mouth, wailing like a siren, opened wide, then wider still. He saw her lips flatten and retract, watched in horror as rows of sharp, jagged teeth protruded from her pink gums.

Her ink-black hair moved with a life of its own, swirling around her head in a fury. As he stood staring, she slid over the side of the bed.

When the creature who had once been Marina dragged herself across the floor, leaving a trail of blood behind her, Lord Henry's small mind snapped from shock. He fainted, fell, and hit his head on the side of the heavy porcelain tub. In an instant, he was dead.

Marina continued her desperate crawl to the tub. Weak from blood loss, she knew she would never reach Cordelia in time. Just as she was slipping out of consciousness, Mrs. Clarke and Bridget burst into the room.

"The tub!" Marina managed, then went silent. Bridget screamed to see the beautiful woman, herself once more, lying on the floor and covered in blood.

"My God in Heaven!" Mrs. Clarke exclaimed, staring down at the tub.

Bridget wrenched her gaze from Marina's body. "Is the baby alive? Get her out of there!"

Instead, Mrs. Clarke stared, transfixed, at the tiny body in the tub. "She's alive, and she's breathing." The two women watched as the baby slept peacefully in her saltwater bath, tiny slits on her sides opening and closing as she took in the precious oxygen.

Sam Hardy had driven the horses at a leisurely pace, since Marina was in no hurry to see Dr. Collins. When they finally arrived at Harrowhold, the doctor pronounced Lord Henry dead of a heart attack. "That's what comes of having a child at his age," the doctor said. "His heart couldn't stand the stress, or the sight of blood." He examined Marina, who had been tucked into clean sheets by Mrs. Clarke and Bridget. "She is weak, but she will recover," he said. "I am sure her hysteria will be cured now, and her uterus restored to health since she has borne a child. The hydrotherapy was a great success," he declared.

"I agree," said Mrs. Clarke. Bridget covered a laugh with a cough.

Dr. Collins took a cursory glance at baby Cordelia, bundled once again in Mrs. Clarke's arms. "She looks to be healthy," he said. "I'll send the undertaker for Lord Henry." With that, he took his leave, and was never again called to Harrowhold.

Marina soon regained her strength and spent her days tending to baby Cordelia, who was a happy, healthy baby despite her unusual anatomy.

One fine spring day, as they sat around the table—for Marina had requested they all eat together now—she said, "I've been thinking about sponge cake, with lots of cream, and perhaps strawberries. For the wedding."

Mrs. Clarke and Bridget looked up with a start, and Sam Hardy, bouncing Cordelia on his knee, stopped, and stared. "What wedding?" Bridget asked.

"Why, yours, of course," Marina said. "If Sam ever gets up the nerve to ask you."

Bridget's face went as red as her hair, and Sam roared with laughter. "I've been waiting for the right time, but I suppose I've waited long enough. What do you say, Bridge? Will you have me?"

Bridget gasped, "Yes!" and ran to throw her arms around Sam. Cordelia laughed and clapped her hands.

"Write home to your sisters, Bridget," said Marina. "There's a place here for them if they want it. And, Mrs. Clarke, place your orders with the merchants in town." She smiled. "Tell them there is to be a wedding at Harrowhold."

Delectable little wolfsbane
Cultivated for beauty
Left to rot on society's hill
They don't know her power
But soon…soon they will
More than a pretty face
Deadly reverie oozes from
Her every word, her mind
A nightmare to Byron's
Lustful grace
Let them look, let them see
Set their withering, aristocratic
Gaze upon she
Whose mind knew witchcraft
Should take her to the stake
So science combined with man's greatest fear
Modern Prometheus she did make
History is hers, future too
You'll remember the glorious
Flower and all it could do
Her finest act, greatest
Illusionary trick shall be
You never pass a thought
To those who wished her to
Wither, the men who thought her
Petals were theirs to pick

Now…it all began with a dream…

Melanie Whitlock

II
The Devil's Servant
Judith Crow

I, Reuben Fancroft, am an old man. I am told that old age only comes to those who are fortunate, and that I should be grateful to count myself among that number, but it is difficult to be grateful for the feeling that good sense and mobility are leaving you, that you are reverting into a shell of the person you once were.

Since taking that post in India when I was first married, I have embraced the habit of sleeping after luncheon, but now find that I cannot help but fall asleep at any time in the day, while finding it hard to sleep at night. My bed is cold without my wife, and the house is quiet without my children. The servants believe they do me a kindness by muffling their steps and conversation, but instead they leave me in a world washed in a nauseating layer of silence, which I must seek to penetrate if my voice and thoughts are to be heard.

I find that the pen has become my greatest companion, allowing me to record my thoughts in a way which I feel is noticed. My daughter encourages me when she visits, bringing new quills and journals, which I fill with the increasingly feverish ramblings of my mind. But I am driven to share this story of something I witnessed as a much younger man, something which has ever preyed on my mind as a mystery I am unable to explain.

It took place in the summer of 1851, a year I remember more clearly than I can summon my own daughter's face. There is something of writing about those days which evokes memory in each of my senses, neither sight nor sound more permeating than the recalled scent of so many people thronging together to ogle and admire the vision which was the Great

Exhibition, or the taste of food snatched when possible, between meetings with one genius or another.

I had always spent my money wisely and had recently invested in the work and wanderings of a certain Mr. Dickens, whose literature had taken him to places beyond the reckoning of so many before. I had always thought him a haunted man: so confident in front of a crowd, yet awkward and unforthcoming when conducting any private conversation. Still, I was happy to promote his work and watch as the reading public lapped it up with all the enthusiasm of a spoiled cat at a saucer of cream. For my part, I was grateful to always find myself in the circle of people who made it possible for me to indulge my interests and, as a bachelor of thirty-three years, I enjoyed the company of others like myself.

It was at the Crystal Palace one late July afternoon that I happened to spy a familiar face in the crowd. I had returned for a private look at the majesty and might of the British Empire, portrayed so boldly under one roof, and the time alone allowed me to notice the individual I might have missed had I been with anyone else. The dark eyes were familiar at first, then the pale face around them, and finally I realized I was looking at none other than Henry Giles, who had been a companion of mine over a decade earlier when we attended the same college at Oxford. Henry seemed to have less difficulty recognizing me than I had in recognizing him. No sooner had my eyes started to narrow than he had raised his hand to wave in my direction. Fortunately, by the time he made his way through the bustling crowd, I had recalled his identity and was spared the embarrassment of searching for some clue as to who I was addressing.

"Fancroft!" he exclaimed, dropping his slender hand on my shoulder with a surprising weight for one so thin. "I should have known I would meet you here! Of course! Where else would you be?"

"Giles!" I hoped my own voice sounded as enthusiastic as his own and, judging by the broad smile which never left his features, he was happy enough with my response. "I have meant these past six months to send you a letter. I hope you received my condolences on the loss of your father last year?"

Giles nodded. "I did. Thank you. I find I miss his good sense more each day. I fear I wasn't cut from the same cloth as him, for I'm not made to be the master of my own house. But it has given me the chance to further embrace my interests." He paused for a second, and his brow creased into deep furrows before he shook his head and his eyes lit up again. "But you must come and see it for yourself, Fancroft. I have my carriage outside, and you can stay with me at the house while you are in London."

I had not the heart to tell him I had my own house in London, despite that my parents still lived in theirs. Instead, I graciously accepted his offer and, an hour later, we were traveling through town together, with him regaling me about all that had happened since we had been at university together. We had maintained a sporadic contact through letters but, after his sister died suddenly, we had not seen each other. He was required to return to his parents' house after the tragedy, while I had completed my studies and been distracted by the business which had become my world.

"Here!" Giles said brightly as the carriage came to a stop. I looked out to see the house and found it much how I remembered, having visited as a young man. I realized a smile must have crossed my lips, for Giles nodded enthusiastically.

"I see you're pleased to be back. Come in and see my own humble exhibition."

I had no idea what to expect after those words but followed him into the building. I had thought to find the house as I saw it thirteen years earlier, although in my mind I may have confused it with the one owned by my paternal grandfather. What I came into, however, was more like the thing I had just left. It was indeed an exhibition.

Portraits of familiar faces lined the wall: Lord Byron, Percy Bysshe Shelley and his wife, and John Keats. Glass cases packed the halls so tightly that, in places, I had to walk sideways so I could fit through, although Giles had no difficulty slipping between them with his slender figure. He ran his hands lovingly over the glass, a warm, paternal glow radiating from his face as he gazed at their contents. Here was a sardonic letter from Lord Byron to a friend; there, a much scribbled-on draft of a poem by John Keats. A lock of hair in another of the cases professed to have been cut from the head of the infant William Shelley and treasured by his mother in the years since his death.

"You may remember my interest?" Giles whispered, sweeping his hand toward some of the exhibits.

I nodded, but in amazement at the sheer quantity of what I was seeing, I found myself speechless. Somehow, it had not seemed strange to admire the many wonders of the Crystal Palace, yet I will not deny I felt overwhelmed by how this house had become smothered with the presence of so many objects. Even as we went into the study, I noticed there was not a single portrait of anyone from Giles' family, save for a miniature of his sister which rested on the desk. Every other face that stared at me was a stranger.

"My interest has given way to a passion," Giles said, sitting down behind the desk and gesturing for me to take the other seat in the room. I sat down and looked at him, waiting for him to go on. Eventually, under my keen gaze, he did. "I doubt there are any in London who have such a collection as mine."

"I doubt it too," I agreed. "But I suppose it is difficult to entertain with your house so full?"

"Indeed," Giles laughed. "But I have all the companionship I require. I have paid for it, I admit, and it has cost me more than I had any intention to spend. Even the house itself is mortgaged to pay for the items which fill it."

"Are you sure that's sensible?" As soon as I spoke, I knew I had overstepped the mark, but Giles only smiled again.

"I could not help it, Fancroft," he said slowly. "You know surely that Mrs Shelley died earlier this year? I could not allow her estate to go to anyone who would love it less than I."

"But I believed her son outlived her," I pointed out. "Indeed, I know he did. Our paths have crossed on more than one occasion."

"Yes," Giles said, "but you don't understand. No one could love them like I do, and God knows I paid enough to prove it." For a second, his voice sounded troubled, but then his face lit with the same enthusiasm he had exhibited since I met him in the Crystal Palace. "Six weeks ago, I acquired possession of something which I consider to be the crowning jewel of my collection. Would you care to view it?"

I nodded, beginning to formulate an idea of what I expected to see. Giles walked over to the bell pull, then took his seat again, watching me with a look I could not fathom. At last, the door opened and one of the servants walked in, a small man with a dour face and greying black hair that hung long around his shoulders. He looked rather scruffy, I thought, and I wondered when Giles had last taken his staff to task. I nodded at him and waited expectantly to see whatever he had brought but was surprised to hear Giles' laughter.

"No, my dear Fancroft," he said amid his amusement. "You do not understand. O'Connell has not brought any object. He is the object. My most prized possession, who served Percy and Mary Shelley themselves for four and a half years from 1818."

O'Connell bowed slightly, and I forced a smile onto my face, trying not to imagine the lengths Giles had gone to in achieving such a connection with the writers he so admired. He was sent away once I had congratulated Giles on his find and agreed on the time for dinner.

We ate in a room adorned with yet more portraits of those from the same era and, when I went to bed, I was somewhat relieved to discover it was in a place decorated with nothing more than wallpaper. As pleased as I was to be spending time with an old friend, I found the contents of his house, not least the dour old servant who had been employed solely on the basis of a previous master, somewhat disconcerting.

I lay awake for some time, wondering how an interest had descended into fanaticism and trying to work out how long I would have to stay without my escape seeming rude. However, I eventually managed to find some sleep and dreamt of the wonders I had seen earlier in the day, and that I was having a tour of the Exhibition by none other than Dickens himself who, for once, wore a genuine smile on his face.

The dream was so harmless and amusing that I nearly leapt out of my skin at the shrill, terrified scream which echoed from elsewhere in the house and brought me violently back to my senses. I lit one of the candles and hurried out of the room to follow where I thought the sound had come from. Panicked sobs guided my way. I knocked on the door and let myself into the room to find Giles huddled on his bed, staring alternately between his knees and a dark corner of the room. Instinctively, I followed his gaze and, taking my candle over to investigate, found it contained nothing but a moderately-sized spider, which scurried away from the candlelight.

"I didn't know you were afraid of spiders, Giles." I tried to hide the laughter in my voice.

"Spiders?" Giles repeated. "Spiders? Can you not see it, Fancroft?"

"I saw the spider," I replied, feeling confusion get the better of me. "I will kill it if you want?"

"No." Giles pointed back into the corner. "The Creature is there! Her Creature!"

I looked again, not knowing what I expected to find but unsurprised that there was nothing there at all.

"It was a nightmare," I said at last, hoping it would reassure Giles, but his horrified look became only more intense as I moved into the corner and took up a stance there.

"Is it a nightmare?" he demanded, his hand pointing shakily where I stood. "When I can see it with my waking eyes?"

Although I was certain Mary Shelley's Creature could not possibly be in the room with us, I felt a sudden urge to be somewhere else, so I suggested we return to the study and have a drink to calm my friend's nerves. Within a few minutes of our arrival, the door opened, and O'Connell came in, bringing a box of cigars with him. He offered one to Giles and another to me before he returned to his master and lit the cigar for him, as Giles' hands were still shaking violently. Then, much to my chagrin, he took up a position in the room and stood there, shamelessly listening to what Giles and I were saying to one another.

"I do not remember you being troubled by nightmares at Oxford," I said at last.

Giles looked across at me and shook his head, taking deep breaths to visibly steady his hands and mind.

"Nor was I ever," he replied, "until last month. Since then, I have seen what was hidden from me before. They do not always come at night, but that is when I am mostly troubled by them. And they are not nightmares, Fancroft, for they are not all when I am asleep."

"Mr. Shelley had the same." It seemed strange to hear O'Connell's voice when he had not spoken before. "Many times, he brought the house down with his screams."

"Perhaps I should be comforted to be in the company of such a great mind," Giles said, pushing his chair back and letting his head loll slightly. I saw his eyes follow the smoke which rippled through his lips and danced up to the ceiling.

"You say a great mind," O'Connell muttered dourly. "But there are plenty who saw only the madman."

Somehow, I felt as though O'Connell was judging me, and I suggested he leave us to talk, which he would not do until his master bade him the same. The man's attitude grated with me, and my usually long patience suffered as a result.

The days and nights which followed only made me more convinced my friend was suffering from some malady of the mind. At most times, he was his usual charming and enthusiastic self, but sometimes his eyes would slide towards a dark corner of the room, and the same look of horror would cross his features. Almost every night was peppered with the same screams and sobs which had awakened me that first night. O'Connell was always there, although he never set a foot in Giles' room, and would encourage my friend to believe he shared the same grave curse which had claimed the life and sense of Percy Shelley. For my part, I cancelled my appointments and dedicated my time to caring for my friend, who I saw as needing someone to support him during whatever darkness had descended upon him. My own dreams became darker, and I found that living in the house with all the strange portraits and artifacts was beginning to take its toll on me too.

It was to that end I made the suggestion to Giles that we should leave the house in London and travel to Lincolnshire, where his family held the estate of which, since his father's death, he was now the master.

"I have not been back there for the best part of the year," Giles said, uncertain, but then nodded his head. "No, you are right, Fancroft. London is close and stifling at present. I think the fresh country air will do me the world of good."

"Excellent. We can travel tomorrow. Shall I tell the servants to prepare?"

"No," Giles replied. "I intend to take only O'Connell. And you too, Fancroft. If you'll come?"

I nodded and said I would, but I couldn't hide my disappointment at his decision to take the servant with him. If I had not warmed to O'Connell to begin with, I was finding him ever more irritating and, dare I say it, even loathsome. He seemed always on hand to encourage Giles to believe in whatever he claimed to see, whilst simultaneously making comments about how Shelley's visions had been put down to madness. Still, I attempted to be a good friend to Giles and went along with his plan to travel to Lincolnshire with only the two of us as companions.

We traveled by railway for much of the journey, which always pleased me, as my father had invested a great deal of money in the development of the transport links which facilitated our rapid travel from London to Lincoln. From there, we took a carriage to the estate at Broughley Abbey, some distance to the south of the county. O'Connell said very little. He traveled in third class on the train and sat up top with the driver when we traveled by carriage, so I did not need to worry about his influence on my friend. For his part, Giles was as excited as a boy traveling home from school and watched out the windows with an eagerness which brought a smile to my face. It had become my dearest wish that the country would allow my friend to regain his mental composure and, as he excitedly hurried into his house at Broughley, sweeping the dustsheets away from the furniture himself, I felt I may have succeeded.

The housekeeper was somewhat flustered by our sudden appearance, but we assured her we would require only minimal service so, within a day, everything was as it should be. That evening, O'Connell served us at dinner but then left, which had not been his wont in London, and I enjoyed the meal more for his absence. I went to bed with the same feeling of dread which I experienced in town, waiting for the penetrating scream to tear me from my dreams, but it never came. To the best of my knowledge, Giles slept peacefully through the night, and for the next thirty nights too.

His newfound mental fortitude led to a greater physicality, and we enjoyed a number of country pursuits together. I found I had rather lost my touch at shooting, while Giles remained an excellent marksman. I remember that month as one of the most carefree of my life. I rarely even wrote letters, although I was careful to ensure Mr. Dickens remained aware of my continuing interest in his work, and I assured him I would meet him again when next I was in London.

However, one month to the day since we arrived at Broughley Abbey, Giles refused my invitation to go shooting, which I thought was strange. Instead, I went alone, taking my gun with no real intention of using it. I took in the magnificent view of the house and the haunting ruins of the abbey in the grounds, and I wondered why Giles spent so little time in such a place. Indeed, my imaginings led me to lose track of time, and I hurried back to the house as dusk fell around me and the sky became busy with a host of bats whisking their way overhead.

"I am sorry for my absence all day," I said jovially as I stepped into the drawing room but stopped when I saw the dark figure of Joseph O'Connell slip out the door at the other side of the room. Giles was sitting on one of the large chairs, a glass of brandy in one hand and a cigar in the other. His face was completely ashen, and I felt my spirits plummet as I considered the possibility we had returned to where we had been in London.

"Did you see her?" Giles asked, taking a sip of the brandy but never turning to face me.

"Mrs. Rhodes?" For a second, I wondered if the poor housekeeper had absconded somewhere under the pressure of our descent on Broughley Abbey. She always seemed to be rushed off her feet, and I could only assume O'Connell was as much of an annoyance to her as he was to me.

"No," Giles said. "By the lake. O'Connell said he saw a lady there."

"I saw no one," I replied, moving over and taking one of the chairs. "I assure you though, there is no reason to believe you would have any trespassers."

"Not a trespasser." Giles leaned forward in his chair and, for the first time since I entered, fixed me with his intense gaze. "The lady by the lake. My sister."

I paused, trying to work out what to say. In truth, I knew very little of Giles' family, apart from that he lost a sister shortly after she visited us at Oxford, and that both his parents died during the years which had elapsed since then. And, of course, for him to have inherited both the townhouse and the estate, he must have been the eldest or only son. It hadn't crossed my mind to ask whether he had any other sisters or younger brothers.

"If it is," I said with a smile, glancing out of the window, "then I'm sure she will be just behind me. I can't see why she would go to the lake and not come into the house. Oh, Giles, I feel remiss now! I wish I had met her. What if she saw me and thought I was ignoring her?" I wasn't sure whether I was talking to him or just rebuking myself for being so wrapped up in my own thoughts that I ignored the sister of my host.

"But maybe she can't come in the house," Giles said. "What if she cannot leave the lake?"

I feel now that I should have immediately challenged the question, but instead I just laughed.

"Did you have a quarrel with her, Giles? I am certain if she's come as far as the lake, then it won't be long before she makes it to the house. Just be sure to welcome her with open arms if you want her to forget the past."

I got to my feet and walked over to pour myself a brandy and my friend another one, but Giles got up too and moved to the window, staring out onto the darkening estate.

"No, Fancroft," he muttered. "Twelve years ago, Henrietta, my sister, took the boat out onto the lake to sketch the landscape. She was a wonderful artist, you may remember?"

I nodded but said nothing, hating every syllable my friend was uttering, as I felt it leading to the conclusion I now expected but did not want to hear.

"She drowned in the lake that day, Fancroft. I was called back from Oxford, and Mother died from the grief. Perhaps Father too. So why would she come back now?" He turned to me, and his face lit up, although there was something almost frantic in the wideness of his eyes. "Do you think she might come to the door, Fancroft? Perhaps you are right."

That night at dinner, for the first time since we arrived, O'Connell took up his old position by the table and did not leave. I had little appetite after Giles's well-intentioned ghost story, but found I was too preoccupied to feel hungry as I went to bed. I half expected to wake to the sound of screams as I had every night in London, but fortunately it was an unbroken night's rest. The following day, I did not go out but, as the mist had rolled in from the nearby fens, I did not feel I was missing anything. Instead, I told Giles about the exploits of Mr. Dickens, and he read to me from Childe Harold's Pilgrimage and then Endymion, each word clearly a delight to him. We ate dinner under the watchful and disconcerting gaze of O'Connell before both retiring to bed.

That night, I was not awoken by any screams, but by a quiet footfall on the landing, followed by the sound of Giles's boyish laughter a little distance away. I listened hard to hear another voice, hoping it would not be O'Connell's, but there was no other sound. I snatched up a candle and hurried out of the room, trying to work out where the noise had come from. For some time, I wandered through the extensive corridors until I heard Giles's voice.

"I will endeavor to keep still, my love."

I was taken aback at the term of endearment and froze for a moment, trying to determine whether I would be interrupting some secret rendezvous if I opened the door. The words were followed by more of Giles's laughter, but with no other voice joining in. I placed my hand on the door and felt it swing into the room, then walked in to find the place in near darkness, apart from a candle clutched in Giles' hand and the one I brought in myself.

"Tell me what you think." He gestured to the other side of the room. I glanced across to find nothing more than a fireplace, adorned with beautiful ceramic tiles.

"It is very handsome," I said, nodding approvingly. "But perhaps just as much so in daylight as in the middle of the night."

"Would you say it is a good likeness?"

"Likeness?"

"To the subject. To me. Tell me, will this portrait take its place alongside Lord Byron on the stairwell at the house in town?"

I had no idea what to say, so I stood still for a moment, trying to puzzle out what was going on.

"Don't take his silence as displeasure, my love," Giles said, directing his comment beyond me. "He has always had a most critical eye." He smiled across at me as he spoke. "But I believe he can recognize beauty when he sees it."

"Who is it painting the portrait?" I asked, unsure whether I was doing the right thing in playing along with his hallucination.

"My sister, of course. Henrietta."

I could not help the shudder which rippled through my body as I remembered how he told me yesterday that his sister was at the lake she drowned in over a decade earlier, and of his concern that she might not make it to the house. Fear gave way to fury as I wondered why O'Connell would lead his master to believe something so damaging and impossible and, as though my anger had summoned him, the servant appeared in the doorway and moved over to Giles.

"Many times, I've done the same for Mr. Shelley," he explained, and Giles's face slipped into a kind of stupor at the apparent closeness to one of his idols. "All those nightmares and visions. We are not all blessed with such sight."

Although I am by no means a violent man, my fists clenched as he spoke. I followed while he guided his master to bed and then, once I had ensured Giles was sleeping, rounded on him.

"Why did you tell him that?" I demanded. O'Connell appeared surprised I was addressing him directly.

"Tell him what, sir?"

"About his sister at the lake."

"I told him nothing of the sort, sir. When would I have said such a thing? I have not been to the lake since we arrived."

"Yesterday," I replied, although my anger and conviction were leaving me as I considered the possibility Giles had been mistaken. "He said you told him there was a lady at the lake. He took that to mean it was his sister."

"No, sir," O'Connell protested, confusion on his face. "I tell you, I had no conversation with him about any lady at the lake."

My brow creased as I tried to think of something to say which would excuse my rudeness. I decided, since he was so keen to talk about his former master, that could be a good topic of conversation.

"You cannot have been very old when you worked for Mr. Shelley, O'Connell?"

"I was neither man nor boy, sir."

"You were a youth then?"

"Sir."

O'Connell clearly did not want to engage in conversation with me, and I cannot say I blamed him after my accusation that he had caused the return of his master's madness. I bid him goodnight and returned to my room, guilt and worry striking me with every step. Once again, I was both relieved and surprised I was able to sleep and awoke in the morning to discover the fog had gone and a bright late-summer's day stretched before me.

Over the next few days, I tried to keep Giles busy enough to take his mind away from thoughts of his sister but, every so often, he would look across the room and past me. A smile would appear on his face which made me certain he believed he was looking at Henrietta. O'Connell was never far away from his master and, despite my impassioned accusation that he had somehow ruined his master's mind and the subsequent feeble attempt to create conversation with him, he behaved in the same muted way towards me as he had since my arrival at Giles's London house.

During the nights, I would hear my friend's footfall on the landing and his accompanying laughter as he followed the vision of his sister into the empty room, where he believed she painted his portrait. But God forgive me, he always sounded so happy that I let him undertake the task uninterrupted. I always heard O'Connell guiding him back to his room an hour later, sharing hushed stories about the wonder of Mr. Shelley's visions.

For my part, I committed to helping Giles during the day. In my attempt to engage my friend, I learned more of the poets he idolized than I ever believed possible to know of any one man, especially those who had been dead for nigh on thirty years. He talked about them as though they were old friends and left me only able to nod along, sometimes trying to decipher who he was talking about. He explained he had recently written to the artist, Joseph Severn, to paint a posthumous portrait of his sister and, when I asked why, he smiled broadly at me.

"You know so little of them, Fancroft." He patted my arm as though to demonstrate some great sense of sympathy. "Joseph Severn nursed Keats on his deathbed. Who better than he to understand the beauty in death?"

I tried to hide the grimace I felt twitching across my features, but perhaps I should not have attempted to conceal it with a yawn, for Giles's face fell slightly.

"Are you not feeling well, Fancroft?" he asked. I recognized there was no concern in his voice, but a definite note of annoyance. "I can have Mrs. Rhodes make you some tea?"

"No tea," I said quickly, then took in a deep breath, trying to draw in the steel I would need to say what was really on my mind. Instead, the same muted words I had been speaking for so many days came from my mouth, avoiding the real issue. "But the miniature you keep of Henrietta? That is a fine piece of work and a great likeness as I remember."

"Indeed." Now Giles's boyish smile returned. "She painted that for me to take to Oxford. But does she not deserve more than a self-portrait in miniature? She was a beautiful woman, Fancroft. The sort who could have persuaded you into marriage."

I laughed and assured him I had no need to be persuaded into marriage. I had no intention of remaining a bachelor for the rest of my life, but I was still busy with my work and did not want to take a wife only to leave her alone for great lengths of time. However, Giles's comments must have entered into my mind, for that night the young lady I remembered from her visit to Oxford and the portrait on my friend's desk appeared in my dream and took hold of my imagination.

We were together at Giles's townhouse but, instead of the portraits, the house was alive with those who had formerly been there in paint only. Lord Byron stood at the top of the stairs, watching the thronging people below him with an unimpressed smirk on his face; Percy and Mary Shelley, now separated significantly in age, for she was an old lady, and he was the same young man who had died nearly thirty years earlier, crouched to listen to what a small red-haired child was saying to them. Keats, Haydon, others I did not recognize, they were all there. And Giles stood in the midst of them all, holding his arms out like a priest declaring a blessing on everything he could see. The young lady at my side whispered in my ear that she must go to where Severn would be painting her and, as may happen in dreams, I heard the door close before I even noticed she had left my side.

I woke up suddenly, looking around me and relieved to find I was alone. A slight draught crept under the door and caused the temperature in the room to drop. I remembered the sound of the door closing in my dream and wondered whether some element of reality had penetrated my sleeping mind. As I had done every night since my friend's madness had returned, I lit my candle and waited to hear the familiar tread of his feet on the landing.

There was no sound at all.

I had woken feeling fully rested, if slightly unnerved after my dream, so wandered to the window and looked down onto the grounds. I cannot describe the sense of panic I felt at the sight of the white figure below, walking purposefully away from the house. I recognized it immediately as Giles and, without thinking, hurried out of the room and ran towards him. But something was different in his countenance this time, and he did not seem to notice I was there. I followed him on his determined walk through the estate, whispering his name but unwilling to take him by the hand and guide him back to the house.

At last, we reached the lake where his sister had drowned and, holding his hand towards some waiting individual only he could see, Giles began to walk calmly into the lake. A great panic seized me and, dropping my candle, I ran towards him and pulled him forcefully from the water. He faced me and, in the split second it took his candle to fall from his hand into the lake, I saw his expression change into the same look of horror I had witnessed so many times in London. He collapsed in my arms, spasming for a moment before lying completely still.

The doctor diagnosed Giles's collapse as the result of a great shock to the heart, doubtless after being rudely awoken from his sleepwalking to find himself in the lake. He did reassure me, as did Mrs. Rhodes when next we met, that I could not have done the wrong thing as, without my intervention, Giles would surely have followed his sister to the same fate. My friend was physically weakened by the events of that night and, for nearly a week, I sat by his bed and read him the poems he loved so much. When I slept, Mrs. Rhodes, or sometimes O'Connell, would take the role of watching him and, as days passed, his strength began to return.

I awoke from the chair by his bed one morning to find him deep in conversation with O'Connell. For a moment, I had no idea what they were discussing, so I simply sat and listened to the conversation, wondering where its macabre bent was leading.

"...his hands and face all gone," O'Connell said. "Believe me, for I saw it with my own eyes. And then, dear God! the stench when they exhumed those bodies and placed them, one after the other, on the pyre. It was an ungodly sight, Mr. Giles."

I frowned at the discussion, wondering how it could possibly be an appropriate topic for a sickroom. I must have made one move too many, as Giles noticed I was awake and looked across, his warm smile returning and directed towards me.

"Percy Bysshe Shelley, Fancroft. He drowned and was buried where he was found. Then his friends exhumed and cremated him."

"His friends?" The recent return to waking dulled my senses so I could not hide the disdain in my voice. Then I remembered I was attempting not to upset my friend, so I smiled slightly and looked at O'Connell. "I am certain I read somewhere that Mr. Shelley's heart would not burn."

"No," O'Connell replied. "For a man may persuade his heart into stone if he has any such wish. And why should he not? Stone is far stronger than flesh."

This time, I made no attempt to hide my distaste at the man and directed he should leave immediately. Giles seemed distracted by his servant's words and, once the door had closed behind O'Connell, he shuffled into a sitting position and looked at me with a desperation which pulled at my heart.

"I believe, since Henrietta's death, that I have willingly turned my heart to stone, Fancroft. But I cannot believe O'Connell when he says it is better than flesh, for it has led my mind into utter darkness."

"It is impossible for a heart to become stone," I said. "You just have to find the person who will remind you that it is flesh. The person who will break it and mend it again. Then you will know no part of you is made of stone."

"She is the only one who can do that," Giles muttered. "The lady of my dreams."

I smiled and rebuked myself for not realizing all this madness and obsession was just Giles' way of dealing with an unrequited love.

"Then you should go back to her," I said, placing my hand on his shoulder in what I hoped was reassurance. "As soon as you are well enough, you should go and find her."

I shook his hand and took my leave, spending the rest of the day reading some of the manuscript I had instructed Mr. Dickens to direct to Broughley Abbey. I lost myself in the depth of his characters and the twisting plot until it was dark. Before going to my own bed that evening, I looked around the door to Giles's room to find my friend sleeping soundly with a look of peace, almost serenity, on his face.

My own sleep that night was the best I had enjoyed since my friend's madness returned a few weeks earlier. I felt as though a weight had been lifted by Giles's admission that his heart was broken over a woman, and my own unconscious mind strayed to where I might, one day, find a wife of my own.

I awoke the following morning feeling refreshed and went straight to Giles' room to check on him but was surprised to find it empty. As I turned around, I nearly bumped into O'Connell, who looked at me with the same dour expression which was ever-present on his face.

"Sir?"

"Where is he?" I demanded.

"Mr. Giles has gone out, sir. He left early this morning to paint the house and gardens from the lake."

The lake? As soon as those two words were uttered, I felt my heart stop in my chest. Without a word, I ran as fast as I could from the house towards the lake, driving myself on and pleading that I would be spared from finding what I knew was inevitable. I realized as I ran that the lady Giles had described was his sister. Who else had he dreamt of these past weeks? I must have known it, and yet I had been responsible for counselling him to seek her out at his earliest possible opportunity.

The paints, brushes, easel and canvas were beside the lake, but there was no sign of my friend. It is impossible to describe the emotion which gripped my body as I considered that he was gone. For a moment, my voice escaped me, but then I forced my lips to form his name and called it over and over again, in the certain knowledge that it would now never be answered.

That moment began the long wait I endured to find Giles again. I informed the authorities, who sent men in boats with long sticks. They plunged into the water in an attempt to persuade the body from where it was believed to be resting in the lake. O'Connell and I watched it all in silence, never speaking to one another. for my part, a fierce anger built up in my heart that this man allowed my friend to be driven to such an end.

On the tenth day of the search, Giles's body was brought to the surface. One of the men advised me not to look upon it, saying there must be pike in the lake, for the flesh of the face and hands had been completely eaten away.

"But this was in his pocket," the man went on, moving slightly to block my view of where Giles's body was being brought to the side.

I looked down at the object and found myself staring at a face preserved in oils, the smile unbroken by the ten days it spent in the water. I will not deny I felt strangely relieved to know she had been with him at the end.

I marched up to the house, spurred on by a fierce determination to dismiss O'Connell and take pleasure in the act. Whether he was responsible or not, I felt he had never allowed Giles to escape from his obsession, and I did not want his constant presence as a reminder any longer. There was no sign of him in the house when I went in, but Mrs. Rhodes was standing at one of the windows, weeping into a handkerchief.

"Have they found him, Mr. Fancroft?" she asked, and I nodded. "I'm sorry, sir. Only, I knew him and Miss Giles from birth."

"Where is O'Connell, Mrs. Rhodes?"

"O'Connell?"

"Mr. Giles's manservant who came with us from London."

Mrs. Rhodes looked at me for a moment. "I have not complained and, heaven knows, I will not complain now. But Mr. Giles and yourself brought no one from London. For these two months, I have been the only servant living under this roof."

To attempt to describe my horror at her words would be impossible. Her tone and manner proved she was in earnest and, in truth, she had no reason to lie to me.

I spent as little time as possible at Broughley Abbey, although I did oversee the burial of my friend in the Giles family vault at the nearby church of St Francis. Then, upon realizing he had died intestate, I took it upon myself to redistribute the strange collection of portraits and artifacts which filled his London house.

Only when all that was completed did I begin to fully consider the impact of Mrs. Rhodes's words and question who O'Connell had been. If Giles alone had spoken of him, I would have believed him to be nothing more than a symptom of his madness. But hadn't I also seen him with my own eyes? Spoken with him and, on that one occasion, held a conversation with him? And those parallels which he had time and again drawn between Giles and his former master? And then for them both to end their days in the same way?

Since old age has taken me, I have found myself entertaining Giles again. He has not aged as I have done, and his boyish smile and laugh are unaltered by time. We sit together in my warm living room and share stories of the days we spent together in Oxford, while the miniature of Henrietta, the only object of my friend's I took from his collection, sits on my mantel and smiles down upon us.

But there are days when I dare not even rise from my bed and open the door to my room for fear of who I might find there. A creature. Not of Mary Shelley's creation, nor man, nor boy. For these days, as death draws closer, I am haunted by the idea of O'Connell as much as Giles was captivated by him, and the very idea of seeing him there is enough to spark terror into my heart.

I set a fire to cleanse my soul
Bound to you
So I'll watch you burn
Hair from root
Blood turned cold
This is a mixture
Only nature knows
Tears from eyes
Painfully shed
For all the torment
This love has bled
Dark and twisted
Cursed are we
Heart in palm
I toast to thee
Each valve replacing
All you broke
boundless ties
Forever shook
I ingest you here,
Always mine
Now purified,
this valentine
A soul now cleansed
Ever free
As I watch you burn
away from me

Fiery Valentine
JayLynn Watkins

III

The Wig Maker

Catherine McCarthy

Ninety-eight, ninety-nine, one hundred.

Alice Webb set the gilt-handled hairbrush on the dressing table and smiled at her reflection in the looking glass. She smoothed a hand down the length of chestnut tresses that tumbled to her waist before resting it on her stomach. Her white cotton nightgown, gathered beneath the bosom, displayed the small bump to perfection. Sixteen weeks pregnant. Already past the most dangerous stage, the stage at which she had previously suffered three miscarriages.

In the warm glow of the candlelit room, her glossy locks looked more luxuriant than ever. They were her crowning glory and best feature. A tremor of excitement rippled through her torso at the thought of becoming a mother. For five years, she and Jonathan had tried for a baby, and she had begun to believe it might never happen.

The sound of the bedroom door opening jolted her back to the present. In the mirror, she watched her husband enter the room. His expression spoke volumes: a look of feigned cheer accompanied by a shifty demeanor.

She turned to face him. "Please don't tell me you're going out again."

He strode towards her and planted the lightest of kisses on her bare neck, sending a shiver of excitement down her spine. If only she could make him stay home, but her sexual power had dissipated a long time ago, scattered to the wind and replaced with an urgency to bear a child.

"I must, darling," he said. "Business, but I shan't be late."

Alice knew there was no point arguing. His late-evening escapades had become all too frequent, but whenever she tackled him about it, he would assure her she had nothing to worry about. Besides, she was so tired. She had to admit she was not the best company of late. She glanced at the clock. It was too early to retire, but she could think of nothing better to do. Her copy of Jane Austen's *Persuasion* lay in wait on the bedside table. It would have to do, since she had failed to persuade her errant husband to stay home and keep her company.

She lay on the bed and watched him dress. Double-breasted waistcoat in deep gray and matching trousers showed off his athletic frame to perfection. In the full-length mirror, he granted his appearance a nod of approval before donning his jacket and approaching the bed. As he leaned to kiss her, the heady scent of sandalwood wafted, warm and sensuous.

And then, like a genie, he was gone, leaving her to spend yet another evening alone.

It was during her morning ablutions that Alice first noticed the swelling. Small, round, painless, the lump sat at the entrance to her vagina. Her heart sank. Careful not to slip, she hobbled towards the dressing table, leaving a trail of soapy footprints in her wake.

Taking hold of the hand mirror, she hoisted a leg onto the stool and examined herself. To her alarm, there sat a small swelling, a chancre of sorts, dark pink and blistered.

Syphilis. The word slipped onto her tongue with the ease of a serpent before hissing and slithering a pathway to the pit of her stomach.

She tried to convince herself the lump must have something to do with the pregnancy, but her heart raced, and a cold sweat broke on her forehead. She would wait a while and see what, if anything, came of it. She had always been faithful to Jonathan and was certain the trust was mutual. Or was she? Could his evenings spent away from her have something to do with this? She thought back to the last time they'd had sex, certain his own body had borne no sign of disease. It had to be hormonal, or else he would have a similar mark, wouldn't he?

Over the weeks that followed, Alice monitored the vaginal chancre as closely as she did her husband's behavior. At first, she noticed little change in either, which worried her to the point of sickness. Torn between not wanting him to notice her ailment and longing to scrutinize his genitals, she could not be certain whether she was glad of his sexual disinterest in her. Of course, he kissed her regularly, albeit without passion, so she was at least reassured that he bore no sores around his mouth. Nor was he shy about undressing in front of her. In fact, he strutted naked around the bedroom like a prize-winning cock. But close up? In those most intimate body parts? She couldn't be sure, because the opportunity to look did not arise.

She was being silly, of course she was. Both of them were thrilled that at long last their marriage would be blessed with a child, and apart from the late nights, Jonathan's attitude towards her had not really changed. He remained as conceited and superior as ever, but wasn't that one of the things she had fallen for? His lack of modesty and air of dominance? Alice cast her gaze around the sitting room. She should count herself lucky. As an astute businessman, the house he provided in Grosvenor Square was palatial. Some would consider her spoiled, her every wish his command, at least when it came to material possessions.

And yet, the niggle of doubt continued to override her sense of joy.

When a month later the chancre began to heal all by itself, Alice's sense of relief knew no bounds. No more than a pale scar to remind her of its misdemeanor, the area around her vagina appeared otherwise normal apart from its heightened fullness. All part of the territory, she was assured by her sister Elizabeth, who also happened to be mother to three young children. Alice had made no mention of the chancre, of course. The snippet of information, regarding the tendency for the vulva to swell during pregnancy, had been awarded by Elizabeth voluntarily. She blushed again, remembering how embarrassed she had been by her sister's crudeness. They were so different, her and Elizabeth. Chalk and cheese, as Mother used to say.

"Look at your hair, darling!" Elizabeth had crooned when she'd visited the previous week. "So voluptuous! And it's not the only part of you that's blooming." Elizabeth had placed a hand on the swollen curve of Alice's belly and laughed. "And those breasts! I imagine Jonathan can barely keep his hands off you."

Alice had been horrified and embarrassed by what she knew to be the truth: Jonathan had not attempted to lay a finger on her for at least two months. In fact, his sexual appetite had disappeared as soon as she told him about the pregnancy. Weren't most men the same, though? Yet he hadn't been like that with the other three, just this pregnancy. She cradled her fingers and nursed the curve of her belly protectively. Of course, he was afraid intercourse might trigger another miscarriage, that was all.

Alice's reprieve from worry was short-lived. Some six weeks after the disappearance of the chancre, and in the twenty-sixth week of pregnancy, a reddish-brown rash broke out on the palms of her hands and soles of her feet. At the same time, she suffered violent headaches and bouts of weakness so severe she could barely stand.

Jonathan insisted her tiredness was due to the pregnancy and assured her there was no need to see a doctor. And the rash on her hands and feet? Hadn't he caught her barefoot in the garden just a week or so ago? It was probably some kind of allergic reaction.

But some three days later, when she gave her hair the usual hundred strokes before bed, Alice was appalled to discover that a handful of her luscious locks remained in the bristles. She took hold of the hand mirror, swiveled on the stool so the larger dressing table mirror stood behind her, and gasped. A thinning patch on the crown of her head stared back at her: wispy, pathetic, forlorn, just like her state of mind.

Alice broke down in tears.

As soon as she had discovered she was pregnant, she asked Jonathan to appoint an *accoucheur* to look after her. He declined, declaring it an unnecessary extravagance. Now, at Alice's insistence, he grudgingly agreed to a visit from their physician, a friend of the family named Doctor Hillings. Her stomach churned at the thought of an ulterior motive behind Jonathan's reluctance.

She awaited the doctor's examination in her chambers, dismayed to hear him and Jonathan speak in hushed tones in the hallway. Doctor Hillings had, on occasion, been invited to dinner, and she knew all too well that should any indiscretion on Jonathan's part be to blame for her ailments, the doctor would be unlikely to admit it.

A cursory examination of the rash on Alice's hands and feet was followed by a more thorough examination of her swollen belly. Doctor Hillings's expression grew more and more concerned with each passing moment. "Have you been aware of the baby's movement these past few days?" he asked, twiddling the corner of his carefully curled moustache.

Alice considered her answer. Since becoming overwhelmed by fatigue, the hair loss, and the rash, she had paid little attention to the flutters and swishing movement of the baby. "I–I, come to think of it, no, not for at least a week." Tears threatened, and her throat constricted. Was he implying there was a problem with the pregnancy?

He frowned, and her breath remained captive while he listened again to her stomach. "Have you suffered any loss of blood?"

"No, Doctor, none at all. It's just that I feel so unwell at times."

"Then let's not jump to conclusions," he said, examining the swollen lymph nodes in her groin. "It's possible the baby's just having a rest."

To Alice, his smile seemed disingenuous and did nothing to alleviate her concern. Before he left, he handed her a jar labelled "tincture of iodine and mercury," upon which sat a small skull-and-crossbones. My future, she thought. A prediction of what I will soon be reduced to. She failed to hear his instructions that she was to administer the tincture to the rash twice daily.

Six more days passed before she bled, by which time Alice was at her wit's end. In the twenty-seventh week of pregnancy, she was forced to endure the pain and heartbreak of delivering a stillborn son.

Her hopes of becoming a mother to a healthy child was stripped along with her crowning glory, which grew thinner and thinner by the day. Jonathan tried to pacify her, saying there was plenty of time for her to conceive another child and that the hair loss was due to stress and hormones, but she was beyond comfort.

"Why don't you visit the wig maker in town and treat yourself to something special," he said. "No expense spared."

Alice's mouth fell open at the suggestion. "A wig? Do you want people mistaking me for a whore?" She clenched her fists and gritted her teeth to prevent herself from lashing out.

Jonathan flinched at her sudden outburst. "Then perhaps a hairpiece, just until your own hair grows back." He read the indignant look on her face and sprang to his own defense. "Don't tell me they're outdated too. I see many fine ladies about town wearing them."

Alice burst into tears and fled to her room.

However, whilst on an errand in town the following Wednesday, she found herself turning down a warren of small streets and passageways until she reached Artillery Lane, where she stopped outside the wig maker's shop. The sign above the door read, *La Petite Salon, Hairdresser, Perfumier, and Wig Maker*. She looked left and right, furtive as a mouse peeping from its hole, relieved to see no one else about.

The shop window displayed a selection of what looked to Alice like severed heads carved from wood in a variety of skin tones, upon which perched a bonnet wig, a tie wig, and a scratch wig, to name but a few. Interspersed between the mannequin heads lay a variety of jeweled and beaded hair combs, decorative pins and barrettes, and exquisite bottles of scent labeled in enticing French script.

Alice peered into the glass frontage to determine whether or not the shop had customers and was dismayed to see her haunted reflection staring back: sallow skin, sunken eyes, and a pretty blue bonnet which belied the wispy, bald-patched head hidden beneath. Her spirits sank. She almost turned on her heels and fled, but just as she was about to do so, the tinkling of a bell announced the opening of the shop door.

"*Bonjour, madame.*" In the doorway stood a middle-aged woman wearing a gown of arsenic green with a lace cap tied beneath her ample chin. What struck Alice most was the woman's smile, which seemed to light up her whole face. That and the scent of amber and lily which drifted towards her through the open door.

Alice smoothed the front of her skirts and adjusted her bonnet in an attempt to regain her composure. "Good morning," she managed, in a timid voice.

"*Chère fille*, you look as though you've seen a ghost. Why don't you come inside? I've no customers at present." The aroma was intoxicating, and when the woman beckoned Alice inside, she obeyed.

Perched on a high-backed chair in front of the glass-topped counter, Alice examined the perfumes and hairpieces displayed beneath the glass. The whole arrangement was so enticing, she could not peel her eyes away. Her hands trembled in her lap, though her shoulders relaxed.

"Now then, I'm Mademoiselle Durand...and you are?"

"Alice. Alice Webb."

The woman stood behind the counter, palms pressed flat against the glass. She was older than Alice first thought, for the lines and pigmented patches on her hands spoke of centuries rather than decades. A gold ring adorned every finger, complete with colorful gemstones that caught the light. An enameled ring with a little face at the center caught her attention. She cast her gaze to the wig maker's face. Yes, the face in the center of the ring was a miniature replica of Mademoiselle Durand. Even the bonnet was the same. As she watched, the right eye of the ring winked at her encouragingly.

"*Maintenant, ma chérie,*" the wig maker said with a wide grin and a strong French accent. "Why don't you and I partake in a drop of gin, and you can tell me what's vexing you." With that, she padded her way over to the door, locked it, and flipped the sign to *Closed* before rejoining Alice at the counter.

An hour later, Alice left with a face flushed with gin and passion, and a heart full of vengeance. What incited her to spill her deepest, darkest secrets to the wig maker, she could not say, only there was something about the woman which emboldened her to bare her soul.

She emerged with no hairpiece or wig, though. In fact, Alice came away with one hair fewer than she had going in. The wig maker needed to pluck it from Alice's head, bulb intact, in order to perform her feat of alchemy.

The wig would follow in a week or two's time, once Alice had carried out a little detective work and reported her findings back to the wig maker.

Disguised in servant's apparel and a hooded cloak, Alice stood in the doorway of a coffee house, which had shut its doors for the night, and watched. Across the road, the gentleman's club was well enough lit to allow her a view of Jonathan and three other men she did not recognize. His behavior appeared benign and business-like, and as time passed, she began to think perhaps her fears were unfounded. She would not give up yet, though. Drunk on adrenaline, Alice watched for more than thirty minutes as the men sat and talked.

Soon, her back ached from standing and the night air chilled her to the bone. Her thoughts returned to the comfort of home. She blew into her hands in an attempt to warm them and stepped into the street, only to come face to face with a woman dressed in a ruby red gown tightly corseted at the waist and plunging at the neckline.

"Oh, excuse me," Alice said, startled by the encounter. "I do apologize."

The woman said nothing in return, but gave Alice a haughty look before continuing along the street with an air of superiority which belied her appearance. A whore, judging by her manner and clothing, she had to be. The absence of a shawl and bonnet suggested such, and the way her jet-black ringlets tumbled loose and abandoned from her updo confirmed Alice's suspicions.

A little shaken, Alice stepped back into the gloom of the doorway and watched as the woman paused outside the club, every now and then glancing up at the window behind which Jonathan and his peers remained deep in conversation. Alice's heart beat a hasty retreat, but she refused to pay heed. Instinct suggested she remain hidden. She lurked in the shadows, her gaze fixed on the scene. Before long, the woman crossed the street and proceeded to walk in the opposite direction, away from Alice. She would stay no longer. Once again, she emerged from her hiding place, but as she was about to take her first step, she heard a shout.

"Sophia!"

The unmistakable sound of Jonathan's voice caused her to stop in her tracks.

Alice froze as she watched Jonathan cross the street and hurry after the whore who stood, hands on hips, waiting for him to catch up. He planted a kiss on her cheek, hooked her arm in his, and the two of them strode off into the distance. Sick to the stomach, Alice could not bear to watch any longer. She had seen more than enough for one night.

Back home, she comforted herself as best she could with a hot bath and a gin and tonic. As she soaked in the tub, she summoned to mind the whore's face. Alice had not been mistaken. On her upper lip, too close to the center for it to be a fashion statement, she had faked a beauty spot—the hallmark of someone attempting to disguise the pox.

With a newfound sense of urgency, Alice repeated the surveillance the following two evenings with the same results, except on both occasions Jonathan emerged from the club a little earlier before proceeding to walk further along the street, turning down an alley, and disappearing from view. Within minutes, he was followed by the whore she had seen that first evening.

On the fourth evening, and at a safe distance, Alice followed, arriving just in time to see the swish of the woman's gown enter the basement apartment of an impressive townhouse. Jonathan must have rented the apartment for the sole purpose of betraying her. In doing so, he had inflicted the pain of syphilis and stillbirth on Alice, for she was now convinced the disease was the cause of her symptoms. Jonathan, of course, was one of the fortunate few who carried the disease yet showed no sign of it. How typical of him. She would have her revenge, though. The man had no clue as to the punishment that awaited him.

As she reached the end of the alley and was about to turn back onto the main street, she spotted a crossing sweeper. "Young man," she said, causing the boy to stop working and frown in her direction. With a finger, she summoned him over. "If you promise to meet me here one week from now at ten minutes to ten, I will reward you with a shiny shilling." From beneath her peasant's cloak, she pulled out a jeweled purse and gave the boy a glimpse of what was inside.

For a few moments he stared at her, open-mouthed. Alice's state of dress conflicted with the way she spoke and the contents of her purse. Though noble in appearance she might be, the length of her vowels suggested otherwise. His eyes lit up. "Right you are, miss," he said.

"Don't be late, mind, or you'll receive nothing."

The boy tilted his cap and nodded in agreement.

The following morning, Alice returned to the wig maker and described in detail the hairstyle of the whore.

"Revenge shall be yours, *ma chérie*," the wig maker said, grinning from one emerald earring to the other, "and sweet as strawberry soufflé."

The crossing boy failed to recognize Alice until she plucked the purse from the bosom of her ruby red gown and pulled out a shilling. "Now then," she said, smiling at the boy who stared up at her in awe. "In about ten minutes' time, a woman dressed almost exactly like me will walk down this street." From the purse, she pulled out an envelope addressed only with the word, Sophia. "You are to hand her this and explain that a gentleman asked you to deliver it with strict instructions that she open it immediately. Do you understand?"

"Yes, miss," the boy said. "But what if she can't read, miss?"

Alice gasped. Why had she not considered such a possibility? Her face flushed and a sweat broke out on her upper lip. She dabbed lightly at the place where she had drawn the fake beauty spot and considered what to do. "Then you shall read it for her. Are you able?"

"'Fraid not, miss," the boy replied with a sniff.

"Then listen carefully, and I shall tell you what the letter says so that you might pretend to read it."

The boy nodded and rubbed the snot from his nose onto his sleeve, all while his eyes circled Alice's soot-lined eyes and rouged cheeks.

Alice opened the envelope and read:

"My darling Sophia,
Something urgent has occurred, so I shall have to cancel.
Please accept my humble apologies, Jonathan."

Alice held the shilling between forefinger and thumb, twirling it round and round like a magician. "Repeat it back to me," she said, glancing towards the street corner in case the whore should arrive earlier than expected. Three times she needed to read the message before the boy was able to repeat it back. Once she was satisfied he would be able to deliver the words in a convincing manner, Alice hurried down the narrow alleyway and on towards the basement apartment.

Should she knock? Suddenly, she felt overwhelmed by the task ahead. Think, Alice, think! Reflected in the gloss-black lacquered door stood the silhouette of a woman she barely recognized: tiny waist, puffed-out shoulders, and above all else, a bountiful head of hair which tumbled free of any constraints. The Queen of Hearts in a suit of playing cards. The image rewarded Alice with a sense of empowerment. She took a deep breath and, without knocking, entered.

"In here, Sophia."

The voice which carried from a room at the far end of the corridor was unmistakably Jonathan's. The smell of whiskey and cigars grew stronger as Alice approached the room. Before entering, she took hold of a ringlet and twirled it round her finger, summoning the voice of the wig maker to mind. "*Chère fille*, his punishment is just. Now take this wig and summon the strength of Samson. All you need do is believe!"

Jonathan stood with his back to her, pouring himself a drink. "You've brought the night air with you," he said, shivering as he turned to face her. Then he headed towards the bed and sat on the edge. "Come, sit on my knee and let me warm you." His dark eyes glinted in the lamplight: lustful, rapacious.

Alice was surprised to find him not the least bit curious as to who stood in front of him. Surely he should recognize his own wife, even if she was disguised as a whore. But the wig maker had assured her the magic would work. She simply needed to believe.

Jonathan held out a hand, and Alice took it. In the other hand, he held a whiskey glass, its amber glow dancing in the firelight. She reached out and took it from him, downing its contents in one gulp. He seemed to find the gesture amusing and tickled her about the waist, causing her to shriek with discomfort.

With a forefinger, he stroked her pale throat and laughed. "You have a wicked streak about you tonight," he said. "You naughty, naughty, girl."

At his words, Alice grew bolder. He didn't recognize her false appearance, nor the change in her voice. Pushing him backwards onto the bed, she hitched her skirts towards her thighs and knelt on the floor in front of him. With the skill of a whore, she unhitched his braces and wriggled him free of his trousers, amused to discover his penis quite flaccid. Perhaps he is beginning to tire of the whore, she thought.

"Lie back," she whispered, clasping her hands behind his knees and maneuvering him onto the bed so that he lay flat. She spread his legs and kneeled between them before pushing both his arms back until he lay sprawled like Da Vinci's Vitruvian Man. Only then, once it was blatant, she was in control, did he stir.

Alice untied the lace of her bodice, freeing her breasts from their bounds. He raised his head, his gaze greedy, and made to grab her. Still, he failed to realize she was not Sophia.

"No," she whispered, leaning over and licking his ear. The wig's ringlets tickled his cheek, and he blew the hair away with whiskey-tainted breath. "Tonight, you do as I say." She leaned back, straddling his thighs, enjoying the sense of power. Then, without another word, she raised her eyes to the ceiling and howled. Guttural, animalistic, the noise seemed as though it came from somewhere else, someone else. The time had come to ignite the wig-maker's spell.

Like a lash from a whip, the tumbling ringlets uncoiled, each lock of hair six feet long and with the strength of a serpent. Strands twisted together, forming rope-like braids, which fastened each of Jonathan's limbs to the bedposts. He jerked and cried out in surprise as the braids pulled tight.

An unearthly scream rose in Alice's throat. She thought only of the pain and suffering she'd endured over the past months, the loss of her child, her health, and of the vengeance she sought. Jonathan opened his mouth to speak, and as he did so another braid whipped from her head and twisted around his neck.

Alice watched mesmerized as it spun tighter and tighter like some sinister vine, until he choked and spluttered and his eyes streamed tears. Within seconds, his face purpled, his tongue lolled, and the expression in his eyes was one of pure, unadulterated fear. The greater his fear, the more powerful her magic. She only needed to think it, and the wig obeyed. He gasped for breath as another braid reached out and snaked around his tongue, coiling like a spring before squeezing tight. Another lassoed his semi-erect penis, constricting like a black serpent and cutting off the blood supply within seconds.

All the while, Alice's exposed thighs rocked in rhythm to her heartbeat. "You stole everything from me," she said, staring into his eyes. "My health, my pride, my one opportunity of becoming a mother."

With what little breath remained, he continued to moan. White knuckles gripped the hair which tied him to the bedposts by his wrists, but his efforts were futile. Dilated pupils fixed on her, and she saw the moment of recognition in them. His whole body deflated, any hope of self-preservation instantly snuffed, and for the briefest of moments, Alice knew a twinge of remorse, and she turned her face away. He was beyond words, unable to utter her name even if he wished to, but he knew who she was.

She needed to see his suffering, to look into his eyes to determine whether or not he felt remorse, so turned to face him. Eyes locked, she sensed his heart rate slowing and knew that soon he would take his final breath. The damage could not be undone on either side. It was too late for him, just as it was for her.

Her skin was soaked with perspiration—his too—and the whites of his eyes glowed blood-red before closing for the final time.

It was over.

As his body relaxed, Alice pulled the wig from her head and gasped as the ropes of hair shrank back in surrender. She stared at her husband one last time. Pathetic. That was how he looked. No longer the strong, domineering man she had married. Purpling ligature marks scarred his neck, teary streaks glistened a silver trail from the corners of his eyes, and the skin beneath his nails turned blue.

Alice climbed from the bed, spent. The wig lay beside him, an innocuous dark mass. Its job was done, its penitence evident in its innocent demeanor. Her hands shook as she picked up the wig and threw it onto the fire. Voracious flames spat and hissed as it melted before her eyes, emitting a rotten, sulfurous odor into the air.

She laced her bodice, straightened her skirts, then took a large swig of whiskey, relishing its fiery scorch as it trickled down her throat and burned her lungs. Then, without so much as a backward glance, she picked up her purse and set off into the still night air, leaving the front door wide open.

Like the weeping willow,
Long, contorted limbs stroke the earth
Of verdant fields
Under storm-kissed silver skies
Howl like the wolves at bay
Beseech the moon above
To forgive your many decadent sins
Ones of spectral pleasure
And sinister, impalpable love
Be still, oh bleeding heart
Lest you drown the foliage
In sanguine tears of blood.

WEEPING WILLOW
AYSHEN IRFAN

IV

It Will Come

Olivia Claire Louise Newman

"My imagination, unbidden, possessed and guided me...I saw the hideous phantasm...and I wished to exchange this ghastly image of my fancy for the realities around...the dark parquet...the moonlight struggling through, and the sense I had that the glassy lake and white high Alps were beyond. I could not so easily get rid of my hideous phantom; still it haunted me."

—Mary Shelley, Introduction to Frankenstein

I often dwelled upon the mysterious inner workings of such a poetically obsessed man, who, even now, sat next to me, enthralled by the darkness of his chaotic, ceaseless mind. He was unmoving, his chin resting upon his hand, his lips pursed and his hair devilishly askew, as he fell away from me like so many times before. He was far away from me, engulfed by his inspiration—his poetic muse—and while his eyes held a deep concentration of the page before him, I loved him with a certain desperation and obsession that consumed me, for while his muse was the darkness, mine was him.

As a young girl of eighteen, I was true to who I had always been, and those fundamental, most intricate idiosyncrasies lulled me towards the heartbreaking but destined reality of loving a man who was a chaotic energy of passions. It burgeoned literary desires within me, seducing me towards the darkness where inspired writers dwelled. I had always known I was a writer, even when life hollowed me out with its simpleness and prosaic mundanities, but the other bits—the filler, the little ivy of inspiration which would grow into the cracks of my façade—had not yet developed. So meeting him—the glorious man who knew himself all too well, and, most importantly, knew what he wanted—was the catalyst I needed to flourish from the obsession my muse inspired and fill the gaps of my psyche with the intricate crawlers of emerald ivy.

We met in the most unforeseen circumstances, when he entered my father's bookshop in search of tutelage from a great writer of the time, who just so happened to be my distant and brooding father. My father, needing both the money and perhaps the company of a fellow published writer, took him under his wing with the assurance that he would share with him all he knew. But their partnership came to an end when pride and possession stoked the flames between them. The poet and I fell in love, and we decided to leave my father to his dusty books and old philosophies so we could pursue the deeper meaning behind our shared inspirations. Our imagination was hungry, and we would feed it with travel and adventure. While normally the prospect of a young man—one he held great respect for, who, most importantly, was heir to a fortune—wooing your daughter was an appealing one, my father, who had the curious habit of both loving and despising his only daughter, rejected our elopement. Under the disguise of darkness, concealed by the night-mist which filled us with unfettered excitement, we disappeared and never returned.

As I wrote, he squinted and pursed his full lips in concentration, remarking upon his face a look of consternation or amusement, and I knew he was away from me, fallen into the abyss of inspiration. Yet I could still recognize, like all the times before, the himness that characterized his features. He was sensitive, intelligent, thoughtful, a man of so much passion and feeling that thoughts came to him like a wave to consume his mind. He was often possessed by the poetic spirit, and from that thrilling possession came forth a collection of poems that enraptured anyone who read them. In our togetherness, we enjoyed sharing literature, music, and poetry. We took inspiration from the world we observed and brooded upon the desperation we felt for our toils. I knew our only recourse as writers was to write, and because we both knew and shared a love and affection for writing, an all-consuming, inspired writing overtook the majority of our time and our minds during that haunted summer.

What I had not expected was for it to overtake him entirely.

That evening, we had all been tasked with writing a ghost story. But while he dabbled in a short story he felt was going nowhere, I was possessed by a terrible story that would frighten and enrapture.

I sat before the window, writing fervently and watching as the ghostly mist blanketed the lake before me and danced like wispy faeries beneath the moonlight, stirring in me all the darkness and monstrous desires that were eager to escape. I wrote a story so novel and horrifying that its lines prickled my skin and quickened the beatings of my heart. And all the while, my beloved sat across the room, entranced by his own imagination.

My stepsister sat before the grand piano in the corner of the drawing room and played a dreary but atmospheric sonata. Our friends lounged on the sofa, looking both stressed and bored, but I sat at the desk and scribbled as fast as my hand would allow, cursing the page with the horrors of my imagination. The room was hot and stifling, and the open windows let in a little breeze from the lake, so the oppression we felt was sticky in the air. I could tell my dear man was thinking deeply across the room, his eyebrows furrowed, his eyes closed, the paper before him slanted to accommodate his hand, so his disappearing before my eyes did not come as a shock, but rather an eventuality we all could expect from a man so deeply embroiled in his own macabre fascinations.

As a nice breeze blew in off the lake, we were all startled by a precipitous eruption of energy.

"My god!" my poet shouted, leaping from his chair and staring at me in horror. His eyes were manic, his hair wild, his face frighteningly pale. All I could tell in that instant was the severity of the fright, not why nor how, but that it filled his bones so completely, he shook with its immensity. And then he wailed, threw his hands to his head, and ran out of the room, leaving us all staring after him in disbelief.

I looked to my friends to see George, our host, shake his head and chuckle, as if dismissing his behavior as the usual antics of a writer obsessed. George was known for his own outbursts of emotion, so he must have suspected my beloved's behavior was normal for a poet. In contrast, my other friend William, looked deeply concerned and followed him from the room. My sister had stopped her playing and sat on the piano bench, her face shrouded in fear. She was known for her delicate sensibilities, so any outburst was bound to affright her as well. When she saw my own confusion, she rushed to me and hugged me tightly, whimpering under her breath to keep up appearances in front of George. He already regarded her with an apathetic indifference that both vexed and excited her, so she was loath to allow him to see her more childish tendencies.

"What do you think that was all about?" she whispered to me.

"I truly have no idea. But you know him—he is often so caught up in his poetic ideas. He likely had to run out to expel the ghastly visages of his imagination. Don't worry." I stroked her head so she might feel a little comfort. I was her elder by only a year, and although she irritated me quite often with her ever-presence, I still cared for her like a friend and did not wish her unwell. My stepsister had, at her behest, accompanied my beloved and me on our elopement several years prior, and this summer, she had orchestrated our staying in Geneva with George, a rather notorious poet—and a man whom she had only just met—by enticing him with my and my husband's reputation and a potential acquaintanceship. He had accepted, and we followed him here to his rented estate overlooking the lake, where we spent the summer in a blossoming haze of reading, writing, and sailing. My husband and George got on capitally from the start, developing a close friendship over their mutual obsession of poetry and an indulgence of the mind through languid observation, romantic ponderings, and the use of whatever substance would produce the torrent of inspiration required by a poet obsessed. Their penchant for getting into all things luxurious and indulgent was what knitted them together in a friendship profound, and it was often that their antics produced a great show for the rest of us.

Therefore, the way George acted following his friend's outburst was not unordinary, nor did it irritate me. His lack of concern stemmed from their knowing each other well. But I knew my beloved better than anyone, and his outburst was far from ordinary. Therefore, while I comforted my sister, I sat with a deep concern that did not go away until William reappeared. He nodded to me with a reassuring smile, and I let out a breath I had not realized was trapped within me.

"What possessed him?" my sister asked upon William's return. She asked with both a curiosity and a certain reluctance to know the answer.

"A ghostly vision, it seems," William replied, taking his seat in a chair opposite the sofa. I trusted William completely. He was a respected doctor with a calm countenance that provided others an ease that made him pleasant to be around. William was deliberate, gentle, and kind, and I admired him immensely. His look of unconcern eased me now as he crossed one leg over the other knee and clasped his hands in his lap. He portrayed a subtle confidence, but I knew him well from our time together that summer, and he was both shy and unassured, a stark contrast to his friend George across the room. "He saw something quite curious and was in a deep haze when I found him. He's lying down in his room now."

"See?" I said to my sister. "His thoughts got the better of him. No need to worry."

"A poet obsessed is a poet consumed," George mused in his usual theatrical style, characterized by a lifting of the eyebrows and a devilish glint in his eye. Standing, he lifted the book in his hands and declared, "The almighty imagination has vanquished our dear poetic friend! Beware! The imagination is powerful because it is fearless!" Jumping onto the sofa, which made my sister shriek, he looked around wild-eyed, as if possessed. "We all must allow the poetic imagination to consume us! A sound poet is a mighty god! But a poet obsessed is God himself!"

"Oh, you're positively crazy!" my sister shrieked.

George jumped off the sofa towards her and growled like a beast, making my sister squeal and giggle as he grabbed her up and fell backwards with her onto the cushions. They lay there together giggling and flirting as William looked on with a certain indifference, and I, seeing my sister was well out of her fright, left the room in search of my poet.

The halls were eerie and dark, lit only by candles along the walls that slanted shadows along the floor, allowing my imagination to implant monstrosities into every dark crevice. The oppressive heat from the drawing room diminished as I walked, and a damp chill overtook my senses, spreading an illusory haunting through my bones. My footsteps were the only sound as I walked, but I listened keenly for any haunting sound. Our ghostly stories had not just infected my poet, it seemed, but had also allowed my imagination to run wild, and I quickened my pace so as not to linger in the enfolding darkness.

As I entered the foyer, I was glad to see the housekeeper, Sara, who was busy sweeping the entryway and muttering under her breath. When I greeted her, she looked up, startled, but smiled when she saw me. "Miss, are you looking for your husband? I am afraid he just ran out the door in the most alarming of manners. He looked like he had seen a ghost."

My mouth went dry. "Did he say anything? He was not feeling like himself earlier in the drawing room, and William said he had taken him up to bed."

"No, miss. But he looked odd indeed. Would you like me to fetch the doctor for him?"

"No, no. I will go myself. Thank you."

When I entered the night air, I grew resolved and straightened my spine. For in the world, there was no monster but man, and my man, whom I saw walking possessed towards the lake, was the only man of my concern, and I knew his monsters like my own. I quickened after him, calling his name. He paused his stride and turned back. When I looked upon his face, a ghostly chill possessed me, and I saw with my own eyes the emptiness within the beautiful depths of his soul. I did not recognize the blankness in his stare, nor the thin, determined line of his mouth. It was as if he was not himself, lost in the encroaching mist, sunken into the depths of his mind.

I said, "What is the matter? Tell me—I must know."

His reply made me fall into his arms. He held me tightly against him, and I felt his warmth and heard his heartbeat, and I knew he was him—the poet by whom I was consumed. "I saw myself there upon the dock, and I watched him from behind the glass. He looked at me forlorn—his face betrayed his desires. I thought I could join my doppelgänger in his grave-cold melancholy, but when I came out under the moon, he had vanished."

I knew his meaning well, having heard it many times in our time together, but I resisted the tears which rose to my eyes and looked up into his. There was no way for me to ease his burden, to take away the all-consuming obsession that tore at his mind and caused many a sleepless night. The fright which had overcome him was a deadly possession that would threaten his sanity, and the pain I saw in his eyes, which were silvered in the moonlight, granted me the solemnity to take his hand and lead him into the house, up the stairs and into our room, where I ran my hand through his hair until he fell asleep. But I could not quiet the voice in my head urging me to take him away from this place, that something was truly wrong inside of him, and the himness I had fallen in love with was leaching out of him, drawn out by the haunting moon and corrupted by fear.

It was not long after he had fallen asleep, and I had closed my eyes to the silvery haze, that he stirred, and like a man possessed, he rose to a sitting position and stared at the window.

Growing still, I choked out a hushed cry, "What the—?"

But he made no response, just stared with eyes trained on the open window, which let in the familiar sounds of nighttime crickets and the peaceful stirring of the lake. Before I could let out a breath of calm, he stood and advanced to the window. Following, I seized his arm to direct him back to bed—I knew trying to wake a somnambulist was rather dangerous—but something beyond the glass caught my eye, and I grew still. There was an apparition on the dock, where he said he had seen someone earlier. The man stood with a familiar air, a proud countenance that also held a slumped sadness, a dejectedness I was all too aware of in my own man, and I watched the apparition with a desperate fear that clutched at my stomach and quickened the beatings of my heart. His face was upturned towards where we stood behind the glass, and his eyes reflected the moon's glow like two iridescent owl eyes. His features were familiar, much like the man standing next to me, and I knew it was the doppelgänger my husband had seen earlier. I would have stayed at the window to investigate had my beloved not started murmuring the enchantments of a madman and walking with purpose towards the bedroom door.

I delayed only to grab my night coat, then rushed to follow his sleeping form. In the foyer, I met William, who was calling my husband's name as he, possessed by sleep, exited the front door.

"He is gone from me," I said to the doctor. He nodded in reply, and we both followed our poet out the door and into the night. The wind had picked up, as if it too were possessed, and with hair obscuring my view, I pressed across the cool grass.

"What is that?" I heard William call. I looked up to see the apparition ahead on the dock, this time with his head turned towards the water. Closer, it was easier to see that his features were less concrete than I had imagined, and he perhaps floated with the breeze, translucent and pale, as if he were trapped in a singular moonbeam.

My sleepwalker must have seen him too, for his pace quickened, and with an anxious exclamation, I followed, pressing my hair out of my face. I meant to catch him, to grab his arm and steer him back to the house, but William caught up to him first and grabbed both shoulders from behind. He pulled him into a tight embrace, whispering words of calm, as if to subdue the monster that possessed my dear poet.

"Careful not to wake him." My voice trembled.

Looking back at the dock, the apparition had once again vanished, but the night spirit still held firm to the somnambulating poet.

Once inside, William took him up to our room to put him back to bed as my sister stopped me in the hallway. "I saw the most peculiar thing. It was your dear husband standing on the dock a few moments ago. He looked likely to disappear into the water—the look on his face was pale and haunted. Is he all right?"

Instead of explanation, I nodded and followed her back to the drawing room, where our host George was seated on the sofa reading aloud to himself. It was a familiar passage, one of the ghost stories we had read earlier in the evening, and upon hearing it, my sister shook her head in protest.

"Please, no. I cannot take another fright this evening."

"Ah, but what is life without fear? Your sensibilities give you away. You must not be conquered by fear, but harness it for your own pleasure," George said. "Your sister metamorphoses courage from fear. Isn't that right?" He turned to me, but when I did not answer, he continued. "Her pedigree has prepared her for the potent emotions of a writer, and so she is crippled by neither ghost nor monster, but instead uses her self-possession not to shriek in fear, but to observe that which lurks in the night and that which romanticizes itself in her mind. You could stand to learn from her, darling." His sarcastic tone made my sister frown and turn away, no doubt embarrassed by his words.

I did not answer, for he was wrong in saying I had courage. My fear was as potent as a fire raging unfettered within me, but I did not want to admit it. My sister spiraling into hysterics at my poet's odd behavior was the last thing I wanted, and George laughing off any concern I had for my husband, treating it as the normal imagination-possessed wanderings of a poet obsessed, would surely irritate me. My man was sensitive, and with that sensitivity came emotions that were like electricity within him that ignited his passions to life. But that sensitivity had never before manifested as a spiritual possession, where I could not recognize his haunted gaze. It was William and I alone who could help him, who could recognize the seriousness of this grave-like chill spreading over all of us. Leaving them both out of the imminent darkness, neither discussing it nor indulging my horrid imagination, would help the issue at hand. Rather than let George in on my fear, I murmured an excuse and left the room.

In the darkened hallway, I once again met William, who looked at me with a grave expression that sparked the foreboding within me I was loath to indulge.

"When we entered the bedroom, he awoke from his stupor. He was rather agitated, and when I placed him back into bed, his nerves overtook him. He shook, and his voice trembled as he inquired what had happened, having no recollection of the night's events."

"What is the prognosis? I have seen him in stupors, seen him afraid and sleepwalking, but never have I not recognized him. It felt as if the man I know was gone, and in his place an imposter. And what was that apparition outside? You saw it. It was as though his spirit stood on that dock, like his body meant to reconnect with it."

"It could be stress, lack of sleep. It could be any number of things. Perhaps an evil has taken root in his mind and is burning out all that we know of him. I've always been a skeptic about these things—being a man of science—but I cannot deny what I saw outside. I fear for your husband."

At his words, I sunk against the wall, and the doctor placed his hand on my shoulder in a gesture of comfort. I knew William held a deep tenderness for me, and I could tell by the sad way he always looked at me that he knew I did not return his affections. And while I often did not reciprocate his friendly gestures, something within me sought the comfort of his arms, and there against him, I allowed myself to shake with the fear and sadness I felt for my husband.

But the comfort did not last long, for as I pulled away, brushing the tears from my face, we were startled by a shattering scream that carried through the hallway. I almost collapsed as my heart beat with a force that knocked the breath from me.

As the scream carried through the house, harrowing in its intensity, I heard my sister scream too, followed by George's angered yell. "Oh, shut it!"

William and I rushed to my bedroom, where we saw the most horrifying of sights. My poet—my beloved husband—was thrashing in bed, as if trying to fend off an invisible attacker, and was screaming with such raw emotion that it set my ears on fire and brought tears to my eyes. We rushed to grab him, to subdue him, to wake him from his terrible nightmare, but his screaming only progressed, getting louder and more tortured as the seconds passed. I could not hold him down, as his thrashing was too strong, and I fell off the bed and onto the floor. George entered then, his face finally conveying a severe look of concern, and he too came over to try to wake my husband, holding him down to prevent injury.

"What the devil has gotten into him! Good God!" George bellowed, struggling with my husband's right arm. William was atop the bed, trying to hold his shoulders down, but my husband convulsed like a man possessed. I tried to stand, but my fear was like a weight on my chest, and I just wept.

"Douse him in water—quick!" William called. I was startled at the command of his voice and rushed to the water basin, scooped up the bowl, and flung its contents on my husband. It had the intended effect, for my husband's screams immediately hushed, and his eyes opened with a savagery I had never before seen in my gentle poet.

"What the—?" He was angry and confused, and struggled under the weight of his two friends. "Get off of me!"

They both let go, and my husband sat up, annoyed, breathing heavily. Sweat dripped from his brow, his face a shade of pale that gave him a sickly countenance, his wet nightshirt clinging to his body.

"You were having a terrible nightmare," I said. "You were screaming and thrashing about."

"Death had come for me." His voice was thick with emotion, raw from the screams, and carried a desperation that caught in his throat. His eyes were a hollow reflection of the moon beyond the pane. "I felt the iciness of his grip—there was no escaping his decaying flesh, skeletal fingers, ghastly eyes—" He rubbed his forehead, as if trying to dispel the afterimage of his nightmare.

"You're okay now—perfectly safe," William said, gently patting his shoulder. "Perhaps some laudanum to put you to sleep?"

My husband only nodded, and after drying off, returned to bed, where I sat beside him as William gave him the sleep aid. When everyone but I had left, I took his hand and stroked his pale, sun-freckled skin.

"I'm a wretched soul, aren't I?" he asked, casting his emerald gaze downward with a shadow of sadness that expelled the relief I felt after finding him returned to me. "How can I condemn you to this existence of darkness and not call myself a monster? You are as Eve, and I your deceiver. I cannot even subject you to the horrors of my imagination. They are visceral, unholy, terrifying. You are best left out of this darkness."

I almost smiled at his overly dramatic interpretation, but instead I shook my head with a whole-hearted vehemence. "No, you did not deceive me. I am not fearful of the darkness—I want to join you in its cold embrace. It was my own thirst for knowledge that led me to you, and I walked into your destiny with open eyes."

"My destiny has led to madness." His resigned countenance only further broke my heart, and I pulled him to me, wiped the sweat from his brow, and kissed him tenderly. "I am a man stitched together by death-like darkness, thrown together haphazardly, and awoken anew to a strange and unfamiliar world. All I want is to discover what lies beneath..." He trailed off, his eyes captured by something outside.

"You are stressed, overcome with emotion, exhausted—that is all. With some sleep, you will feel yourself again. Come." I adjusted so he was lying in my arms. "Sleep now, my dear. Stay with me. I will keep you safe from whatever unknown lurks in your mind."

Sometime in the darkness, the house was once again rocked by a terrified shriek. This time, it was my sister whose cries echoed through the walls. My husband, in his drugged slumber, did not stir as I rushed from the room, following the sound of the screams.

In the hallway, I met with Sara and her state put me into a terrible shock. She had a ghastly cut on her forehead, and blood streamed profusely down her face. She was distraught, the look in her eyes betraying her usual reservedness, and I called desperately for William as she began to sway, her skin a pale sickliness that looked stark in contrast to her black nightdress. I was without help, alone in the hallway, only my sister's screams filling the chilly air. I once again called for William as Sara slumped against me, her face falling into my shoulder, smearing the crimson blood on my white gown. This time William appeared, rubbing the sleep from his eyes, and startled when he saw the state of us two women.

His strangled question came as a surprise, and the fear almost sent me and Sara both to the ground.

"Did you see the man?"

When I did not answer, William helped me by taking the poor girl from my arms and carrying her down to the kitchen to be looked after, and I followed my sister's cries down the hall.

In my sister's room, I saw her in bed beneath the blankets, staring with horror at the window. When she saw me, her shrieks became less vehement, resorting to moans and whimpers.

"What is the matter?"

"There—" she broke off, struggling to lift her finger towards the window. "There was a man climbing into my window." The tears flowed down her face in hysterics, and I moved over to the window to investigate. The window was half open, and outside the pale moon reflected off the lake, but otherwise, the night was empty and still.

"What happened to Sara?" I asked.

"What? I do not understand you."

I joined my sister in bed. "Everything is okay. There is no man; I checked. You are safe. No one can climb through the window on the second floor."

Through her tears she looked at me angrily. "But I saw him. He had a nasty smile, terrible eyes, evil eyes, so cold. At first, I thought it was your husband, but when I saw his eyes, his terrible smile…" She hiccupped and wiped her nose on the sleeve of her nightgown. It was then she noticed the blood on my own gown. "What on Earth?" She sat up. "What's happened? Are you hurt?"

I looked down and saw the blood that coated my arm, a sickly nausea swelling in my throat at the sight.

"No, it is Sara's. She had a cut on her forehead. That is why I asked you about her. I thought your screaming had something to do with her."

My sister shook her head, her confusion and worry growing. "What is happening this evening? It seems everything has gone so terribly strange and frightful since reading that ghost story."

I shrugged, thinking of a reply to subdue her worries, but William entered, blood smeared down his face. "George will not wake."

In George's room, the three of us stood over where he lay in bed, the candles casting slanted shadows on the walls, lighting his face with a warm glow that emphasized the terrible pallor of his complexion. It was quite frightening to see his face void of the usual spark of character, the twinkle of delight that always marked his handsome features. He looked dead. The only relief was the small rise and fall of his chest.

My sister held his hand tightly and stroked his arm, whispering little urgencies.

"What do you think has happened?"

"Perhaps he has taken too much laudanum," William said. "I was not here to help administer the correct amount. If he has taken too much, I fear he may not wake."

My sister buried her face in George's chest.

"And Sara?" I asked.

"I left her with Roger, but she was still unconscious when I left her."

"Why weren't you here when he was taking it? You are his doctor!" my sister cried.

A shadow of guilt passed over the doctor's face, and he looked afraid of revealing something. I took his arm and pulled him into the hall, shutting the bedroom door behind me, fearful my stepsister's hysterics would send us all spiraling into madness.

"Tell me."

He sighed, running his hand through his hair. The blood smear on his face was clearly not his, but it sent a jolt of concern through me anyway. "I saw a man in the house. I fear that may be who attacked Sara. As George retired, I said I would join him shortly to help administer his sleeping draught as I do every night. I wanted to look out at the lake again and finish my drink. Through the open window, I saw a flash of movement, but before I could ascertain what it was, there came footsteps in the hall behind me, going in the direction of the kitchen. I first thought it was Roger, but they returned, and then returned again, as if pacing the short length of hallway by the drawing room door. Looking out, I saw a figure in the foyer as he ascended the stairs. I only saw his back, but I pursued him, expecting to see Roger, or perhaps your husband, at the top of the stairs. There was no one. It was then that Roger came behind me from the kitchen and inquired about his own retiring. I told him to go on, that I would assure the windows were shut and the doors locked. But as I was making the rounds, I heard the footsteps again, this time directly above me, perhaps coming from the hallway. So, once I had blown out the last candle downstairs, I went upstairs to see who was roaming the halls."

"Who was it?"

"It was your sister. At first, I thought she was sleepwalking, but she spoke to me coherently. When I asked why she was roaming the halls, she admitted she had just come from George's room. She said she wanted to spend some time with him, perhaps read to him, but he dismissed her without allowing her inside, and she decided to walk a bit before retiring. I saw her safely to her room, then went to George's and knocked but heard no response. I figured he must have been asleep, or perhaps enwrapped in his imagination—you know how he is—how he cannot be disturbed—so I left and retired to my own room. I was asleep some time before I was awoken by you calling me—you know the rest."

I slumped against the wall, my skin prickling with fear. There was something happening here, something I did not think any of us could explain. Either we were all mad, clutched by the same darkness that wrapped itself around my husband, or, most harrowingly, there was a man in the house.

"My suspicion was confirmed when I opened the door to find you and Sara in the hallway. I thought perhaps he had attacked her. But you did not see anything?"

I shook my head. "I was awoken by my sister's cries and found Sara in the hallway, bloodied and dismayed. I did not know what to think—still do not. What are we to do? Search the whole house for this mysterious figure? He was last seen by my sister, climbing into her bedroom window. I found no sign of him. Maybe he was not climbing in but climbing out. Perhaps we should shut and lock all the windows, search the house, then call it a night."

"Close the windows in this heat?" the doctor complained. "It is sweltering even with the nice breeze off the lake."

"Are we to let him back in if he has indeed left? Let us be methodical. We must search the house. I will close the windows upstairs; you close them downstairs—and perhaps see if Sara is awake too."

As we parted, I saw the first look of irritation on his face that I had ever seen on the good doctor. He was always so reserved, constrained, repressed, and now, at the prospect of shutting the windows so we could all have a bit of peace of mind, his display of emotion was surprising.

I did not allow it much thought as I went from room to room, shutting the windows. I locked my sister's, checking again that no one was in the room, and went into George's room to shut his.

But my sister had already beaten me to it. "I saw something outside. I was scared," she explained.

"We are shutting all the windows in the house and searching to make sure there is no one about. You should stay here with George."

"You really should change your gown, or perhaps throw on your overcoat. You are walking amongst men, sister, and you look a mess."

She was back to her usual uppity self, so I let her criticism reassure me rather than annoy.

"What are you doing in my room? Why are you covered in blood?"

"George!"

He was sitting up in bed, looking no worse for wear, simply groggy after having woken. His dark hair was askew, and he rubbed at his eyes, but the pallor of his skin had diminished, the warmth in his cheeks returned.

My sister ran over and hugged him, and I saw the look of bewilderment on his face as he acquiesced and returned her affection. "What is going on?" he asked.

"Oh—a terrible, terrible thing, George. First, I saw a man in my window, a terrible, ghastly man, and then you would not wake. Even the housekeeper seems to have been terribly injured—that's her blood on my sister's sleeve—please excuse her untidiness."

George gave me a look that spoke of complete confusion, but seeing he was all right, I left to continue my search of the house.

I ran into a rather haggard and bewildered William in the hallway. "The downstairs is clear. Sara is awake. She did not see what happened, just felt a terrible pain in her head and then was bleeding so profusely—she must have hit her head on the candle sconce. She is all right, though. I have bandaged her up and Roger is taking her to bed."

"George is awake too."

His eyebrows lifted in surprised relief. "That is so good to hear. I must go check on him. But rest easy. The house is clear, the windows are closed, and everything seems in order."

Despite my relief, I could not help but still feel frightened and terribly worried for my dear husband, who still slumbered in our bed. His madness was palpable, a strange possession that crippled him and stole his mind away from us. I only hoped he too would be well when he awoke.

Before climbing into bed with my husband, who beckoned me with sleepy murmurs of affection, I changed my gown and washed the blood from my skin.

In bed, I said, "Good night, dear. Everything is all right."

He smiled sleepily.

It was near dawn when I felt the emptiness, and the cold chill that penetrated my bedclothes. The sticky, hot summer air had turned into a dewy dawn, and the breeze from off the lake made my bare skin goosebump. I knew at once, without having to open my eyes, that something was wrong. I most assuredly forgot to shut our bedroom window.

My poet was no longer in bed, and I felt a sick sense of dread spreading like a disease through my bones.

I sat up and saw the room empty. I felt a certain devastation, as if he were already lost to me. Moving towards the window, I saw a figure on the dock. The impending sunrise was visible on the horizon and this time, the figure was the man who left my bed, for his bedclothes, rumpled and skewed, shone like a white beacon in the night. I tried to call out, but my voice caught in my throat. I no longer felt like myself, as if my mind were disconnected from my body, and all that I observed was unfamiliar, unprocessed by my exhaustion-riddled faculties. I watched with a strange, vague confusion as my husband simply stood there on the dock, watching the water.

I did not move—I could not, so I stayed there, silent, framed by the casement in a portrait of torment. Keeping my eye on him was my only relief from the rising devastation within me. My bare feet were rooted to the floor, my eyes ceaseless in their determination to keep hold of my poet, to never let him disappear from my gaze. I could not fail in my task to protect him from himself—could not bear the guilt that was penetrating my soul.

Everything was still, only the breeze deceiving the silence of the world.

Then, in a flash of movement, he disappeared into the lake.

I have swallowed your
love letters in the
name of forever.
Sometimes, love is violent.
It chokes you
While caressing
Your face.
It burns you
While peppering
Kisses on
Your skin.
It makes you
Wild,
Blind
And
Afraid.
Unwittingly,
You start cultivating a monster.

V

The Fruits of Wartime

Rebecca Jones-Howe

The Porter Estate was once full of life, but no longer.

At night, Jacqueline walked in bare feet. She slipped out of the housekeeper's room, her toes curled over the cold hallway floor. It might have been wrong, but she delighted in digging through the places where the late Philip Porter was rumored to store secret piles of cash. He'd been a gambler all his life and his death left his wife, Cecelia, nearly penniless.

The rooms of the mansion echoed now, but the cash flowed for Jacqueline on a good night.

She ventured into the library and held a candle to the shelves. She pulled books out, one by one, cracking the spines, shaking the bindings. An odd bill slid from between the pages.

She stalked back to her room with a smile, hiding her windfall beneath the loose floorboard in her closet.

The future seemed so uncertain since the war's disruption. Men returned disfigured and often Cecelia complained about how women were losing their proper place in society, but Jacqueline didn't mind.

She returned to her bed, reaching beneath her mattress for the metal toffee hammer that kept her inspired in the worst of times.

Cecelia poked her fork into the crepe Jacqueline made. "Philip didn't even eat this," she said. "Why didn't he eat it, dear?"

Jacqueline swallowed, taking the plate away. "Perhaps he wasn't hungry, ma'am."

Cecelia shook her head. "Nothing feels right. Nothing is ever right. I hardly see Philip, and Peter never comes by anymore. He used to play the piano so beautifully. It always used to cheer me up."

"I know, ma'am." Jacqueline fought the urge to admit the truth about Peter, the firstborn Porter son. Cecelia often forgot he was one of the first to valiantly serve in the war, only for news of his death to return just a month later. "Maybe a nap would help, ma'am? Or we could play a game of chess?"

Cecelia shook her head again, this time more vigorously.

Jacqueline observed as the woman glanced about the room, at the unpolished silver that always looked blemished and green, much like the windows. Vines crawled over what little light managed to seep in through the stained glass. Cecelia never commented on the house's slow descent into desolation. She didn't notice the dust on the vases or the lack of staff. She didn't even notice the pair of trousers that Jacqueline had purchased the last time she went into the city.

The trousers allowed for more movement, more freedom. Women often wore them while bicycling, but Jacqueline wore them while doing all her household tasks. She'd even stopped wearing her corset. Without it, she could take deeper breaths, giving her more energy to pry into Cecelia's memories.

"I just wish Peter would come," Cecilia sighed.

Jacqueline pulled up a seat. "You often speak of Philip and Peter, but what about Matthew?"

Cecelia scoffed and pounded the table. "That boy is dead to me! He's gone! He's nothing!"

"That's not true," Jacqueline pressed. "I've heard things. The former servants told me things, ma'am."

All Jacqueline knew of Matthew was that he was the younger son who never appeared at the mansion, either in person or in photos. She'd only heard of him through passing rumors, none of which spoke in his favor. "Some of the servants told me that he was married."

"Oh, he is!" Cecelia spat. "Some Vaudeville strumpet, her face covered in rouge and lipstick. He sent me a photo once, her posing on stage like some common whore on the street." Cecelia struggled to get out of her chair.

Jacqueline moved to help.

"Never speak of that man again!" She pried her arm out of Jacqueline's hold.

"I'm sorry, ma'am. I won't do it again."

Jacqueline was only ever good at making toast or sandwiches. She often tried to replicate some of Cecelia's favorite meals, only to struggle and curse herself for failing at womanly chores. She could clean well, but she was much better at meddling, and sometimes, when the occasion was right, protesting.

She sliced a chunk of meat from an overcooked chicken when she heard a car pull up in the gravel driveway outside. She peered through the window at the black vehicle crawling into view. She hesitated, throwing out the entire chicken before answering the knock.

The man who stood at the door gawked at Jacqueline's trousers. "She's got a gardener answering the door now?"

"I'm not the gardener," Jacqueline said. "I-I'm the housekeeper."

The man narrowed his gaze. "Forgive me, but you don't look at all like a housekeeper."

"I-I know," she said, tightening her grasp around the doorknob. She shifted under the new scrutiny. She'd never had a man see her in trousers before. "We've been rather short-staffed."

He pushed past her into the hall. "She wrote to me a while back," he said, surveying the dimmed gas lamps and the dusty vases. "I'm sure she thought she was writing to Peter, but that alone was a sign things weren't going well here."

Jacqueline shut the door and turned. The guest had dark eyes and brown hair, his chin unshaven. The growing stubble cast a shadow over his jaw. He set his suitcase down and Jacqueline glanced at his left hand. No ring.

"Are you Matthew?" she asked, her throat going tight.

He nodded.

"Your mother hasn't been herself since the deaths," Jacqueline explained. "She reads the paper, but often forgets about the war."

He expressed no concern for Cecelia, ducking instead toward the library. The sun slipped through the stained-glass windows, but the mahogany shelves made the room seem darker than it actually was.

"Do you want me to call her?" Jacqueline asked.

"Not yet," he said, picking a frame with Peter's photo off the mantle. He stared for a while, then set it down so hard, the other frames shook.

"You didn't even attend the funerals," Jacqueline remarked.

"I'm sure my mother appreciated that." He turned to her, cocking a smile.

"Didn't you want to pay your respects?"

"Neither of them ever paid me much respect," he said, looking at her for too long, enough to make her shift again. Then he turned his gaze toward the shelf she'd searched the night before.

"I don't know much about you, sir. People gossip but—"

"You're quite forward for a servant," he said. "You're asking questions that you probably shouldn't. Why would she keep you, out of everyone else?"

Jacqueline made a fist over the shelf, straightening her spine as though she still wore a corset. "I was the last-hired maid. In the end, I was the only one she could afford to keep."

He pushed into her personal space, his gaze settling over the tapered leg of her trousers, where the fabric clung to her ankles. "So, you do all the cooking and cleaning?"

"I try." Jacqueline tried to stand firm. "I try to make things seem as normal as possible. She barely has enough money to keep the gas running."

He smirked again, nodding at his suitcase in the hall. "Well, if you're a half-decent maid, then I suppose I can trust you to take my things to a vacant room upstairs?"

His stare hardened her, but it still made her chest flare inside. She drew a breath, a bigger one than a corset would allow.

"I can do that for you, sir," she said.

His smile quickly faded. "Matthew," he said. "You asked for my name. Go ahead and use it."

"Yes, sir—sorry, Matthew," she said, turning, hurrying to oblige.

Matthew's old room faced the now overgrown rear garden. She pushed the burgundy curtains open and the room seemed to moan beneath the light, the deep reds and mauves swelling like an open wound.

She turned back to the suitcase, fondling the latches.

It was what servants did. They pried.

But then the piano started. The melody worked through the empty mansion like birdsong. It hypnotized Jacqueline for a moment as she fingered the latches. Then Cecelia's door creaked open down the hall. She hobbled, one hand on her cane and the other knocking the paintings, tilting them askew as she rushed to follow the sound.

"Peter?" she called. "Peter, is that you?"

Jacqueline left the suitcase and followed.

"Hello, mother," Matthew said.

His voice felt heavy. It echoed against the walls of the servant's corridor, where Jacqueline spied.

"Why are you here?" Cecelia demanded. "What have you come for?"

"I wanted to help," he said, getting up from the bench.

"What could you possibly do to help?"

"I've brought money. A bit of money." Matthew's voice slipped an octave, his tone submissive and meek. Still, he took a step toward her. Even though he stood taller, he came to her with his shoulders sloped and his head hung.

"And where is she?" Cecelia asked.

"She's gone, mother."

"And I suppose this money you have must have been hers?"

"We settled, mother." He fumbled with his pocket watch before pushing his hands into his pockets. "It was amicable."

Cecelia sighed. "Of all the men that could return to this house, it had to be you, bringing your sin and shame with you."

"I want to help, Mother."

"What good can you do here?"

"I want to prove myself! Please, give me another chance."

She scoffed, taking a seat on her chair. "Send for the maid. Tell her I'd like some tea."

Matthew nodded slowly, then lifted his head, his pained gaze making contact with Jacqueline's prying eyes. A glint slipped over his expression. Then his lip curled. Gentle. Subtle.

It made her flush.

His footsteps moved about the house, heavy and frantic as the day wore on. Jacqueline wasn't used to the sound of a man stalking the halls, either above her or below. He fussed about the rooms. He moved things. Rustled things. She was certain now that he'd only come for the money, and she smiled to herself whenever he stole into a hiding place she'd already raided.

For dinner, she prepared two servings of fillet cod with lemon and garlic. She lit a fire and positioned the candlesticks. But when it came time to bring the plates to the table, the dining room stood vacant. Jacqueline found Cecelia still sitting in the parlor. She placed her hand over Cecelia's shoulder, startling her from her daze.

"I've made you some dinner," she tried, but the old woman sulked over her embroidery.

"I refuse to eat with that boy."

"Can I at least bring your dinner here?" she asked.

"No. I'm afraid I've already lost my appetite."

"There's no need to keep up appearances simply because he's here," Jacqueline said. "I'm sure he'll leave just as quickly as he came."

Cecelia's expression shifted when she finally took notice of Jacqueline's trousers. "He's fond of women of ill repute, you know. The war is over. It's about time you found your place again."

Jacqueline swallowed. "Ma'am, I'm sorry, but I don't imagine things will simply go back the way they were."

"They will," Cecelia insisted. "And don't think I'll let you go back to those silly meetings in town when they do. I need you here."

The footsteps moved frantically upstairs. Jacqueline made a fist, fighting to maintain composure.

"It's foolish," Cecelia said. "You're being foolish thinking you'll ever have the same rights as a man."

Jacqueline swallowed. "Yes, ma'am."

Cecelia pressed the needle into the fabric, making little red Xs in a long line that looked like stitches struggling to hold reality.

Jacqueline went to clear the dining room after putting Cecelia to bed, only to find Matthew sitting at the table's head, his plate half-finished. She caught herself, swallowing as her heart throbbed against the heat of the fire. Matthew nodded at the other plate of food.

"Sit and eat," he said.

The silver fork was tarnished, but she pulled out a seat and pressed the tines into the over-buttered fillet. She bit into a long fragment of bone.

"Please tell me you haven't made her this fish before." Matthew snickered as she placed the bone on her plate.

Jacqueline shook her head and took another bite. Too much butter. Too much lemon. "I like working for your mother," she said, the slippery sinews of meat turning sour in her mouth.

"She lets you get away with far more than you ought to." He nodded at her trousers.

Jacqueline put her fork down, reaching for the glass of white wine. "She trusts me."

He smirked. "She shouldn't. Nobody should trust a maid. Not now."

"Why?" she asked.

"Because you're desperate."

Jacqueline gathered a breath.

"Don't try to pretend that you're not."

The wine numbed her throat on the way down. "I'm hardly a maid, sir."

"So, she admits it, now?" He picked up his own glass.

Jacqueline couldn't help but give a little, her cheeks burning. "I'm trying to survive."

Matthew leaned in, his smile now a grin. "So, I can safely assume that those are your fingerprints all over that shelf in the library?"

This time, it was Jacqueline who curled her lips, finally shedding the burden of what it felt like to pretend.

He had a book of sheet music from the Ziegfeld Follies 1919 show on his nightstand.

"Do you play often?" she asked, fingering the crisp pages.

"Better than Peter," he said, snatching the book out of her grasp. A photograph slipped from between the sheets and Jacqueline bent down to retrieve it.

"Is this her?" she asked. "Is this your wife?"

The woman in the photo was dressed in a Follies costume, her hair cut short and her body scantily clad with fringe and feathers.

Matthew took her wrist in response. He twisted her arm behind her back and snatched the photo. "She's not my wife anymore," he said against her ear.

Jacqueline groaned, her heart beating as he walked her toward the fireplace. He tossed the photo into the flames. The paper crumpled and twisted in the building heat. Her breaths deepened as he held her. She felt his lips curve against her skin, his breath vibrating. His fingers tightened around her wrist, and he forced her arm more firmly behind her. She winced in resistance, but then gathered a deeper breath than before, the fire's heat touching her throat. Its burn worked its way down her chest.

Matthew swayed, his arm encircling her. His fingers caressed her neck, pulling out a gentle moan. "You like this."

She nodded, swallowing against his hand. He turned her toward the bed, his voice deepening, his hold tightening. He pushed her over the mattress and shoved her face down.

"Bastard!" she cried.

"Oh, she has a tongue now!" Matthew said, leaning over her.

Jacqueline turned her face against the covers, struggling under his weight as he pulled the pins loose from her cap. Her hair spilled down, and he dragged the curls down her back as she bucked against him. She freed her arm and grabbed the lapel of his jacket and pulled his aggression against her ear.

"She likes a good ravishing, too," he growled.

"My name is Jacqueline," she moaned.

"Jacqueline!" he said. "Jacqueline with the pretty name and the luscious chestnut curls." He kissed her neck and her jaw, moving his hand down to her waist. He undid her trousers and tugged them down her hips. Jacqueline shuddered, her breaths deep as she wrestled against the firming evidence of his arousal. His grunts built as he struggled to pull the trousers off her knees.

"This is why women should wear skirts," he said. "A man shouldn't have this much trouble—"

"A man always makes trouble." She finished the job for him, pulling each leg free.

He unbuttoned her shirtwaist, then tugged at the neckline of her chemise, exposing her breasts. Her nipples hardened and he twisted them both in the pinch of his fingers.

She shrieked in response, but he buried the sound in the sheets as he pulled her drawers to her knees. His palm caressed her skin, softly at first. He clawed her flesh before striking her buttocks with an open palm. The sting drove her into a frenzied scramble across the bed, which only made him grasp at her flesh like a starving predator in pursuit.

"Is it so shameful?" he asked, pulling her back against his chest. "Is it so wrong to enjoy this? Everyone seems to think I'm some horrible brute, but you, Jacqueline, you suffer so beautifully for me."

"Save your breath," she gasped. "Stop talking. Just fuck me."

"Oh, I'll talk while fucking you, Jacqueline," he said as he guided himself inside. "I'll make you know it's me taking you, that it's me who's making you writhe like a fish on a line! Now, say my name."

She bit her lip, but then he tightened his grasp over the curve of her hips.

"M-Matthew," she sputtered.

"Again," he said, and she obliged. He covered her mouth, holding her tight as the friction worked her into a fury of release. Her cries spilled between his fingers. She twisted her face to catch her breath, but he flipped her onto her back and sealed her mouth with his, suffocating her with kisses until she beat her fists against his chest.

"Kiss me, darling!" he laughed, offering her his cheek.

Drunk with euphoria, she obliged. Then he turned his other cheek. "Again," he said.

This time, she resisted, but he gripped at her curls and held her still.

"The other cheek, Jacqueline!" he growled. "Kiss me like you love me! Like you mean it!"

Her breath caught. She looked at him, searching for his smile, but it was gone now. His gaze turned hard. Determined. Willful.

Jacqueline swallowed. She stilled her gasps and kissed his cheek, unable to hide her hesitation.

He lowered his head and withdrew.

"Matthew?" she tried.

"You can act for my mother, but not for me?" he asked.

She struggled to catch her breath, but Matthew got off the bed and paced toward the bathroom. The faucet squeaked. Water gurgled against the sink basin.

Jacqueline hesitated, swallowing back the tightness in her throat. "Y—you just caught me off guard."

The faucet squeaked again. The pipes moaned, but he didn't respond.

She glanced at the bedroom door, thinking of the cold that lay beyond it. The fire cracked and she shifted her attention to the nightstand as she pulled on her clothes. Only the book of sheet music remained.

"You'd Be Surprised," she read beneath her breath.

"That song was my favorite." Matthew stood in the bathroom doorway now, his robe pulled over his sulked shoulders.

Jacqueline swallowed, suddenly feeling sour, like the sourness was her doing. "One day I hope to see a Follies show," she tried. "I've always wanted to live in the city, to have my own apartment."

His lips curved with a new smile. "I could play it for you tomorrow, if you'd like."

She straightened her spine and raised her chin to address his approach. "I would," she said, feeling sick with herself, with the heat inside that spoke for her. "I'd love to hear you play, sir."

"Sir," he laughed. "That's so impersonal, Jacqueline." He put his hand over hers and squeezed. "Please, call me Matthew."

Jacqueline woke at dawn, splashed her face with water, and confronted her reflection in the mirror before digging out her maid's uniform. She pulled on her stockings and tied her garters. She hooked her corset over her frame, hating how its woven cording held her shoulders up and her head high when she knew she could do both well enough on her own. Her heeled footsteps clacked down the cold servant's stairwell and into the kitchen, but the hob had already been used and the kettle already boiled.

"Mother, I'd do anything to get back into your good graces."

Jacqueline followed Matthew's voice through the dining room. A plate with a half-eaten crepe sat at the table's head.

"Where did Eddie go?" Cecelia cried from the parlor.

"I'll play again!" Matthew said. "I'll play for you, Mother! Remember how much you loved it?"

The piano came to life moments later, bleeding a soft melody through the mahogany halls. Jacqueline's hesitant footsteps sounded on the offbeat, much like her heart did when she kissed Matthew the night before.

Like she loved him.

Like she meant it.

She passed through the library, where new fingerprints now marked every shelf. Her chest pounded. The corset restricted. She pushed the parlor door open to find Matthew seated at the piano yet again. Cecelia sat slumped in her chair, struggling to poke a needle through the cloth.

"This is your favorite song, isn't it, Mother?" Matthew asked, only to change chords and tempo when he made contact with Jacqueline's gaze.

Cecelia shook her head. "This is wrong. You're playing it wrong!"

Jacqueline parted her lips but Matthew's gaze only darkened. "This is right, Mother. This is just how I played it for you before."

Cecelia stomped her foot. "This is that Vaudeville filth!" She took her cane and tried to stand, only to stumble over the corner of the rug. She took a knee and faltered, the cane skittering across the floor.

Finally, the piano stilled.

Matthew rose from the bench and lifted Cecelia. She begged for the cane and Jacqueline rushed to retrieve it.

"I ought to call your father!" Cecelia said, swatting at her son.

"Oh, there's little good he can do now," Matthew seethed.

Cecelia huffed, her eyes turning red. She leaned over the cane and slapped his face. "Get out of this house! You're no son of mine!" Tears streamed as she lifted her cane to hit him, but Matthew managed to block her strike with his arm.

"All you've ever done is hate me, Mother," he said, his voice wavering.

"It's all for a good reason!" she said, trying to swing her cane again.

Jacqueline took hold and pried the woman back. "Ma'am, stop. There's no need!"

Cecelia fought, but Jacqueline patted her shoulder, calming her as best she could before helping her up the stairs. She got her a glass of water and helped her into bed.

"I don't feel well." Cecelia said. "It feels like waves. It feels like when the news of Peter came."

Jacqueline swallowed, pressing a cold cloth to Cecelia's forehead.

"Rest up, ma'am. You'll feel better after a nap."

The piano started again. Matthew played the song he'd promised to, singing along. "He's not so good in a crowd but when you get him alone, you'd be surprised! He isn't much at a dance but then when he's taking you home, you'd be surprised!

"He's brought sin to this house again," Cecelia muttered. "I want him gone."

"He doesn't look like much of a lover, but you can't judge a book by its cover..."

His voice found the rebellious parts of her, but Jacqueline stood at Cecelia's bedside until her confusion wavered and her sobs eased. Closing the door behind her, Jacqueline wrung her hands in her apron, her heart beating beneath the layers of clothing that held her strict and rigid.

"He's got the face of an angel, but there's a devil in his eye!"

He'd closed the piano by the time she returned to the parlor.

"Where did you learn to make a proper crepe?" she asked.

He rose from the bench and buttoned his jacket. "I'm not some pompous rich boy, Jacqueline. I doubt you'd simply fuck any man who was."

She drew a breath, feeling the restriction.

"You're toying with her," she said. "You're toying with me, as well, and I'd rather you didn't."

He hesitated, shifting his glance toward the window and the overgrown vines outside. "I told her my name was Eddie, that I was a new servant. I made her breakfast. I made her tea. She was happy."

"Eddie?"

He blushed, glancing down at his shoes. "After Eddie Cantor."

Jacqueline kicked at the carpet where Cecelia tripped.

"I'm not the man she makes you think I am," he said. "Surely, you must believe that, Jacqueline."

"You lied to your own mother."

"She hardly considers herself my mother." He swallowed. "By the time she wakes, she'll remember even less of me."

Jacqueline stepped back, still tasting the fish she'd ruined.

"I do like you, Jacqueline," he said. "I like talking to you. You make all of this less painful."

She looked at him, longer than she should have. The wound in him lingered behind his smile. She tried to soften her posture, but the corset wouldn't allow it.

"Why would you come back, other than for money?" she asked.

"I thought that if I played the piano, maybe it would trigger a memory. Maybe she would think differently of me. Maybe she'd put me back in the will. This estate has to pass to someone, and if it's not Peter, it has to be me."

"You can't take advantage of a lost old woman," Jacqueline said.

He scoffed. "But isn't that what you're doing? She thinks just as little of you as she does of me!"

"That's not true."

"She doesn't pay you," Matthew countered. "You're not staying here out of the goodness of your heart."

Jacqueline shifted.

"You're toying with her too, Jacqueline. Don't pretend."

She turned away, slipping down the servant's wing. The door swung behind her, but Matthew didn't follow.

His footsteps crept through the house all afternoon.

When Cecelia woke, she asked to play a game of chess, which Jacqueline set up in the parlor.

"The king is the weakest piece," Cecelia said, moving her white pawn across the board. "He's the biggest piece, but all the other pieces move around just to protect him. It's so silly."

Jacqueline moved her knight, setting things in place.

"I never loved Philip," Cecelia said.

"No?" Jacqueline asked.

"He gave me all this, but at what expense?" Cecelia moved her pawn again. "Don't be like me, Jacqueline."

"I…I never planned to," Jacqueline said.

Upstairs, something clattered. Footsteps sounded, moving into the room that once belonged to Peter.

"There's darkness everywhere now," Cecelia said. "Can't you feel it?"

"It's because we have to keep the lights down, ma'am," Jacqueline said, sliding her rook across the board. "Check, ma'am."

Cecelia moved her pawn a third time, doing nothing to prevent what was about to happen. "Philip promised me the world and left me with nothing. Well, save for Peter, but then the war…"

Jacqueline hesitated, glancing at Cecelia's bare left hand. "I'm trying to fight for a better future for myself, ma'am."

"You're naive," Cecelia said. "The war might have changed some things, but it won't change them all."

Jacqueline hesitated before picking up her bishop. "Checkmate, ma'am."

More rustling sounded above them. Cecelia smiled in spite of it.

"I do love that new cook! Eddie, isn't it?"

Jacqueline swapped her bishop with the king. She clutched the white cross of the figure's top, pressing her fingers into the marble until they turned white with it. "His name is Matthew," she said, but Cecelia didn't hear her.

Matthew insisted on making dinner. He cooked much better than Jacqueline, so she kept to the corners of the kitchen, listening to him sing tunes as he simmered and broiled.

"He looks as cold as an Eskimo, but there's fire in his eyes!"

He arranged a slice of brisket on a plate with potatoes and vegetables. He poured a glass of wine and placed the freshly-polished silver around each plate.

But when Cecelia entered the dining room and saw Matthew, she shrieked and raised her cane again.

"Where's Eddie?" she cried. "Where's Peter?"

"Mother, please," Matthew begged. "I'm here. I'm trying to help!"

She struck his shoulder.

Matthew staggered, but Cecelia swung again, barely missing the cheek that Jacqueline had forced herself to kiss.

Jacqueline calmed Cecelia in the aftermath. She bathed her, dressed her, and pulled the covers over her again.

"What did I do to end up with him?" Cecelia cried. "Why did the wrong son die?" Her sobs worked through the halls like a trumpet before the war. There was nothing Jacqueline could do to console her, so she left the room and found Matthew in the main hall, sitting before the fire with a glass of brandy.

Cecelia's cane cracked in the flames.

Jacqueline parted her lips to confront him, but Matthew rubbed at his shoulder and she found herself taking the other seat before the fire instead.

"Why does she hate you so much?"

"Because I'm just a shadow," he said, taking a sip of his drink. "I could never be better, so I sought different influences, none of which she approved of." He lifted the bottle and poured a second glass. "I've worked. I've bled and I've struggled, Jacqueline. I know what it's like to have no other choice."

He slid the second glass toward her.

She took it and he smiled.

He rubbed his shoulder again.

"Is it bad?" she asked.

"It's nothing a drink can't fix," he said. "Nothing you can't fix." He rose with his drink and knelt before her chair. Jacqueline pressed her hand beneath his jacket, her warmth to his bruise. He winced, then eased his hand up her skirts.

"You're a proper maid today," he said, sliding his reach between her thighs, up her drawers, into her folds.

She gasped and pushed at the bruise, but his grasp only firmed with delight.

"Don't pretend you don't like it," he said. He set his drink down and cupped her chin with his free hand. He forced her to look at him, pinching at her lips, manipulating the sounds that came from her mouth like he did with the keys of the piano.

"Matthew, not here—

"I like when you say my name," he said. His pressure burned at her, forcing her to writhe until he pulled his hand from beneath her skirts.

"I know, Matthew."

He climbed over her, pressed his fingers against her lips and crooned. "I like how my name feels on your tongue, Jacqueline. Say it again. Please say it!"

She did as best she could, only for his fingers to hook at her lower jaw, prying her mouth open. She choked, tears slipping down her cheeks. He held her face and kissed her, wiping at her tears, smiling down at her. "You don't have to pretend around me, Jacqueline."

She found herself shaking her head, which somehow felt wrong and awful, considering she was agreeing with him.

The fireplace raged in his bedroom. Afterward, she kissed him on one cheek and then on the other, her insides burning from the shame of what she now assumed would be ritual.

"Tell me you love me," he said. "Like you mean it."

Jacqueline furrowed her brows, unable to hide her reaction.

"Say it!" he said. "Say it now!" He shook her, rattled her.

"I'm not an actress!" she cried.

Her words dismantled him. He pulled away and groaned aloud, doubling over on the side of the bed, his fingers pulling at his own hair. He breathed heavily, frantic. His shoulders rose and fell and Jacqueline scrambled off the bed, reaching for her clothes.

"Please don't go," Matthew begged.

Foolishly, she turned.

"I know I can be a bit much at times," he said.

Her better instincts told her to leave, but then she'd be alone again, in the cold again.

Matthew drew closer. "If you want the truth, I'll tell you. I know how to cook because I worked at a restaurant in New York when I first left home." He touched her back, his hand wet. She wasn't sure if it was with her own lust or his tears. "I'm really not so hopeless," he said.

She glanced at the nightstand, taking notice of the flimsy dog-eared book that now sat where the sheet music once did.

The Way of a Man with a Maid

The author was anonymous. She reached for the book, but he didn't stop her.

"My former wife wasn't so happy when she discovered that printing in the back of my dresser."

Her fingers shifted over the worn pages. Some of them were stained with fingerprints, the corners folded over to mark specific passages of the narrator's ravaging of a helpless woman. But it was the photo tucked into the book's sixth chapter that put her face to face with his former wife again. It was a different picture, this time with her eyes blacked out with ink.

"One would think that for an actress, she would have been more willing to entertain my preferences. Instead, she treated me just as Mother does."

Her eyes skimmed the page, depicting a scene where the narrator forced his captive to give him a kiss. Jacqueline pressed the photo back into the book's spine. She closed her eyes and willed her heart to stop throbbing.

"My wife thought it was in her best interest to rid herself of me." His voice cracked. "I had nowhere else to go. I had to come here. And there you were, waiting for me. I know it's fate, Jacqueline." He touched her shoulder and kissed the tender flesh of her neck. His stubble scratched it. Then, firming his grasp, he bared teeth.

Jacqueline shrieked, but Matthew clung to her as though she were an object, a possession, a comfort toy poised to give a child a blissful night of sleep.

"You act every day, Jacqueline," he said, licking her, tasting her. "You're good at it, except with me."

"I have no other choice," she said. "I have no skills and soon, I might have nothing."

He pulled her legs over his lap and embraced her in his arms. She thought about fighting, but she didn't. Couldn't. He clung so tightly that his hands shook and his breath vibrated. "You could have me, Jacqueline, if you wanted me."

"Wanted you?" Her body stiffened.

"I'd take good care of you," he promised. "I'd give you whatever you asked for."

"I'm not an actress," she said again.

"But you play a mighty convincing maid," he said. "Playing a wife would be second nature."

Her throat tightened. "I can't."

"You can," he said.

She climbed off him, but he remained on the bed, naked, all of his desire exposed. "Please, Jacqueline," he begged. "You know me. You've felt me. Please don't think ill of me."

She put on her clothes and backed herself against the door. "Truthfully, you scare me a little."

He rolled his bruised shoulder and shifted, gathering his book off the bed. His gaze darkened. "It's much scarier out there, Jacqueline."

"I've been out there before."

"Oh, have you?"

She felt for the knob, its cold metal stealing heat from her palm. "I—I honestly don't plan on staying here that long. I want to live in the city. I want to take care of myself."

He set the book back on the nightstand. "I'm a good man," he said, positioning it just as it was before she picked it up. "I'm a careful man. Most wouldn't think so, but I hoped you would. I thought you did."

The fire cracked and she twisted at the knob, her bare toes curling over the cold floor. She waited in the dark for him to protest, but she heard nothing except the sound of him putting a new log on the fire.

She woke in the morning and splashed water on her face. "He's just a man," she said to the mirror. "He's a stupid brute of a man. Don't let him get the best of you."

His music rang through the house and Jacqueline took Cecelia out to the gardens to escape. Without her cane, she stumbled on the rocks littering the paths, forcing Jacqueline to thread her elbow through hers.

"Eddie plays such delightful music," Cecelia said. "And he has a watch that looks just like Peter's."

Jacqueline clung to the old woman's arm. "There is no Eddie," she said. "There is no Peter, either. I'm afraid there's only me, ma'am."

"Oh, nonsense." Cecelia laughed. "You've been so distracted, Jacqueline, with all your meetings."

Jacqueline hesitated, her foot skidding over a loose pebble on the walk. "I haven't gone to a meeting in months, ma'am."

"It's all for the best. The city streets are no place for a proper woman."

"What if I don't want to be a proper woman?" Jacqueline asked, but Cecelia slipped out of Jacqueline's hold. The overgrown brush slapped her cheeks and caught her hair. Crows squawked above, leaving Jacqueline with no choice but to bring the old woman back inside, where Matthew's song lulled Cecelia back into her chair.

When it came time to pay the bills, Jacqueline found the bank account entirely dry. She dimmed the gas and struggled to warm Cecelia's hands and feet near the parlor fireplace. Cecelia's numb fingers barely managed to poke through the fabric of her embroidery, and the roses she attempted to stitch grew distorted.

Matthew cooked a lamb and vegetables, and the three ate dinner over candlelight.

"I hate when the darkness of fall creeps in," Cecelia observed, struggling to cut through her meat.

"Would you like some help, ma'am?" Jacqueline asked.

"I've got it," Matthew said, pulling his chair closer. "Here you are, Mother." He sliced her meat, then lifted her fork to her lips.

"I can do it myself, Eddie."

"Don't you remember, Mother? I'm not Eddie. I'm Peter, your son."

Cecelia's expression slipped, her smile waning, giving way to the bite of lamb that Matthew pushed past her lips.

Jacqueline reached for her wine.

"You know what I miss?" Matthew asked. "A good corset. I appreciate the way a corset can make a woman sit up straight and proper."

"Yes, Peter!" Cecelia said. "You're so right. These women now, they have no dignity left."

Jacqueline found her spine in response.

"Just like that," Matthew said, pointing.

Beside him, Cecelia laughed. "Oh, Jacqueline, you have become quite foolish with all your meetings."

"Meetings?" Matthew asked.

"She used to ask for evenings off, twice a week." Cecelia struggled to chew.

Matthew picked up her glass and held it to her lips, giving her a sip of wine.

Cecelia smiled, patting Matthew's hand in gratitude. "She kept saying it was to visit family, but I figured it out. She made posters, even! You would have laughed if you were here when I confronted her, Peter. She still thinks it's worth all this time and effort just for a silly vote!"

Matthew's face lit up in the candlelight.

Jacqueline raised her glass, easing the tension with inebriation.

After putting Cecelia to sleep, Jacqueline passed through the empty halls and into the narrow corridors of the servant's wing. No footsteps. No hunt. She set the candle on the nightstand, only for its light to touch Matthew's shadow, which emerged from behind the door.

"You startled me!" she said.

The candlelight flickered as he took her. He undressed her desperately, her layers shedding like skin to the icy floor.

The springs of her narrow bed squeaked beneath her back as he took her, toyed with her. Her lungs drew in full breaths of air, relieved breaths of air, but relief only lasted so long. Then, when she refused to kiss his cheek, Matthew turned to her dresser.

"No!" she cried, but he immediately found her suffragette sash and hat, decorated with stripes of white and gold.

"Why would Mother even let you leave the house in these?" he raged.

"Because she respects me," Jacqueline spat.

"Respects you?" His fists shook over the ribbon. "She laughed at you!"

He draped the sash over her frame, set the hat on her head, and pinned it into place over her tangled locks. "If I could just have a picture of you. If I could show it to her, show her what you really are. Just a filthy suffragette who steals and lies and forces her husband to do all her work!"

Jacqueline went to take off the hat, but he shoved her back.

"I'm fighting for myself!" she cried. "There's nothing for me! I have no rights!"

"Oh, and getting a vote is going to change that?" He clutched at the sash, bringing it around her neck so the stripes coiled and cut her breaths. Her heart raced, and she beat her fists against his chest, adrenaline, and lust, and fury heating her insides. Matthew fought back. His anger always brought her drive, but he managed to reach past her and beneath the mattress, finding the little toffee hammer that she often clutched at night, hoping its cold touch would help her one day shatter her own glass.

"She doth protest!" he mocked, shaking the hammer before her face.

"I'd never use it!" she croaked. "I've only ever marched, Matthew, I swear!"

"Then why have it?" He released the sash's hold on her neck.

She coughed and sputtered, blinking tears. "Because it—it inspires me. It gives me hope—"

"I was wrong about you, wasn't I? You want nothing to do with me. You don't want to marry me, or give me children, or bless me with the love that I deserve!"

She froze beneath him. She flattened her palms against his chest and tried to push him away. He tightened the ribbon around her neck again.

"I'm scared," she choked. "You're scaring me, Matthew."

"Then kiss me!" he cried. "Tell me you want me! Tell me you love me!"

And she did, with the sour stench of brandy and tears between them. One cheek. Then the other. Then on the lips, his sobs filling her throat, making her cling.

"I love you!" she cried in shame. "I do love you, Matthew." She rubbed his bruised shoulder until his heaving breaths eased.

He laid his head between her breasts, and she held him until his hands stopped shaking. "I promise I'll take care of you," he said. "I'll give you all the things a proper woman deserves."

She glanced at the pile of clothes on the floor, dreading the morning when she'd have to put them all back on again.

"You're better than this," he said. "You don't belong in this room without comfort."

She shook her head again. She agreed with him again. "I love you, Matthew," she said again, her mouth sour and awful and stained.

Then he lifted the hammer and slammed it against the window, shattering the glass to let in the cold of winter.

"He's just a man," she said, staring at herself in his bathroom mirror. She used to shout in the streets at the drunk men who mocked her as she marched, but now she walked downstairs into the library, where Cecelia sat at the desk with a newly-drafted will.

"No, Mother. Peter doesn't start with a P. It starts with an M."

"Don't be silly!" she insisted, trying to write her favored son's name. "It can't start with an M."

"I'd never steer you wrong, Mother," he said. "It can and it does. Now just write the points." He directed her to spell the rest, then lifted his gaze, making contact with Jacqueline's prying eyes. A glint slipped over his expression. Then his lip curled. Intent. Sinister.

It would have made her body go cold if she wasn't so cold already.

On the day of the first snow, Matthew went to the bank to pay the bills.

Cecelia watched him drive off through the parlor window. "What a good man he is, that son of mine."

"That's not Peter, ma'am," Jacqueline said. "That's Matthew and he's just as vile as you made him out to be."

Cecelia laughed, stabbing the needle into her hoop. Her rose was just a massive span of red that bled in all directions. "Matthew died, dear. Don't you remember? He's always been dead to me."

Jacqueline wanted to scream, but she couldn't, not when she was wearing a corset and a proper amount of petticoats. She struggled to kneel, adding another log to the fire. Even her hands were cold now, but she warmed them in her skirts and squeezed her way up the servant's stairwell to her former room. She dug into the floorboards, only to find that Matthew had taken all the money she'd stored away.

She cried until her insides burned.

The door squeaked open and Matthew's gasp fogged in the cold.

"Come here, Jacqueline," he said, lifting her off the floor and into his embrace. He carried her through the threshold of his room, where the fire raged. He buried her in his covers, then tossed her suffragette ribbons over the flames.

"You took my money," she said.

He knelt over the bed and smiled. "It's in an account," he said. "It's a part of the estate now."

"You took everything!" she cried, making fists.

"I'm giving you everything!" He reached into his jacket and pulled out a tiny hinged box.

"No," she said. She shook her head, but he grabbed her left hand and forced Cecelia's diamond ring onto her finger. She fought and writhed, but he persisted, wrestling the cold metal over her knuckle.

"Say it, Jacqueline. Make me the happiest man in the world. Do it, now!"

"It was my money!" she screamed. "It was mine!" She'd always thought herself a formidable foe against Cecelia, always several moves ahead, but Matthew twisted the ring, bending her finger until the flimsy bones threatened to break.

"You'll never have to leave!" he said.

Check.

Checkmate.

She withered in his arms, held so tight and dear that the storm of kisses he showered over her left her weak and empty and with no other choice but to do as he demanded.

She splashed her face in the morning and tried to pry the ring off her finger. "He's just a man," she said, but the ring was too tight and it clung to her swollen knuckle.

She left Matthew's room and approached the house's grand staircase. She thought back to her first day at the Porter Estate, when she looked up the carved mahogany banister and imagined herself descending just like a proper woman would. Now, she curled her toes over the steps.

She closed her eyes, lifted her skirts and took the first step, only to scream when she noticed Cecelia.

The old woman lay at the bottom, her mouth contorted, her body stiff and her gaze solid and cold, staring at Jacqueline with a face of permanent confrontation. Around her body lay the scattered pages of the book of sheet music she'd slipped on.

You'd Be Surprised.

Matthew's music rang through the house at Cecelia's funeral.

He'd invited friends from New York and hoarded them all into the parlor. Jacqueline took her time getting ready, struggling to pin her hair back like the women in the fashion magazines. She didn't want a lady's maid. She didn't need someone prying. Someone judging. She pinned her black hat into place and made her way toward the stairs.

Matthew switched tempo and tone at the bottom. Classical to Vaudeville.

Jacqueline clung to the banister, desperate not to slip as he sang.

"I may look simple but I want you to know, I've been to college. I'm full of knowledge!"

The crowd laughed in the parlor. They kept laughing when Jacqueline entered. Matthew continued to play, to sing. He smiled and beckoned her forward with a tilt of his head.

"Oh, the dumber they come, the better I like 'em, 'cause the dumb ones know how to make love!"

His fingers worked over the keys, much to the crowd's delight. Then he turned on the bench and pulled Jacqueline over his lap. The crowd of strangers whistled and hollered and cheered.

"I'd like to introduce you all to my wife, Jacqueline," he announced. "She loves me despite everything. Oh yes, she does!"

The crowd crooned and chuckled as Jacqueline did as was their custom now, kissing him on one cheek, and then on the other.

Love like a cellar
Dark and dim and cold
A creeping crawling lust
Dirty and rotten and bold
Desire and need in an oddly form
Forging an unbreakable bond
Soulmates bound forever
Into the grave and beyond

ROTTEN LOVE
GINGER LEE

VI

Vera

Helen Whistberry

Rough manual labor. Hard worker wanted. Discretion a must.
Most balked when they answered the newspaper advertisement and discovered the exact nature of the job, but Martin Breedlove was a towering figure of a man and laconic beyond measure, so the work and its peculiar requirements suited him fine.

In truth, he never felt so completely at home as when he walked through the cemetery gates under the cover of night. The dead welcomed him, never lied to him, didn't judge. Their bones and gristle thrummed with the sounds of decay, a quiet energy that hummed up through the soles of his hobnailed boots as he hunted for newly dug graves. Corpses were simply vessels that had hosted a life from start to finish and were now at peace. Most of the time, at least.

This night was different. As he stood chest-deep in muck, knocking the mud from his shovel against the coffin lid at midnight, the coffin knocked back. He uttered a loud curse in his deep baritone, then swore again silently at himself. Body snatching was a stealthy business. The authorities were paid well to look the other way, but only if he was discreet and didn't draw unnecessary attention to his activities.

Breedlove stood listening as long minutes ticked by, debating whether to abandon the grave and start anew, but that would mean hours wasted. It would be nearing dawn by the time he unearthed another body, and he didn't get paid if he came back empty-handed. He balled one filthy, rough hand into a fist and rapped his knuckles against the coffin.

A faint scratching came from within.

That decided him. He'd never seen any evidence of it himself, but he'd heard tales of tormented souls buried alive, found with fingernails torn off and splinters in their hands from a desperate struggle to free themselves from their underground prisons. He wasn't about to rebury someone who might have suffered such an unimaginable fate. He pulled a pry bar from one of the deep pockets in his greatcoat, methodically levered up the top of the coffin, then shoved the lid aside.

Abundant, dark amber hair flowed loose and wild down to a sharply corseted waist. Breedlove swept his hands against his thighs to wipe away the worst of the grime before gently pushing strands of hair away from the face. Staring up at him, all soft brown skin and unblinking hazel eyes, was the most beautiful woman he'd ever seen.

Her skin radiated heat as though she burned with fever. He could feel it even through the heavy satin gown she wore. Cream and French lace and pearl buttons. Not a dress for burying. A wedding dress. He noted the thick golden band on the ring finger of one of the hands arranged so carefully across her chest, a chest that never moved. No sign of breath or life.

Breedlove was not a superstitious man, nor an imaginative one, but rarely had he witnessed so uncanny a thing. He examined the inner lid of the coffin. There were thin scratches, though her hands were pristine, her fingernails undamaged. He sensed movement from the corner of his eye. One white-booted foot flicked and shifted, but when he looked, all was still.

A catatonic state, he thought, *or else, I am overtired and out of sorts and seeing things*. Either way, he knew he would not leave her there beneath the cold and muddy ground, nor pass her on to his employers until he had unraveled the mystery.

She had a womanly figure, no fainting sack of bones here, but he had hefted much larger prizes from the earth and had no trouble lifting and setting her gently aboveground. He swiftly followed and turned to read the headstone. He rarely spared the markers a glance, uninterested in the person that once was, but he had to know her name:

Vera Masterson. Beloved wife and sister.

Vera. An unusual name, yet it suited her. It reminded him of verity, truth. There was a pureness to her expression that fascinated. Even her gown, though constructed of such fine materials, was simply cut and unadorned with the gaudy beading and excessive ornamentation that had lately come into fashion.

He glanced back into the grave and noticed a flash of white. He jumped down to investigate and found a filmy veil edged round with tatting in a simple looping pattern. Hair pins were scattered around the casket. Another puzzle. He assumed her hair had been carefully arranged, the veil attached when she was buried. How had it come undone?

Time was growing short. Dawn approached, and light was not a friend to such furtive work. He slid the lid back in place and returned to the surface, setting to work on pushing the mound of dirt into the grave to hide his handiwork. He couldn't help glancing over at the bride between nearly every shovelful as though he might catch some sign of life, some movement. But she remained inanimate, skin softly glowing in the moonlight, eyes glistening.

After patting down the last of the soil, he retrieved an old tarpaulin he used to hold the dirt so it wouldn't disturb the grass around the grave. Usually, he would wrap the body in it, but he couldn't bear to sully her dress. He removed his greatcoat instead and wrapped it round her like a shroud, buttoning up the front until it swallowed her whole.

Breedlove folded the tarp and threw it and the bride over his shoulder, his long strides making short work of the walk back to his handcart. He lay her in reverently, setting the empty baskets he used as camouflage against prying eyes gently atop her swaddled form. Instead of heading north toward the medical college, he turned east to the grimier side of town where those "less deserving" spun out their brutish and all-too-short lives.

An empty garret room awaited there. Its one saving grace was an old skylight with panes missing and stuffed with rags in a futile attempt to keep out the cold—but it was worth it for the light that seeped in even on gloomy days. On bright ones, he would drag his straw mattress into a sunspot and sleep away the daylight hours, basking like a cat until his next midnight mission.

Working men and women arose early by necessity, heeding the call of workshop and household service, but none gave him a second glance as he unloaded his cart. All had learned to keep curiosity and speculation to themselves while out on the streets if they wanted to survive.

Breedlove carried the woman up three long flights of stairs past rubbish and crying babes, arguments and lovers' rendezvous, the chaotic and muddled business of living crammed cheek and jowl like livestock into holding pens. All made way for him, his scowl and silence and size too intimidating to risk asking him what burden he brought into their shared abode.

A mattress and a wreck of a wooden chair were his only furniture. He laid her on the mattress, removing his coat from around the body so he could see her face and form, and sat down on the chair to watch her.

Vera.

He turned the name over in his mind. It felt too intimate to think of her that way, but Mrs. Masterson seemed rather formal for a corpse. *The bride* felt too impersonal, *the woman*, disrespectful.

Vera.

He whispered the name aloud, rolled it round on his tongue to get the taste of it. He swore her eyes flicked over at him as he spoke, but when he bent closer, they were staring straight ahead at the cracked and yellowed glass of the skylight above.

Now that they were away from the earthy, moldy stench of the graveyard, he caught a whiff of something sweeter, like walking past the flower stalls at Hightown Market. He straightened her gown, smoothing out the folds before he arranged her hands. Then he took his old gap-toothed comb and ran it through her fine-stranded hair, gently loosening knots and tangles.

He was no lady's maid, but he'd watched his mother plait his sister's hair many a time when they were young. The pattern came back to him after a few false starts. He tied the end with a strip of cloth torn from the ragged hem of his shirt and lay the braid over her shoulder where it trailed down to her waist.

She looked peaceful enough, except for those staring eyes. He dug two heavy coins from his meager stash and attempted to weigh down her lids, but try as he might, they would not close. He gave up the fight and sat back down so he could gaze at her in what little comfort the rickety chair offered.

No sign of decay or corruption marred her smooth skin, but then her death date was only a few days ago. Give it time. Strange that they had the grave marker already prepared and installed. Almost as though they had anticipated her death and made ready. Perhaps a lingering illness, a slow decline. Her face was remarkably serene, if so. He'd seen enough of the ravages of disease to recognize its signs in the newly deceased.

The impulse to save her from her earthly imprisonment and the cruel implements of his employers' experiments had led them to the tiny piece of the city he called his own, but now what? He could hardly keep her forever, and his masters would be angry he had failed them. But the thought of a scalpel piercing that firm flesh, despoiling her perfect form, was intolerable. Better to lose his job than deliver her up to such a fate.

His body rumbled with fatigue and hunger. It had been a long night. He took one of the coins that failed to weigh down her eyes and bought a few hand pies from a street hawker. He wolfed them down in as few bites as possible, meaning to toss the scrap of old newspaper they came wrapped in, before an irresistible compulsion overcame him. He returned to his loft, fished a small sliver of coal from the fireplace, smoothed out the greasy paper, and began to sketch.

He hadn't drawn since he was a boy. It had been an obsession then. He'd dreamed of being a famous artist, a painter, a sculptor. All daydreams too far out of reach for someone of his humble birth, but an indulgent mother had sacrificed to buy him scant supplies, and a penniless artist come down in the world offered him lessons as a kindness after noticing some raw talent in the boy.

The skill he'd acquired from hours of practice came back to him now. He knelt by the chair, using it as a desk, while he stared at her face and drew. He'd created a pleasing likeness when he was done. Closer to the reality than he would have thought possible, but inspiration strikes that way sometimes. When creation flows through, rather than comes from the creator.

Breedlove felt as if he were but a tool in some greater artist's hand. He stared in wonder from the drawing to his muse, and back again. He had captured something melancholy, yet peaceful in the expression. What had her life been? She had lived long enough to be courted, to marry. *Beloved wife and sister*, but not *mother*. Her time on earth was cut short before reaching that milestone.

His fingers itched and danced. The sketch of black and gray was insufficient at portraying her beauty. He longed for canvas and brush, paints and turpentine, but such items were expensive. He'd need more money, and more money meant more bodies. He lay the sketch beside her, a mirror image to keep her company while he was gone. Then he walked the long blocks to the medical college.

His masters were as displeased as he expected. They'd had to cancel their exhibition, much to their embarrassment and chagrin. But he had never failed them before, as they grudgingly conceded. They were in a magnanimous mood; they would give him one more chance.

Breedlove listened, hat in hand, head bowed obsequiously in acknowledgment of their generosity, all the while thinking that they would be hard-pressed to find another so strong and silent and reliable, as they themselves well knew. If the public ever caught wind of where their specimens came from, these fine doctors might find themselves in a very tricky situation indeed.

He left them with the reassurance that he would redress his failure that very night. All the while they had scolded and rebuked, his thoughts had been with *her*. Had she awoken while he was gone? She would be frightened to find herself in a dirty, unfamiliar room. He never thought about it before, but now he was keenly aware of how unfitting his place was for such a gentlewoman—how unfitting *he* was.

There wasn't much he could do about himself, but the room was another story. He spent a penny he could ill afford on a used and ragged straw broom from an odds and ends stall. It was with a strange mixture of relief and disappointment that he re-entered his home to find the scene exactly as he left it. He removed his greatcoat and laid it over the body to protect her from dust as he vigorously swept.

It hardly seemed to make much difference, but he was satisfied he had done what he could. He gently peeled back his coat and rearranged the amber braid it had disturbed. So tranquil in death, if death it was, yet her skin glowed, and she smelled as fresh as ever. He sat in a corner across from her, watching for any sign of movement or life, eyes growing heavy until he fell into a restless slumber.

She called out to him, *Martin, Martin…* reached out a delicate hand, warm and real in his, a pretty, tinkling sound like a light drizzle of rain against the skylight glass. She placed his other hand around her waist and swayed and twirled, a dance he never learned the steps to, yet in this dream world he was graceful and handsome, confident and bold. Her eyes danced with delight. With love. She reached up on tiptoe, her soft lips pressed to his. A kiss, never-ending, never-ending…

He woke with a start, breath hoarse and shallow, gasping for air, suffocating, and leapt to his feet, panting. A dream, a nightmare, nothing more. Perhaps to be expected in his line of work and with a corpse lying mere feet away only, he had never had one before. Not like that.

The light in the room had grown dim. Evening time. He hated to go out and leave her alone in the dark, but candles were too dear to leave burning. He lay a hand over hers and promised he'd be back before she missed him. He chuckled at himself. Talking to the dead now, was he? Yet he couldn't help one last backward glance as he left.

He was hungry, and digging was tiring work, but he hated to spend money on food. The idea of painting her had taken hold in his mind. He would need every penny for art supplies. So instead, he found an apple, bruised and mealy, that had escaped notice along the street. Breedlove rubbed the worst of the grime on his coat and ate it down, seeds and all. It was hardly sufficient, but it was something.

The city was rife with graveyards, but he knew better than to mine the same one twice in a row. It meant a longer walk, pulling the heavy handcart behind him, but he was used to it. He'd walked the length and breadth of the city many times over. Death stalked its residents with such profligacy, he rarely had trouble finding a fresh grave but tonight, even greater fortune smiled upon him.

A dead drunkard, sprawled in the gutter, starved or frozen or both. He'd never stumbled upon such a fresh corpse before. From the looks of the man's clothes and long beard, he'd been living rough and was unlikely to be missed. If he took this offering, he could get back home all the sooner. Vera was calling to him. He missed her already. He would rather be gazing upon her stone beauty than wandering the streets and shoveling half the night away.

Breedlove glanced around. No one else about. The temptation was too great. He loaded up the body and headed to the college. The night watchman there accepted the package as usual and handed him his wages. When he subtracted his weekly rent and the bare minimum for food, there was far too little left to buy paints and brushes. Art was a rich man's game.

A rich man. He knew of one. A portrait painter, much sought after by the highest ranks of society. He knew where the man lived, the famous studio in the garden often pointed out by guides to gawking tourists. Compulsion directed his feet there.

It took but a moment to vault the high wall, enter a door that had been carelessly left unlocked, and rifle about for what he needed amidst such a surplus that he doubted the artist would notice anything amiss. Still, as he stumbled home with his contraband, he was stunned at what he'd done. Life had been a hard slog, but he'd never stolen before. Except for the bodies, of course, but that was a job, paid for by respectable men even if the work itself was not strictly respectable.

Any guilt or regrets he had fled when he saw Vera lying in the pool of moonlight cast down through the skylight. There had never been anything so beautiful in all the world, and never would be again. It was his duty to record it for all posterity. He arranged his paints and prepared his canvas as he waited for the sun to rise. Debated poses. Decided on a three-quarter view, but those eyes… those eyes should be directed out at the viewer, at the creator, at him.

He began with the undercoating, great washes of shape and color, building layer upon layer upon layer, too impatient to allow time for proper drying between applications. Fumbling at first, unsure, until some long-ago muscle memory surfaced, guiding his efforts. He worked through the day with no thought of rest or hunger, the world narrowed down to brush, paint, and her. The work was far from finished by twilight, but the broad strokes were there. He lit his last two candles to better see as he worked as long into the night as he could before his strength gave out.

He awoke to daylight and a clearer view of what he'd accomplished and was amazed at the details he'd managed in the dress, her hair. There was just the face left to do, the most important part. It flowered on the canvas as naturally as a rose in bloom under his hand. *Uncanny* was the word that floated round his brain as he worked. Uncanny was the effort he'd expended, the speed at which he'd worked, and the skill which was surely far beyond his own.

As night fell again, he added the finishing touches. A gleam in the eye, a slight smile about the elegant lips. He propped the finished canvas in the seat of the chair with a guttering candle in front for illumination. He leaned against the wall and gazed at his work, more than satisfied. Now he would have a memento when her body inevitably decayed. Her beauty immortalized, perhaps even displayed somewhere all might gaze upon it.

The idea disturbed him. No, no one should ever gaze upon her again. No one but her portraitist. He was afraid they wouldn't see, wouldn't understand the wonder that was this woman, this *Vera*, this unfortunate bride. And yet, how fortunate she had been found by one who did appreciate her, who hadn't dressed her in her wedding finery only to discard her in a muddy hole in the earth for eternity.

He chided himself. Foolish thoughts. Lack of sleep, lack of food. Vera Masterson had fled and left this container behind. That's all it was. She was no longer a woman, a personality, a soul. He was as familiar with death and decay as any man living and no sentimentalist. He would doze a little, regain his strength, then take her back, take *it* back to that empty box built to embrace this forlorn object. He'd no right to keep it. What had he been thinking? A temporary madness. A nap, a decent meal, and all would return to normal.

She came to him again in his dream. Brushed her hand along the rough planes of his face, a gentle swipe of her thumb across his lips. Then she kissed him ever so softly along the sharp bone of his jaw. She was dressed all in black now. A figure of mourning. Much more appropriate.

Do not abandon me, she whispered. *I do not want to be alone.*

Smoke roused him. The candle had burned down and set the corner of the canvas aflame. He flung the picture from the chair and himself on top of it, smothering the fire and ruining his waistcoat with the still-wet oils. Anxiously, he held the painting up to the dawning light. A minor black smudge marred a section no larger than his hand. He had done more damage with his attempt to put it out. The face was no longer pristine, the flawless skin wiped away, canvas white as bone visible underneath.

He would have wept in frustration if he was the type of man who wept. Having never shed a tear in his life, he went to work repairing the damage instead, afraid it would never look as good again but determined to try. The hours flew by as he restored her beauty. Finally, he held up the finished work to compare with his model. Perfection.

Breedlove lay a hand against the cadaver's cheek and rubbed his thumb across her lips as she had done to him in the dream. He stopped short at the kiss. His madness did not extend so far as that. She was warm still. Not with the fiery burning she had radiated at first, but the natural warmth of a living, breathing woman. The horror of consigning her back to the worm-infested earth came over him along with a great weariness.

With effort, he tore himself away, nearly tumbled down the stairs to the street, stopped the first pie seller he saw, and bought all she had left in her tray. Returning to his room, he crouched, feasting like a wild animal, crumbs and filling flying, and felt some semblance of sanity return.

A knock at the door brought alarm. Had someone found out? Tipped off the authorities? None of his neighbors would have ought to do with coppers, but perhaps the surgeons had grown tired of him and wished to punish him for his failure. His word against theirs would carry no weight, and he would be left holding the bag.

Ridiculous fears—no one knew, not even his employers—yet he didn't answer the summons. A slip of paper was pushed under the door. Waiting until footsteps receded, he cautiously retrieved it. It was a note from the medical college. They had an offer for a prestigious lecture. Another body was needed without delay. A large bonus awaited if he was successful.

Fools, he thought. *Where do they think I'll get a body in broad daylight?*

His eye fell upon that very thing laying before him. His mind went to war. Here was an opportunity, an excuse to kill two birds with one stone, satisfy his masters and earn more coin than he might see in a week or a month while at the same time, be rid of this relic and the strange hold it had established on his imagination.

It might even be for the woman's own good. If she was in some catatonic state, surely the first cut of the knife would wake her, possibly leading to her restoration to friends and family. What a joyful reunion that would be. A second Lazarus. A miracle. And if she were well and truly dead, then what harm did it do? Her soul had already fled. The woman who visited him in his dreams was no more than a figment of his tired brain.

No less than three separate times, he wrapped her in his coat and lifted her from the floor, on the verge of smuggling her downstairs, but always unable to take the fateful step. He finally decided to go out hunting instead, to postpone the time of reckoning. If he found an opportunity, an out-of-the-way cemetery, he could weigh the risks and take a chance.

Convincing himself this was a more sensible plan than using a corpse ready at hand, he entered the bustling streets. It was no easy task to weave in and out of traffic with his cart, but he knew the city well, the backways and byways that people avoided or ignored. Those alleys and narrow streets where only the desperate loitered.

It was in one such dark passage that he spotted a man. Another drunkard like the night before. A common sight, for who wouldn't drink in times such as these if they had the coin? But this one was very much alive, weaving and singing a seaman's chanty. The sailor stumbled and fell, hitting his head on the rough cobblestones.

The victim beckoned him over, groaning and crying pitifully for help. Breedlove stared at the blood pooling on the ground. He approached cautiously and examined the man's head. The skull was crushed, gray matter showing.

A kindness, he thought.

A kindness to speed the man on the journey he had embarked upon without further pain and suffering. He laid his great palm across nose and mouth, stifling breath. The man jerked and danced under his hand like a marionette on a string, but Breedlove was relentless, fixated on this solution—this alternative to giving up Vera to be butchered like a sacrificial lamb.

In the end, killing proved easier work than hours of backbreaking digging and was seemingly no more hazardous. He expected shouts or questions, accusations to ring out at any moment, but nothing stirred other than a stray orange tabby, flicking its tail as it watched the scene with avid curiosity. He wrapped the sailor up in his tarp and loaded him onto the cart.

At the college, the surgeons came down to inspect the delivery. They looked from the broken skull to Breedlove and back again. They may have had suspicions, but a very important personage was expected. Someone with great interest in the burgeoning science of autopsy and with influence at court. They held their tongues and paid him triple the usual price.

Reaction set in as he wandered home. First stealing, now… well, murder seemed a little strong, didn't it? Mercy killing more like, but lines had been muddied, crossed. It was *her*. He had always got by, kept out of trouble until now. Resurrection men were viewed as a necessary evil these days, rather than the rank criminals they had once been. They were helping advance the cause of science, medicine, to discover cures for the myriad of diseases humanity was prey to. A noble profession, if one thought of it that way.

Breedlove didn't feel very noble. He felt sullied, depressed, and more determined than ever to return the woman to her grave, destroy the painting, and forget the whole thing had ever happened. Maybe he would even move away from the city. He'd heard they needed strong men for farm labor down south, or in the smoky factories up north. Life might be easier away from this city that chewed up and spit out all but the well-to-do.

By the time he walked through his door again, he had made up his mind to have done with her. By the time he strode across the room and gazed upon her face, his resolve had crumbled away.

A witch, he thought.

She must be. No woman had ever had this effect on him. He had been a loner, only occasionally seeking relief where all lonely men do. He turned to the portrait and peered closely. The face was not as perfect as he remembered. The white of the canvas was again showing through on the jaw and cheek facing the viewer.

He felt compelled to repair it, but was too exhausted and downtrodden in mind, body, and spirit to tackle it. He lay down on the cold floor and fell asleep.

She was there again, but this time, she was not alone. The two drunkards were her escorts, one on either side. They were dressed in the finest evening wear, such as he'd seen toffs wearing out on the town, a sharp contrast to their shabby beards and straggling hair. Her delicate hands were curled into the crooks of their elbows as she laughed up at them. They smiled down at her in indulgent admiration.

When they saw him, their merriment ground to a halt. They looked him up and down with contempt, then stared and stared, as still as statues. They did not point or accuse him in so many words, but he knew it was in their thoughts: *There is the man who has done us a grave disservice.*

He awoke, both horrified yet morbidly amused at the strange turn of phrase his mind had conjured up. *A grave disservice.* How apt. How true. He had robbed them all of their natural rest, their dignity, their rights. His head throbbed. He was a common thief, a grave robber, and yes, a murderer. What a long way fallen from the artistic dreams of his youth. Little better than an outcast now, whose one artistic masterpiece was destined never to be seen by an admiring public.

He picked up the painting and examined it closely, sucking in his breath and whistling in wonder between clenched teeth. The white was not canvas. It was very clearly paint. A miniature schematic of jaw and cheek bone, of teeth, of the skeleton beneath the skin. How was that possible? He swore it was an exact likeness of her when he painted it, a mirror image.

A sudden terror struck him, that the cadaver's face would also have decayed to reveal the structure within. He whipped around, expecting to see her beauty gone. But she lay still as ever. A perfect effigy, untouched, unchanged.

With shaking hands, he picked up a brush and painted out the bone, covering it over with blushing skin. When he was done, he curled up in a dark corner of the room, as far from corpse and painting as possible, and slept like one dead.

She did not come to him, but when he awoke, the painting was worse than ever. Bone, tendons, nerves. Like illustrations he'd seen in the surgeons' medical books. Paint flew again. Perfection achieved. He sat against the wall, holding the canvas in his hands and staring at it as little by little, almost imperceptibly, the fresh layers melted away, and the underpinnings that should not have even been there emerged again.

Numb at first, a fury slowly rose in him at this insidious decay. He gathered the will to rise, to act, smashing the painting across the back of the chair and ripping the canvas. He tore the wood framing apart with his bare hands, breaking the longer pieces against his knee, and feeding all into the fireplace, setting it to burning merrily with a lit match and a shaking hand.

A choking smoke, a horrid miasma, filled the room. He climbed the chair, pulling down rags from the skylight, so that the dreadful fumes had somewhere to go.

Night had fallen yet again. How many days since he brought her home? He no longer knew or cared. Tonight, she would go. There was some black magic at work that he would have no further part of. Not even bothering to wrap or disguise her in any way, he swept the bride over his shoulder and barreled down the stairs past shocked faces, beyond caring about any speculation he might engender. All that mattered now was returning her. He would face any consequences later.

Filled with an unnatural energy, his long strides with the heavy handcart made short work of the journey. There had been no rain since last he stood at her graveside, so the soil was still loose and shifted easily. He had never dug so quickly in his life and was soon lowering her into the empty box on top of the discarded veil.

Where once he might have reverently placed her and arranged her just so, he now tossed her in and pulled the lid into place, driving down the nails with the flat edge of his pry bar, driven by an anger that increased with each strike.

Her fault, her fault, her fault, he repeated with each blow.

He vaulted himself out of the hole and scooped the soil back in, smacking it down flat with his shovel and smoothing it so that no sign of disturbance could be seen. He expected relief, and yet he instantly missed her, yearned for her. It took every molecule of strength of will he possessed to walk away as a misty drizzle began to fall.

She would be cold and wet. So alone. No one, nothing to appreciate her beauty but the burrowing insects who feasted. With every step he took, he felt as a man split into pieces, half of him striding the earth above, half of him nestled beside her below.

Not pausing to collect his handcart or tools, he stumbled home. The few pedestrians about in the early morning hours made way, hurried across the street pulling their black umbrellas low as though to hide from him. Some even made the sign of the cross, chilled by the expression on his face.

He paid no mind. His thoughts were with her. The smooth satin of her gown, the soft fineness of her hair as he braided it, the staring eyes that never closed, not even in death. He cursed the ill fate that took him to her grave when he might have set out in a hundred other directions. Unearthed any other corpse but hers.

Whispers abounded as Breedlove climbed the stairs to his room. A bold hand reached out to grab his arm, but he brushed it away as though it was no more than a bothersome fly. He slammed his door, shutting out the mutterings and speculation. He meant to throw himself down on the mattress where *she* had lain, to sleep and sleep and sleep in hopes of escaping to a dream, any dream where she would appear to him in any form, loving or disdainful, spectral or real. He stopped in his tracks.

It was there. Propped up in the chair. The painting. Whole and neat as though it had never been slashed and burned, her face a grinning skull with bare wisps of hair and flesh still attached. A bony hand lay outspread against the surface, as though it reached out to him. He lay his own against it. It felt of warmth and flesh. The scent of spring flowers wafted gently.

The paint was dry and set, but even as he watched, faint cracks appeared in bone. Spidery webs that spread out, forming crazy patterns like the glazing of an old porcelain doll. Decay was not done with her image even now.

Pounding at the door barely registered. The rush of bodies. A melee. He vaguely recognized men, some his neighbors, some from up and down the street. A gang had gathered to demand answers about the gentlewoman he'd been seen with, *plunked over his shoulder as though she weren't no better than a sack of potatoes*, as one old cat screamed in his ear.

Let me take the painting, he pleaded.

What painting? Are ye daft? they hooted, and indeed when he looked again, the portrait was nowhere to be seen.

They pushed and prodded him down the stairs, him too stupefied to resist. But when they reached the street, he heard her calling.

Martin, Martin…

No one had called him by his first name, his true name, since his old ma passed. It was Vera, calling for him. She was lonely. Lonely and afraid.

Breedlove fought back then, throwing massive roundhouses that landed indiscriminately but did the trick. The crowd receded, no one willing to be first in line for this display of brute power. He ran away, ran with a speed none would have suspected given his size and impassive demeanor. He shed his coat as he ran, feeling as though its great weight and the heavy cloth blowing in the wind were holding him back.

Pursuit was quickly abandoned. Not worth the trouble. *They'd given him a right good scare, hadn't they?* The mob all agreed, patting each other on the back in celebration. He wouldn't return to their neighborhood. They'd be safe from whatever evil lingered round him. Let others worry about it now.

Breedlove slowed. Running through the city streets coatless and sweating would only attract more unwanted attention, and he had a mission to fulfill. He slithered and slunk through back alleys and byways until he reached the gates of the cemetery, standing wide open in the morning light. He sauntered in casually, found a quiet, out-of-the-way spot under a massively spreading oak tree and curled up there, dozing amongst its mighty roots until nightfall.

She came to him, her dress shining and bright. The simple veil covering her face was crowned with white roses that pricked her scalp and made blood drip dark and black. He caught a drop on one finger and tasted. It was sweet.

Vera unwound her veil as though it was a shroud, and her face was revealed in its rotten glory, all fine bone china, so smooth to the touch. He kissed her lipless teeth; they tasted just as sweet as her blood. He thought—no, he knew he had never felt such happiness before and never would again.

He awoke at moonrise, filled with the serenity known only to those who have seen a path illuminated clearly before them and mean to follow it to its end without wavering. He was in luck for a change. The shovel was where he had left it in the abandoned handcart. The soil was heavy, rain-soaked, and the effort needed great as he piled shovelful after shovelful on the tarp spread out for the purpose. Long work, hard work for any other man, but his heart was light, his soul sang: *for her, for her, for her.*

He dug straight down to the coffin, leaving as much dirt along the sides as he could without risking a cave-in. The rain helped, turning all to mud and clay more stable than loose, dry soil. Iron nails he had so angrily pounded into place were now gently pried up, the lid propped open once again.

She lay as he had left her, limbs askew, arms open as though welcoming him back. He cupped one hand along a soft cheek. Her skin no longer burned, was cold as ice, but intact and serene. Her eyes watched him closely, and he thought her lips curled just slightly into the whisper of a smile.

Now for the difficult part, a quite inhuman feat for anyone without his strength and determination. His obsession lent him unnatural power as he grabbed the tarp where it hung over the edge of the grave and tugged with all his might. A seemingly impossible task. He groaned in effort and pain, felt muscle and sinew tear in back, arm, groin and thigh, but still he pulled.

All of a sudden, it shifted. So sudden, he fell back into her waiting arms as dirt and mud tumbled down upon them. A poor job, an incomplete job. Insufficient to fill the entire grave neatly and not give rise to speculation and investigation the next time someone happened by. No matter. He would have suffocated long before then, his soul fled to join hers in whatever lay beyond. What happened to the vessels left behind them was unimportant.

He clutched her arms tight around his chest as breath was squeezed out of his laboring lungs. He felt her both above and below him, becoming painfully aware of his own flesh and bone, and understanding how fragile a thing a man was after all.

Panic set in. A natural human instinct to breathe, to fight, to live. The muddy earth was slimy and cold; it filled his mouth and chilled his skin. Had he been tricked? Enchanted by some demon in disguise? It might still be possible to save himself. Scream and claw, kick and dig, leave the madness behind with this temptress of the earth.

He strained half-heartedly against the weight pressing down upon him, all the while knowing it was a lost cause and that his fate was already sealed.

Don't worry, Martin, Vera's teeth chattered into his ear as darkness descended. *I'll keep you safe. You're home now.*

Walking down the dark streets
We are the nightmares
Warned of in children's tales.
The lights flicker
And I remember
When candlelight was the cause.
They say we're cursed,
Damned,
Forever to walk this earth.
Sustaining ourselves
On the life blood of others.
I used to agree
Before I met her.
She is like me,
A lovely creature of the night.
Eternal youth and beauty,
And I will burn the world
For one more kiss
From her.

Burning
K.R. Wieland

VII

Lucia & Tatiana

Alexa Rose

Midnight at Viteri Manor

My dearest Lucia,

I write tonight of my cousin, Emilia. We know her to be in Gran Aran, and we know she sent no word in some weeks. Now, we know why. The murderous inquisitor Amand Leroux has finished his purge of Gran Aran. Now he comes for us.
I am sure my cousin is dead by Leroux's command. I shudder to think of what he will do with us. His faith speeds his feet to the walls of Orena, and the Church follows in his wake. My father speaks of this man as though he is a specter, an impossible enemy. I know not what to do when he arrives, but I hold to my faith in us.

Pray be safe, my love.

Yours eternally,
Tatiana

I fold the letter and return it to my corset. Curious eyes consider me from across the room, but none hold my stare. I motion to a passing thrall for a glass and take the chilled burgundy wine in my hand as he bows and moves toward the next thirsting person.

Some humans know their place in this world.

Around me, the masquerading room swirls to the energetic rhythm of piano and violin. Silk and hair sway as the women dance and the black-clad men clap their hands in time to the music. I lean back on a maroon monstrosity of a couch and raise my wine glass. It is a human vintage with a sickening taste of citrus and wood. It needs iron and that tinge of fear. I swap which leg is crossed over which, and I dangle the glass above the white-marble floor as the music swells.

My mind wanders to last winter as I succumb to the rhythm. Snow settles on Tatiana's black fur cape. A street performer teases his bow across a violin's strings. Humans fill the park around us. They stink of dying flesh, but Tatiana distracts me with a kiss. I feel her fangs with my tongue. Her hand brushes my hair aside. We break our kiss and listen to the mus-

I am pulled from my reverie by raised voices behind me. Eyes on the masked dancers, I focus on what is being said as I gently press a finger against the memory of that kiss.

"I left three at the wells." A bass voice. Confident. Young. Brash.

There is a sharp intake of breath followed by a curse.

"Was this wise? Won't they come for vengeance?" An older voice. Wiser, perhaps. Worry clouds their words.

I smile as I turn toward the two men, setting one bare foot on the couch and propping my arm on the monstrosity's mahogany back. Both men are dressed in their finest black jackets. Neither takes part in the masquerade. The older vampire raises his glass to me. The whelp shows his fangs in a broad grin. Silly boy. I ignore his charms and lock eyes with the elder.

"What's this? Corpses left in plain view?" My voice cuts through the notes. Mother's haughtiness comes from my mouth. Inwardly, I cringe. Age is worsening my attitude.

Both men look away. The elder drains his glass in a long swallow and looks for the nearest carafe.

"It would seem so, Lady Viteri," he says as he placates with a gesture. "Forgive me." Without pause, he starts across the room.

The younger vampire leans over the couch. I smell blood on his clothes. Vampire blood. His hands are rank with it. Curling my lip, I set both feet to the floor and stand.

"You killed our resources and left their corpses in an alley?" I ask the whelp. My finger taps against my cheek as I watch self-satisfaction drain from the creature's eyes. He glances elsewhere and my ire rises.

Reaching out, I curl my fingers into a fist. I feel my power swell as I pull his attention to me. His mouth slackens and a rivulet of wine and saliva drip to the floor.

I stare into his eyes and see crudeness. Bloodshed. Carnal desires. Feasting on the dead. "Answer me."

"Yes."

"Were any of the humans women?"

"No."

Inwardly, I sigh. To the room, I am wrath incarnate.

"Go. Find the corpses you made. Remove them from the city."

I feel eyes upon me. People are standing still. Murmurs rise above the quieted music. I release the creature and turn. He skitters into the dark as I stride into the crowd. Everyone parts for me. Some glare. Some long for me. None speak a word.

"My gathered Ladies and Lords, a moment of your time," I say. My voice carries down here. It echoes, and I hear the sharpness of my tone. Should I break the news gently? I shake my head. What does it matter? Mother would be proud if she yet stood among us. Maybe. I never learned what made her hate me less. She cannot hate me anymore.

Smiling at the memory of Mother's last glare, I draw myself up and eye my guests in their exotic masks.

"I trust you have enjoyed yourselves at Viteri Manor."

A smattering of light claps echo to me. Mostly, narrow eyes watch, waiting for what comes next. Servants pass among the crowd with oil lanterns. The chandelier is lit with a gesture. Light returns to this dark dwelling.

"I fear tonight will be the last festivity I will host. In fact, tonight is the last festivity any of us will attend."

Heads turn toward the doors. My guests back away from my servants.

"Oh, you are safe here, but alas, you must leave. Grand Inquisitor Amand Leroux approaches Orena from Gran Aran. The Church comes with him. I would explain further, but you know how this tale ends for undying people like us."

For a moment, silence.

A guest raises his mask. Others follow his lead. Drunk on blood-wine, the unbalanced crowd totters for a moment and erupts in chaos as panic takes hold. I remain still, my hands clasped at my waist, as my ballroom empties and the stampede of frightful fools flees into the night.

When at last my manor is empty of guests, I venture upstairs. I hear the muffled *shhhhh* of rain through the walls and pause, my hand upon the solid door that separates me from everything vile in the world.

"Lady Viteri?"

I pause, but I do not turn. I recognize the servant's voice, but I cannot recall her name.

"Is it true? Does Amand Leroux approach our city?"

"Yes."

"Will the ancient houses fight the Church?"

"No."

"Why not?" Her voice hardens with anger and defiance.

Such is why she is a servant.

I lift my umbrella from a rack and open the door. "Lock this behind me. Or flee into the night. Whichever grave you prefer."

She says something, but I do not hear her.

Flames rise from the city gates. Distant bells toll their dirge into the dark. Even at this distance, I feel the oppressive weight of holy relics carried by the Church's priests. My skin itches. I ignore the sensation while it is mild. Later, I may not have such a luxury.

Draping a cape around my shoulders, I open my umbrella and step into the rain. The city's lanterns are blurred points of light winding below me. I have not walked the streets of Orena in a long time. Holding my head high, I set off into the storm.

It is a beautiful last night.

Witching Hour at Baran Park

Rain patters against my umbrella as I stop beneath a towering elm's bare branches. I smell smoke, but I ignore it. Tonight is not for worries.

The damp clings to my skin and upsets my carefully arranged hair. If a human dares to look closely, they will wonder why my breath does not fog the air. Bolstered by Leroux's arrival, they might even try to drive a stake through my heart or splash me with oil and set me ablaze. Few humans are in the park at this late hour, but I pull my cape's hood lower and sink into its depths.

Lightning claws the sky, leaving a bright wound for a blink. The world shudders with thunder. Across the way, human lovers laugh and shriek and scurry like rats. I can smell their lust. It is a cloying thing. My tongue catches on a fang as I watch the humans round an alley's corner.

One of them guffaws. I want to take wing and sup upon their delicious bodies. I would drink from the woman first. The man can watch in thrall and be dessert.

That thought barely fades when my Tatiana approaches along the lamp-lit boulevard. She is svelte beneath her cape, and she moves with practiced grace. Her hips sway with each step. Her shoulders bear the confidence of one who knows precisely where they mean to be. She ascends the three steps into the park as though she climbs a queen's dais.

The last of the human lovers pass from the night. I hear the distant boom of something explosive. A second later, fire blossoms over the city's shadowy outline. None of that matters. My Tatiana stares at me, and I see my whole world in her smile. I want to take wing and ravage her delicious body.

She crosses the stone path to stand beneath my elm. As always, lilac and rosehips envelope her. I close my eyes as I take in her perfumes. I feel her hand against my cheek. Her thumb wipes the damp from my skin as her fingers slide into my pinned hair. I lean into her touch. Her lips find mine. Her tongue darts against mine. Keeping the umbrella upright, I wrap my free arm around her and pull her body against me. Our lips move as only passion can inspire. We remain in our embrace until the next peal of thunder.

"I am happy you came," I whisper, my eyes languid and their lids heavy with lust.

"I could never deny you," my Tatiana says. Her hands fall to my hips, and she holds me as lovers do. She smiles, and her fangs show. They are long and beautiful, curved to the finest points. I want to ravish her, but she sees my intent and shakes her head.

"I would dally in this rain all night," she says as her large eyes look up at me. "However, we do not have all night to dally."

Searing malice toward Amand Leroux and the poisonous Church rises in my mouth. My hands tremble with it. Tatiana's touch calms me. Her hands cradle my face, and her smile pulls me from that pit of hate.

"Where you go, I will follow," Tatiana says. Worry clouds her features. Her fingers intertwine with mine. "Stay with me tonight."

In a perfect world, I would lay her on these sodden stones and burn the night with our passion. Alas, this is not a perfect world. I fold my hand over hers and I kiss her lips. I do not need to speak. She has my answer.

Predawn Perch on Emil's Wall

Church bells strike five o'clock. Already, screams carry on the wind. Thralls are put to Leroux's sword. Tatiana's arm is around me as we stand atop the city's upper wall and watch the Church file into Orena in neat procession. Firelight glints on the steel horde. Bonfires burn wood and flesh alike. For now, humans are content to kill humans.

"How long will the gates hold?" Tatiana's whisper is a fragile thing. For a moment, I do not answer. I do not want to break her unbeating heart, but I must.

"The upper city's gate is for decoration, my love." I fold my arms around her and pull her close so I can kiss her cold cheek and lean my brow against hers. "None of this should have come to pass. But the world grows tired of old ways."

Tatiana does not slump as I expected. Rather, she becomes rigid and looks into my eyes. I see the flames of wrath rise within her.

"They are humans. We can push them back. Tear them limb from limb. Feast on their beating hearts and dine on their fear."

She is young. This past century taught her to take what she wanted without repercussion. I slide my hands to her shoulders and hold her at arm's length. Her fury flares and she strains against me. Below, a bonfire blazes as oil is splashed upon a thrall's shrieking body.

"We are legion," she hisses. "They should fear us."

I shake my head, but she presses on.

"It is yet night. We could take wing and drive them from our city. We could fight. We coul—"

"No." There is finality in my voice. The shrieks from below perish in flame.

"Why? Why will you not fight, Lucia?"

I turn my lover toward the fires of Orena. I point to the masses of dead and beaten thralls. I gesture to the hundreds of soldiers and the faithful priests who walk among them.

"Look at them," I say.

She blinks and glances at me. Her mouth opens, but I stare into her eyes and let slip a moment of my power.

"Look at them," I command.

Her fury cannot overcome my will. She looks upon the once-beautiful courtyards and markets of Orena's lower city as they burn and are trampled into mud. I join her in spectating the death of so many hardworking people.

"Do you feel that?" I press my hand over her unbeating heart.

She nods. "I do."

"That is the weight of faith." I feel the same pressure upon me. It is stifling. Oppressive. It is enough to make me fearful. Pointing at the priests below, I continue. "That is the conviction of their faith. We made pacts with devils and swore promises to witches. We danced during the witching hour on All Hallow's Eve. We forsook our humanity. They embrace their humanity. That is their faith. Their power."

My Tatiana slumps against me. Her wrath abandons her. I hold her close and press my lips against her brow.

"I do not want to die," she whispers.

"I do not know how to avoid our fate," I say.

She turns in my arms and sets her hands against my face. Sadness is etched upon her wide eyes and sharp features. She leans forward to set her lips against mine, and she says, "What of the devils? Could we not make new pacts?"

Words come to my lips, and I speak them, knowing they are true. "What could we offer them? They took our humanity. They left us immortal and cursed. We have nothing more to offer."

She glances at the fires below. I feel her shudder, and I hold her tighter. If I could bear the weight of her fear, I would. But I have my own fears to fight, and I am losing. Ancient as I am, powerful as I am, I know my end will come this day.

"Come," I say. I turn my Tatiana from the carnage of the lower city. "Let us return to my manor. They can seek us behind my walls."

She becomes mist and I follow. Orena speeds beneath me as I fly toward the grand granite manor cresting the city's heights like a weather-worn crown. It is my home, and it will be my grave.

The Monstrous Leroux

Amand Leroux wipes his arming sword free of gore and tosses the cloth strip onto the dying thrall. When a priest comes forward with holy symbols raised, Leroux lifts a hand and shakes his head without ever looking at the priest.

"No prayers," Leroux says. "The creature is in thrall to the vampires that feed upon this once-great city, and it does not deserve God's mercy."

The priest opens his holy text and shuffles through the pages, words stammering from his mouth as though their half-formed utterances will afford him time. Leroux walks away, sheathing his sword as he goes.

"I have spoken, Father Ameti. Leave it to die in peace," Leroux calls out.

Around him, pyres burn heretical thralls. Each creature is marked by twin puncture wounds on its neck. Some bear tattoos or stylized scars as further proof of their fall from the Light of God. Soldiers pass him with their swords drawn. No one falters at the screams and pleas of the dying heretics. Death is their mercy.

A captain approaches with one hand on his hilt, the other holding a furled sheet of parchment. A foppish hat of pretentious design covers the man's high-born head. Leroux slows but does not stop as the captain reaches his side.

"Count Leroux, I bring news of our first forays."

Leroux nods once. He glances sidelong at the sweating captain and notes the singular smear of blood across the man's breastplate. Raising an eyebrow, he waits for the captain to share the details.

"All houses in the lower districts have been searched. Eighty-four thralls have been executed in their homes. The rest are being led here. Several houses bore heretical markings and writings, all of which are being delivered to your carriage as ordered."

When the captain lowers his report and says no more, Leroux stops. His feet sink into the churned mud. The smell of urine and blood and charred flesh assails him, but he is no stranger to the stench of fear and death. Scrunching his nose, he presses on.

"How many vampires did you find?"

The captain swallows hard and takes off his silly hat with its two peacock feathers and the steel insignia of his bought rank.

"None."

"None?"

"T-there were markings, of course. And the writings. The heretics have the fiends' marks upon their necks. Perhaps the vampires live elsewhere?"

"Elsewhere?"

"Elsewhere in the city, perhaps." The captain eyes the city's upper reaches with its Noble's Quarter and the manors that overlook the fall of Orena. "Perhaps they even reside within Duke Faustus's estate."

"Oh?"

The captain's voice finds its steel and hardens when he realizes what Leroux wants to hear. "Vampires are here, and that Duke Faustus has not expelled them means he is complicit."

Leroux's mouth curls into a Cheshire grin. He sets his hand on his hip and looks up to Emil's Wall and the Noble's Quarter beyond. For a heartbeat, he sees twin figures standing against the graying sky. When he blinks, they are gone. Tricks and devilry.

"Gather the priests. They must bless every doorway so the vampires cannot gain entry. We will press into the Noble's Quarter at dawn. We will drag them from their homes and stand them in God's Light where He will judge them."

The captain salutes but does not hurry off. Rather, he folds his feathered hat in his worried hands and shuffles from foot to foot.

Turning toward the military man, Leroux's smile falls, and a bitter taste fills his mouth. I know a damning question when I see one.

"Out with it, captain."

"What is to be done with the honest citizens?"

Leroux scoffs and raises his hands toward the heavens, saying, "Why do You challenge me like this?"

"Count Leroux?"

Returning his penetrating stare to the captain, Leroux asks, "Who do you mean by honest citizens?"

The captain stammers and drops his hat. He plucks it from the muck, wiping the filth from the velvet as best as he can.

Frowning, Leroux snatches the fool's wretched covering from between thick fingers and tosses it far to the side.

"Captain? Who do you mean?"

Forlorn, the captain refuses to meet Leroux's glare and says, "The people without the fiends' marks and whose homes are free of markings and signs of devilry."

Leroux's hand closes around the captain's chin and lifts the man's face until Leroux can see the man's ineptitude.

"Look. Harder."

"B-but we searched. They are innocent."

Leroux pushes the captain away, sending the man tumbling to the muck. Soldiers, priests, and heretics alike glance at the commotion then avert their eyes.

"There are no innocents here!"

The captain opens his mouth. A strained sound escapes as he falls to his knees and whispers a prayer to God.

"Get up. Do your job. We will cleanse this city with holy fire. Any who are truly innocent will be judged by God and admitted to Heaven. Unless, of course, you believe you can do God's work for Him."

At that, soldiers and priests turn their attention to the muck-covered captain. True to his station, the veteran soldier rises to his full height and adjusts his sword belt. He steps forward and salutes Leroux, saying, "Orena will be purged."

"To the last man, woman, or child, Captain Hammond. To. The. Last."

"Of course."

Leroux looks to the sky as the captain barks orders and sets off with his sword drawn and his foolish hat forgotten. Dawn fast approaches. With Your Light upon us, we will save this city.

His smile returning, Leroux sets off for Emil's Wall. Soldiers fall into step behind him. The clergy rush to gather around him. Prayers are whispered. Knees rise and fall in genuflections.

"The devil dies today, Count Leroux," a priest says with a fervor bordering on madness.

Leroux nods once. "So it does," he says.

Farther off, screams ring out as the rest of the heretics are put to the sword.

No devilry will remain, Leroux promises himself.

Dawn Comes to Orena

I stand in the quiet ballroom enlivened by dance hours earlier. Glasses remain where they were set. Blood-wine spoils in the open air, lending the smell of iron and rot to the candle-lit room. Ignoring the remnants of my last festivity, I move to the massive portraits along the back wall.

Lord Viteri looks upon me as though he judges my failure. His widow's peak is pronounced, and the artist added prominence to his fangs. In his cursed life, the elder bore small fangs and resented those born with beautifully long fangs like my dear Tatiana.

Thinking of her, I look over my shoulder to see her standing near the fireplace as it crackles with a tiny flame. Her arms are wrapped around her body, and her wide eyes shift from one mess to another. She looks so fragile and elegant for such a misused environment. Giving my elder a parting glance, I cross the room to my lover's side.

"Where did they go?" she asks, her voice a small thing I must strain to hear. A moment later, I understand her question and set my hands upon her arm.

"I imagine they fled."

Hope lights her eyes. Oh, my dearest Tatiana. I pat her arm and say, "They will not have gone far, my love. These are people who have ruled Orena for centuries. They believe themselves immortal. That no one yet slayed them makes them believe they cannot be slain."

She looks at me with profound sadness weighing upon her features. It is a terrible thing, to see a distraught vampire. We are predators. We are the horrors in the night. We are not made to be fearful and pensive.

"Come," I say, pulling on her arm. She follows with a slight hesitation, and I lead her to a back stair that winds upon wrought-iron spiral steps to a bedchamber draped in lilac and scented with roses. Lilies grow in pots near the closed windows. A chandelier of guttered candles stands watch over my possessions. It is a shame the servants did not attend to my chamber.

My Tatiana pulls away and lowers herself onto my bed. She passes a hand over the soft sheets and presses against the plush blankets. Despite her fears, a smile pulls at her features as she looks around.

More portraits hang on my walls. These are of me and of the human women I once loved. Fashion dates each artwork going back several centuries. I have not aged, but I see the burden of time in my eyes.

"I have never seen your personal chambers."

I pause to consider her words. She is right. Nodding, I say, "We had so many places to meet, and my chambers are nothing special."

She does not believe my words. Her smile continues as she points to the nearest portrait.

"Who is she?"

I follow her gesture to an ancient painting of the Marquess Vantre. I cannot recall the details of our romances, but I am sure they were memorable for a time.

"An old friend," I say. When Tatiana shifts her gaze to another portrait, I join her on the bed and take her hands into mine.

"These are faces from my past. People I knew. Lives I touched in some way. They sent portraits as remembrances that I might not forget them, but alas, time ravages all things."

"At the end of things, you bring me to your past?"

I turn toward my love. My fingers intertwine with hers. I gently raise a hand to her jaw to turn her full attention upon me.

"I brought you here because this is my most personal space. This is the me no one else sees. It is my past, but it is also where I feel safest. I hoped you might feel safe here, too."

"In this dark, strangely, I do."

I cannot tell if she means her words or if my aura has drawn those words from her. Regardless, I smile and lean forward. She meets me. Her lips press against mine. Her hands wrap around my neck and her fingers pull at the lacing that keeps my corset tight. I do not fumble with her laces. Rather, I drag my sharp fingernail across the cross-laced silk until her corset is loose and easily pulled away.

We fumble each other out of our dresses. Each mass of fabric pools on the floor. Atop the bed, we roll to the middle as our hands explore one another and our mouths find sensuous purchase. I am reminded again of my lover's youth when she does not relent. Her eyes glimmer in the dark, and the force of her lust weighs upon me. It compels me, and I do not resist.

For hours, we writhe and let loose our desires. By the end, we each bear bite marks and the ragged furrows of passion's claws. The bed is a mess. My wonderful sheets are shredded and torn. The imported pillows have scattered their goose down.

I lay my head upon my lover's breast and languidly draw circles upon her belly with a singular fingernail.

"I love you," I say.

"I love you too," my Tatiana replies.

For a moment, all is well in our world. For a moment, we simply are. But all moments end. Ours does so with the distant crash of a battered door and the dulled voices of intruders into my home.

Tatiana clings to me. I decide there and then I will defend her. My conviction is newfound and uncharted, but it becomes a vow. I feel my power swell like it did centuries ago. I know if I give in to this idea my power will consume me.

I say nothing of this to my Tatiana. Rather, I stand and whisper, "Wait here." I lie and add, "I will return."

Amand Leroux leads a contingent of twenty soldiers through the uppermost manor in the Noble's Quarter. Lighting his torch high, he sees signs of devilry and debauchery everywhere. Blood spoils in wine glasses. Exsanguinated corpses lie in heaps along the walls like so much discarded trash. Behind him, the soldiers mutter prayers and whisper to one another.

A grand stair leads to the second floor. Advancing one step at a time, Leroux tilts his head to better hear the faintest sound. Only whispers come to him.

"Silence your blathering," he hisses. The soldiers quiet down, but they stink of sweat and fear. He turns on the stair to scowl at his best soldiers, but as he does so, their mouths slacken and one among them points to something at his back.

Spinning, his sword at the ready and his torch thrust forward as a ward, Leroux finally sees a vampire in this wretched city. It is womanly and obscenely nude. He fights through his shock to recall the holy lines that might weaken the creature.

"And I walked alone through the night where beast and devil might feed upon me, but such was my faith in God none could come against me, and I bore my flesh and blood to the dawn that I migh—"

Leroux realizes the words have no effect. He screams as the vampire hisses unnatural sounds and simply appears at his side. He thrusts his sword with abandon and scores the banister for his efforts. Behind him, soldiers scream and flee, their steps thundering down the stairs.

To Leroux's horror, his feet betray him, and he stumbles backward. His blade wavers. Prayers die on his lips. God protect me. But that thought feels hollow in the face of the dark beauty who appraises him with infernal eyes and black hair that writhes like serpents.

Biting his lip, forcing himself to fight his fears, Leroux grips his sword hilt so hard it hurts, and ascends the stairs two at a time to lunge toward this destroyer of humanity.

His blade finds purchase. His sword drives so hard against the creature that its tip is buried in the banister behind. The force of his faith washes over him as he smiles in victory. I have defeated this vile creature!

Overhead, a deafening shriek pierces his senses and drives him to one knee. His hand falls away from the holy relic, and he drops his torch upon the stair. He dares to look up. Another vampire leans over the rail. Its face is contorted with rage and . . . sadness? That is not right, Leroux tells himself.

The second vampire falls forward into a puff of smoke that plummets to the stair and reforms into the image of a beautiful maiden. Her long fangs and wicked claws mark her as a creature of the night, but Leroux is without the means to defeat this vampire. He glances to his sword, but he recognizes his defeat and withdraws in a jumble of legs and scrambling hands. Behind him, the vampire wails.

It shouts in the language of men.

"Curse your faith and your wretched kind. Curse every one of you who came to our city and bore steel against us. May your blood rot and your minds break. May your God forsake you and the ground deny your bones!"

In his haste, Leroux slams into a doorway, knocking the air from his chest. He coughs violently and sees droplets of bright blood expel with every heave of his lungs. Panicked, he races as best as he can until he passes through the front door and stands in the daylit boulevard.

Priests and soldiers gather around him. Everyone turns a frightful eye toward the manor. The wails continue. They sound like grief.

"Should we rally, Count Leroux?" a soldier asks.

Shaking his head, his breath still catching up, Leroux says, "No. It is cursed."

Hearing that, the priests balk and call for fire. The first priest to make such an utterance grimaces and coughs bright blood into his hand. Every priest who summons flames bears the same bright token.

Realizing the weight of his predicament, Leroux pushes his people away from the manor's granite walls. He feels it now. An oppressive weight burdens him. Each step away from the manor eases the feeling of suffocation. The creature cursed us all. When Leroux understands his thought, he ushers everyone farther and farther from the manor.

"Away," he says, coughing blood as his lungs finally fill with air. "Away, all of you. It is cursed. Quick, return to the lower city. Seal Emil's Gate behind us that none might enter that place of death."

No one rejects his words. Those who come running with fire in their hands are sent back to the pyres from whence they came. At Emil's Gate, Leroux pauses long enough to twist the key.

The loudest wail yet echoes through the midmorning light. Hearing it, the soldiers flee and the priests give up every pretense of composure. Leroux stares up at Viteri Manor and listens to the pains of lost love.

Breaking the key in the lock, Count Amand Leroux abandons the Noble's Quarter and his mission, leaving both to the damned.

Night's Sweet Embrace

I stand at the balcony of my lover's manor and look at Orena's ruins. The armies have withdrawn, but their pyres still burn. To my horror, all is quiet in the necropolis.

Across the quarter, I see the smoldering remains of my family's estate. Burned bodies kneel with spears through their hearts. My father did not deserve this. The same sight is repeated near every manor but Viteri Manor.

Retreating from the city, I close the doors behind me and move near Lucia's lust-sundered bed. My dead lover lays in respite upon her torn comforts. She is beautiful as ever. Eternal rest does not diminish the love I feel for her.

Sitting at an easel with a plain canvas ransacked from my lover's closets, I dip a brush into her oil paints and begin her portrait.

Let the murder flock down
In my garden of roses
As the sky fills with carnage
This is when I finally become
Who I'm meant to be
Divine
My eyes burn like liquid flames
Skin soaked in ash—crumbling
I've marched through trials, tribulations, and malaise
To reach my pinnacle
I am a goddess
Fire cradles my soul
I finally join my sisterhood
Where I'm meant to be.

GARDEN TO GODDESS
ERIN QUILL

VIII

Death Cry of the Magpie

CARLA ELIOT

Its surface is satisfyingly smooth beneath my fingers.

The afternoon sun shines high in the cloudless, cornflower-colored sky, throwing golden light over our garden which is a long carpet of freshly cut grass. Surrounding fields create a patchwork of greens and yellows. The rapeseed is in full bloom.

I scrape my knee climbing the stone wall, but it is worth it. As I peer into the dome-shaped nest, my heart gallops.

Six eggs, the color of seafoam, sit snugly under the shadows of the tree's leaves. I slip my hand beneath the nearest egg, and with my other hand clutching the branch, I draw it out from its nest. I cradle it to my chest like I'm holding a newborn baby, still precariously balanced on the uneven wall.

I know I should wait until I've climbed down before taking a better look at the magpie's egg, but I can't resist having a quick peek. I bring my arms away from me, just a little bit, and slowly uncurl my fingers. I hear the sharp intake of my breath.

The color of the egg is even more vivid in the sunlight. It's not as bright as the robin's eggs I saw last year, which were a vibrant turquoise color. This one is more subtle and speckled with green flecks that remind me of the olives Mum sometimes buys. It is oval shaped like an olive, too.

I wish I could keep the egg. Add it to my collection of treasures. But I won't. I'll just look at it for a while, and then put it back in its nest.

I'm about to bend my knees, so that I can sit on my bottom and make it easier to get down off the wall, when a frantic flapping sound from above snatches my attention. I'm startled by the rippling cool air created by the magpie's beating wings. The bird's shadow falls over me, its plump body blocking out the sun's warmth as its ghostly twin flutters darkly across the grass. My fingers tremble, heart racing.

Chacker chacker chacker

The magpie's harsh cry fills my ears, and for a moment I lose sense of everything else.

The egg falls from my hands like a teardrop. Unstoppable. I move fast, and although I'm moving in a world that seems to have slowed down around me, I don't make it in time. I'm unable to halt its descent. The egg glides through the air, as if down an unseen tunnel, and only stops when it hits the wall.

The cracking sound as the egg's shell breaks is horribly final.

I watch in horror and shame as the gooey substance oozes out from the once-beautiful blue egg. I step back, covering my eyes, not wanting to see what I've done. I forget that I'm still precariously standing on the wall.

My foot rolls over one of the stones, and my ankle twists. I cry out as the sharp pain shoots up my leg. Once again, the world slows down as I fall backwards, arms windmilling.

I hit the ground with a dull thud that causes my teeth to clatter.

My bottom hurts and my hip is throbbing, but it's nothing compared to the pulsing pain in my ankle. Sprawled on the grass, I contemplate my injuries and momentarily forget about the magpie.

I suddenly feel very warm and realize that the sun, no longer blocked by the bird, is beating down on me. I lift my head, eyes searching for the mother magpie.

My breath catches in my throat. I feel my bottom lip tremble in remorse. And fear.

Perched on the branch by her nest of now only five eggs, the mother's dark eyes regard me fiercely. I feel the heat from her accusing glare at the same time a cold wave of dread ripples through me.

The sun still paints the garden in a golden light, but the warmth I felt just a moment ago has drained away. All that I feel now is the coldness of the mother magpie, though I am no longer draped in her shadow.

My ankle twinges. It's a physical response that afflicts me even ten years after the day I dropped the magpie's egg and fell off the wall. I rub at the knot of bone, certain that as I do, the skin swells under my fingers.

I'm in the kitchen, sitting on a wooden stool. One bare foot is planted on the cold, rough surface of the flagstone floor. The other is propped on my knee as I inspect my left ankle. The room is dark, but the sun streaming through the long window by the door provides enough light for me to study my old injury. The skin appears very gray and growing grayer still as I look at it. The tissue and bone under my darkening flesh seems to writhe and push upwards. I swallow, stomach churning, before I lower my foot to join the other.

I gaze around the quiet kitchen, eyes falling on the empty chairs surrounding the long wooden table. It feels like years since I was last sitting here with Mother and Father, although they've only been dead for three weeks. My ankle seems to have gotten worse ever since.

And that memory keeps resurfacing.

I still have a lingering shame for what I did that day. It was just an accident. I didn't mean to drop the egg. But I could never forget the look in the mother magpie's eyes. Nor my fear of its beady, penetrating gaze. The memory has become like a nightmare that I know I shouldn't be scared of. However, I can't outgrow the childish fear. I'm a twenty-year-old woman, but inside I'll always be that ten-year-old girl.

The day I fell off the wall was the start of everything else that inevitably tumbled around me. Things revealed themselves as no longer perfect and everlasting. Everything was just waiting to crack and break like that egg.

The first bad thing to happen was Mother losing the baby. I'd been looking forward to having a little sister or brother. But whoever she or he was ever going to be, their flame was extinguished before they had a chance to shine. That put a big crack in our family. Mother was never the same after that. She always seemed to have a similar look to the mother magpie when I dropped her egg.

Was I to blame for Mother losing her baby, too?

Then came the rain. So much of it, I remember feeling as if we were stranded in the middle of the ocean. Our tiny little farmhouse became Noah's ark. But unlike the Bible story, God had abandoned us.

Father struggled with the crops, and then the farm animals began to suffer. By the time the weather became drier, we were left with just a goat and a couple of chickens. They're gone now too, of course.

The house is an empty husk of a building. All the goodness has been scooped out and only the cracked shell remains. It's functional but lacking in warmth or love. I'm grateful that I have a roof over my head. And as long as I can keep finding work so I can eat, I'll be fine. The land Father used to farm is now barren. I lack resources to do anything about it, financially or physically.

I watch the dust particles as they hover in the shafts of golden light. They shift and change direction as if moved by an unseen force.

"Charlotte, you're a grown woman."

The words that leave my mouth are quickly swallowed by the silence of the house.

I sigh before pushing to my feet. My ankle is still complaining, but I'm used to the discomfort. I often wonder if the pain is even there at all.

The flame flickers and snaps, throwing distorted shapes against the walls as I walk through the house. I'm doing my evening routine of checking the windows and making sure the doors are locked. My feet are silent on the stone floor as I move. The billowing of my long, white nightdress behind me is a reminder of how quiet the house is.

Cold air tickles my legs and whispers around my neck. Darkness presses against the windows, and shadows bleed from the corners of the rooms like spilled ink. I'll be glad once I'm in bed and asleep. I can escape the darkness of the real world only by entering the darkness behind my closed eyelids.

At the kitchen window, I do what I always do. I stop and gaze out over the once-neat garden, now just a carpet of yellowing bristle, until my eyes come to rest on the tree.

The magpie's tree.

Like everything else, the tree has suffered, too. Naked, skeletal branches claw at the slate sky. No birds have nested among them for a long time.

I start to turn away from the window, but a flicker of movement outside catches my eye. I stop, heart pounding.

On the thickest branch of the tree, the one that hangs over the stone wall, there is a dark shape. It's even blacker than the darkness that surrounds it.

"Mother Magpie," I whisper. "It can't be."

I lean closer to the window. The candle's flame quivers and brings an orange, ghastly glow to the reflection of my face in the glass.

The bird twitches, puffing out its round chest. The silhouette of its bill is sharp with a hooked end. The hollowed eyes of my reflection grow wide. The cold, familiar wave of dread washes over me.

"Ow," I cry, pulling swiftly back from the glass. The sharp pain in my ankle has intensified. It's as if I was bitten.

I shake my head, rubbing at my eyes with my free hand. I need to get into bed and rest. My throbbing ankle pleads with me to do just that.

I glance back towards the tree.

The magpie has gone.

Each step creaks and groans under my weight as I carefully ascend the stairs, candle held high. My shivering shadow on the wall follows close behind. I lift the hem of my nightdress so I can see where to place my feet. Shadows of indiscernible shapes flutter on the ceiling. At the top of the stairs, I turn towards my bedroom. I sleep in the same room I did as a child. My parents' room will always be theirs, even if they are no longer alive.

There's a low shuffling sound as something crawls in the shadows behind me. It is accompanied by a low hum. I don't turn towards the sound. I'm used to it now.

My bedroom door moans as I close it. I bring down the latch to lock myself in before turning to place the candle on the bedside table. I'm pulling back the bed covers, eager to get under, when there's a sudden shift in the darkness to my right. The candle's flame dances as if stirred by an outside breeze. I whirl around.

A scream escapes my mouth before I can bring up my hands to smother it. The sound dies on my lips as my blood turns cold. I watch in horror as the black shape looms large—growing larger still—against the wall at the foot of the bed.

Its shadowy wings beat madly, the whipping sound filling my ears. Cold air rushes at me and lifts my hair.

I scream again, certain the magpie is behind me. Then I realize it's just a shadow thrown against the wall. The wings flutter with a building frenzy. I turn to face it.

And the candle goes out.

I don't scream this time, for the darkness and my fear have robbed me of my voice. Just a strangled whimper is all I can manage as I dive onto the bed. I bring the covers up over my head and curl my knees in tight, like I used to do as a child.

My body shakes with building terror. The sound of my rapid breathing is loud in the otherwise silent room. I draw in a harsh breath, trying to still my quivering chest. I chew my bottom lip, listening.

A loud, familiar cackle shatters the silence. The tiny hairs lift on my arms. I clamp down hard on my lip, and a moment later, I taste blood.

Chacker chacker chacker

The repetitive cackle is clear. It emanates from just above my head.

Chacker chacker chacker

"It can't be," I whisper. "It can't be her."

Chacker chacker chacker

"Please," I plead with the darkness beneath the cover I cower under, clutching it tightly. "Please leave me alone. I never meant to do it. I never meant to drop it."

Chacker chacker chacker

"Please."

My eyes sting, and I realize I'm crying. Warm tears roll down my cheeks and drop to the mattress as shivering spasms take over my body.

Chacker chacker chacker

"Please," I whisper as I close my eyes. Snot oozes from my nose to join my fallen tears. "I never meant to drop it." My hands go slack, fingers loosening from the sheet. "Please leave me alone. It was...It was just an accident. I promise...I promise. I never...meant to..."

The words are barely audible to my own ears as I drift into sleep.

The next morning, I walk to the village. Absorbed in the daily housework I do for elderly Miss Morris, I am almost able to forget the previous night. The day passes in a blur of scrubbing floors and preparing Miss Morris's meals.

Mushroom-colored clouds hang low as I walk back home along the narrow, dusty lane. A sharp wind tousles my hair and tugs at my skirt. I round the last bend, and my family's home finally comes into view.

I'm aware that my heart starts to beat faster. My footsteps falter. I swallow before coming to a complete stop.

I don't want to go back in there. I'm so tired of being alone with only the things that crawl in the darkness to keep me company.

And what if she is waiting for me?

The question forms in my mind before I can stop it.

"You've nowhere else to go, Charlotte," I say. "You have no choice."

I roll back my shoulders, lift my chin, and resume walking. The tree looms tall as I pass by, and a chill sweeps over me as soon as I step into its shadow. When I reach the door, I expect the chill to fade, but it doesn't. My whole body feels cold. The hairs on my arms stand on end as a tingling sensation builds on the back of my neck. I'm about to step into the house and shut out the world when I realize what the sensation is.

I'm being watched.

I turn my head, sharply, eyes searching the garden, and beyond that, the fields. I gasp when I see it.

A dark smudge interrupts the grim horizon, where the brown fields meet the brewing sky. As I stare at the speck, it takes on the silhouette of a man. A tall and broad man who is standing completely still.

Watching me.

Although it is difficult to be sure because of the distance, I am certain I don't know the man. He is a stranger.

A crowd of moths flutter uneasily in my stomach.

Who is this stranger? And why does he watch me?

Chacker chacker chacker

The cry of the magpie makes me jump. I bring a hand up to my chest, as if I can slow my beating heart.

I decide to not hesitate any longer. I push open the door without another glance at the stranger, and slam it shut.

I toss and turn, unable to sleep. The rain drums on the roof and beats against the windows, but that isn't the problem. I usually find the rain relaxing. It isn't the sound of the rolling thunder which bothers me either.

It's the stranger.

Why had he been watching me? What did he want? Does he know that I live alone? Will he come back? Did he even leave?

These questions keep circling in my head, round and round. Picking up pace and gathering more questions like a tornado accumulating debris. I'm not even thinking about the magpie tonight. My ankle hasn't twinged once.

I don't know why I'm so concerned about the stranger. Perhaps it is because he seemed to be watching me so intensely. There's a feeling in my gut—not dissimilar to the sensation I had on my neck when I felt his gaze and when the moths in my stomach panicked. It seems to tell me I'll be seeing him again. And soon.

The magpie had also given its warning.

Chacker chacker chacker

Whenever I've heard the wooden cry of the mother magpie, something bad inevitably follows.

Thunder shakes the house. The walls quiver and vibrate, echoing the malevolent sound. It pulls me from sleep. I sense that it hasn't been long since I finally drifted off.

I listen as the silence returns. But it's quickly replaced by another rumble of thunder and followed by a loud crack.

Bang bang bang

I sit up, the sheets tangled around my legs. The walls are shaking again, and I realize it isn't the storm that's causing it.

There's someone knocking at the outside door.

It's him. I know it's him. I knew he'd come back.

Inside my stomach, the moths' wings beat in an anxious frenzy.

He never left.

I push back the cover and lower my feet to the bare floorboards. Cool air kisses my ankles. Goose pimples pebble my flesh. I search the bedside table with my hand. and a moment later, I strike the match and a yellow flame bursts to life, in unison with the dancing shadows. The flame licks at the candle wick. I feel it creeping up the other end towards my finger and thumb, beginning to scorch the skin. I blow out the match and take hold of the candle. The darkness retreats to the corners of the room where it lingers like hunched beasts, waiting to close in on me once more.

I take a deep, shuddering breath and step towards the bedroom door.

Bang bang bang

The sound grows louder as I open the door. But by the time I reach the top of the stairs, I can barely hear anything above the banging of my own heart. Blood pulses so heavily in my ears that I feel almost lightheaded.

Bang bang bang

The blackness to my right crawls closer, humming towards the light of the candle. I hold my breath. The smell is something I can't get used to.

Bang bang bang

I clutch my nightdress as I descend the stairs. My whole body feels tight, my muscles tense. I'm aware that I'm clenching my teeth—the pain in my jaw pulses in time with the throbbing of my ankle. The darkness at the foot of the stairs heaves and comes to life as I draw nearer. Intimidated by the heat and the light of the flame, the shadows scuttle away.

Bang bang bang

At the bottom of the stairs, I release my breath. I turn to face the door, then hesitate.

What am I doing? It's the middle of the night. I shouldn't be answering the door to anyone.

"You can't stay in bed and hope he'll go away, either." My words tremble around me, and the candle flame flickers. I step over the threshold and into the kitchen.

The window frames nothing but darkness pebbled with fat raindrops. A yellow orb in the center of the window forms as I move deeper into the room, candle held high. The glow expands in the glass, stuttering and blinking as I draw nearer. It reminds me of the amber eye of a cat.

Bang bang bang

I jump at the sound. I'd briefly forgotten about the stranger at the door. The candle almost goes out, and the shadows dance and bend over me, eager to swallow me up. However, the flame steadies, robes of yellow and bright white shimmering bravely.

It might not be him, I think. *It could be anyone. It doesn't have to be the stranger.*

The crowd of moths flutter wildly, bouncing against my insides. I swallow down my rising fear as I grab the door handle. I push it down, but it requires no effort on my part to open it. A great force pushes it towards me, and for a moment I think it's the stranger knocking it back. I gasp and stumble backwards, clutching at my nightdress.

Squinting against the rain and the cold wind, I can see that the man has stepped away from the door, and that he's standing calmly, although his clothes are soaked. I realize it was the storm that ripped the door from my grasp, and not the man after all.

From where he stands, I can't discern his features. His face is draped in shadow. His wide shoulders fill the doorway, and his stooped demeanor indicates his height.

It is the man from before. The stranger who'd been watching me.

How long had he been outside? Had he just been watching the house, waiting? What for? What could he want?

"Hello," is all I say.

"Hello," he echoes. His voice is gruff and easily heard despite the shrieking wind. He takes a step closer, and the light from the candle catches his eyes. The flame shivers in the dark depths as he stares at me.

"I need shelter," he says. "From the rain."

I want to tell him that he's a liar, that I know he was here before. But I realize stating the fact would make no difference. This unfamiliar man is coming in anyway. I won't be able to stop him.

I manage to nod. I hope I appear calm. I avert my eyes from his, afraid he'll be able to see what's going on behind them. He steps over the threshold, bowing his head to avoid hitting the door frame. I move to the side, my back against the wall. Cold, wet air trails behind him when he moves past. Raindrops fall from his clothes to form a river on the flagstone floor. I watch as he stops and seems to search the kitchen shadows.

I'm not sure how long I stand there, studying the dark, damp curls on the back of his head, but he seems to feel my gaze. He turns to face me. Deep lines appear on his brow as his eyes twist towards the door.

"Ain't you closing that?" His deep voice reminds me of thunder as it rolls and echoes in the close confines of the kitchen. Suddenly comprehending his words, I turn to the open door. The rain creates a murky veil as it pushes into the room, carrying with it a strong wind that tugs at my hair. My nightdress billows behind me, and I become acutely aware of my naked flesh beneath the thin cotton.

I think about dashing out the open door.

I could be dead before the morning, I think as I stare at the curtain of rain glinting by the candlelight.

I could be dead if I stay. Another unwanted thought pushes its way in.

I feel the heat of the stranger's eyes on my body. Realizing that I have little choice in the matter, I push the door shut.

"Is it just you here, then?" His voice sounds close—closer than before—but when I turn to face him, he is still standing in the same place.

"No," I say quickly. Too quickly. "My parents are upstairs."

The stranger smiles, as if he knows my secret. His dry lips part to reveal yellow teeth. I notice a couple of teeth are missing. His face looks dirty—not just because it is caked in filth, but because of the stubble on his chin.

"How long have you been outside?" The question slips from my mouth before I can stop it.

His smile drops, eyes hardening. "Too long."

I swallow as the candle flame quivers. I realize that I'm shaking. The man seems to notice, and his expression softens. He lifts his hands, palms facing me.

"Look, I just want a bed for the night. That's it. Then I'll be gone as soon as the sun is up."

I'm not sure that I believe him, but I feel my shoulders relax slightly.

"Okay, follow me."

I walk ahead of him, leading the way through the kitchen and towards the stairs. The shadows part as we move through, dark spectators to this unusual affair. Once again, I am aware of his eyes as I ascend the stairs, him following close behind. I feel vulnerable in just my nightdress. I'll be glad to be back in my bedroom with the door bolted.

At the top of the stairs, I turn to the bedroom next to mine. I'm so used to the crawling little bodies that creep from under the left door that I don't even stop to wonder what the man will think.

"What the hell is that?" The tone of his voice makes me pause. He sounds disgusted. And that's when I remember.

I turn back to face him, opening my mouth to say something that will stop him from entering the room. But it's too late; his hand is already pushing down the door handle.

"And what is that god-awful smell?'

I move quickly through the cloud of rising flies, and a few dip towards the snapping flame.

"Don't go in there," I cry, grabbing onto the man's thick shoulder.

Chacker chacker chacker

"What the..." The man turns away from the door, distracted by the sudden sound behind him. The shadow looms against the back wall of the corridor. He takes a step away from it, his face ashen. Mother Magpie's wings flap wildly. The point of her bill ends with a deathly hook.

Chacker chacker chacker

The rapid movement of her wings stirs the cold air. The flame flickers, writhes, and stutters before going completely out.

I hear the man take another step, and then he gasps.

He doesn't scream when he falls down the stairs. He manages a grunt in between several thuds and knocks as his heavy body makes contact with the steps. But then there's a loud snap, and I don't hear him utter anything else.

I push the door, and it groans on its hinges. The buzzing flies hover above my head, attracted to the new flame of the candle. The smell is thick and sickly, and unlike the flies, I haven't yet grown used to it. I step further into the room, eyes falling to the bed.

I briefly wonder about bringing his body to this room before I dismiss the idea. He would be too heavy for me to drag up the stairs. But that's not the only reason why I can't do it. This is my parents' room. It will always be theirs.

I stare at the bodies on the bed. The flesh around their eyes has shriveled and sunk. Patches of a bluish hue dapple their arms. The skin between their mouths and noses is flecked with something white—I don't want to think about what it could be.

Mother Magpie warned me that something bad was going to happen. The fever took both my parents within days of each other. I thought it was my fault. That the magpie had taken its revenge. But now I understand.

The magpie wasn't something to be afraid of. It was my protector. It had warned me about the strange man and, ultimately, saved me from him.

Mother Magpie is all I have.

A thin strip of watery light streaks the horizon. Shadows slowly retreat under the early morning light. As the sun lifts, the color of the surrounding fields shifts from black to gray, then to a soft green. The rain stopped hours ago, but its scent lingers, mingled with promise.

I give the earth a final tap before propping the shovel against a tree. My nightdress clings to me, sweat sticking the cotton to my back. It's going to take me a long time to clean the soil from under my fingernails. But it was the right thing to do.

I couldn't have kept his body inside the house. It's cramped enough with the three of us.

Besides, I think as I lift my eyes to admire the tree's web of branches. *The soil could do with the nutrients. And so could the tree.*

There's a fluttering behind me. My heart flutters with it as I hold my breath. I feel the rippling in the air. It whispers around my neck and lifts my hair as the shadow falls over me.

I wait for the cry of the magpie.

When it doesn't come, I smile.

Find me in your dreams
By the weeping willows and the moonlit stream
She whispered to him as she died
The river swallowing her in vain
He can still hear her in the rain
Her wails laced in damp earth and lavender
Caressing the misery cloaked stone
Beating, bleeding beneath his rib cage
He looks out to the river behind his home
Where the children play happy little games
Obsidian hair blowing in the wind
And knows
He left his heart across the oceans
In the Land of Sorrows.

A.L. Garcia

IX

Lolita

A.L. Garcia

Every dawn, she wakes at three to swim in the Santa Blanca River, waiting for the sunrise to warm her supple honey skin and awaken the rest of her side of the world. The water is a constant relief, enveloping her limbs with tiny currents and bits of seaweed. She imagines it like one of the many wombs of this earth. She could float there pretending to be nature's babe forever if they let her. She is safe here. It's only about a mile away, but still far enough from the inquisitive piercing eyes and judgement that greet her every morning. She has not been able to sleep past three a.m. since she turned fifteen, the day that marked her womanhood with festivities, but scarred her existence. Her mind wanders back to the day she rejected Hector's first and last attempt to kiss her, the day she lost her oldest friend.

She recalls her crimson lace trimmed dress dampened at her breasts and her face still glistening with sweat from their rendition of the Paso Doble as she gave a deep curtsey and he bowed. *After practicing for weeks, they had executed the dance perfectly.* They were all smiles as they shimmied towards the dessert table, hands clasped. She let go, grabbed two cinnamon sugar cookies, and passed one to him. She hadn't noticed how he was staring at her, waiting for her to finish. In fact, everyone had been staring. As she wiped the crumbs off her dress, she felt one of his hands take hers and the other make its way toward her waist. She stood paralyzed, staring straight into his longing emerald eyes, like a deer caught in the front sight of a rifle. He didn't catch on to her anguish as he leaned into her bosom and placed his mouth ever so gently upon hers.

She'd felt a surge of rage burst out of her like a volcano. The way she shoved him away in front of a room full of their friends was the most embarrassing thing he had ever experienced. She knew that, but how dare he kiss her without asking her first. Her mind raced with a million questions. How could he see her that way? Why didn't he tell her what he was planning to do? He had never concealed his thoughts from her before, or so she thought. She saw him as a brother. She was unaware he saw her as a woman, or as a prospective lover. Even the memory of his failed kiss filled her tongue with an almost palpable disgust. The tiny bit of spit from his lips and his cinnamon sugar covered breath meeting hers had been both shocking and repulsive.

It had been three years since that ill-fated day, but she still recalls precisely how everyone gasped when she pushed him. Her face still flushes red and burns hot with shame when she thinks of it. *Did everyone assume they were already a couple? How could she be so absent-minded and unaware? Did no one care or know that she still felt like a child? She just wanted to run around old buildings with her friend, pretending she was discovering ancient artifacts and making believe random stones were long lost gems left behind by pirates or conquistadors that just needed to be polished. Was it wrong of her to share so much with him, to hug him when she needed comfort, to stroke his hair and let him cry on her lap when he needed her? Was I a tease like everyone murmured that day?* She wonders. *Was it so wrong to think that someone else could like what I like or enjoy my company just for the sake of it?* She snaps out of her internal questioning when her mother calls out to her. She always knows to find her at the river.

"Lolita, get dressed and come to the hacienda. Your father wants to talk to you about tonight's dinner party." Lolita's mother Lupe, short for Guadalupe, was traditional, just like her father, just like the entire small town of El Duelo. Her father, Sebastian Moya, was the owner of the only bank in town. He was strict and demanding, but she was his little girl and only child, so he was prone to spoiling her. Lolita was not a fan of expensive gifts, though she could not deny her varied and eloquent wardrobe often elicited the envy of most other girls in town. Still, this meant nothing to her. The freedom to make her own decisions was what she craved the most, and her father obliged her, for the most part. She was eternally grateful for this, so she was usually quick to address his demands, following the rules of etiquette when his reputation called for it.

Lolita's name is Dolores, but everyone has been calling her Lolita for as long as she can remember. In honor of the Virgin Mary, or, as they say in El Duelo, Nuestra Senora de los Dolores, Our Lady of Sorrows. She gets lost in daydreaming as she dresses in her riding clothes. *Our sorrow is so powerful, so beautiful,* she thinks. *It means you've loved, for what is pain but love persisting past loss. When Grandmother Magdalena passed away, I stayed in my room crying for three days. Everyone thought I was going mad, and all the while I was wondering if anyone loved her as I did. Maybe I did go a little mad. How could I not after losing someone like her?*

She tucks her white chemisette into a pair of dark trousers and pulls on her charcoal riding boots. She pairs it with her favorite redingote, a crimson number that belonged to her father when he was young. She pulls her hair up into a bun and pins it back, adding a black tricorn hat to complete the ensemble. She looks at herself in the mirror, imagining how nice it would be to start over in a new town somewhere. *She could pass for a man, perhaps live the rest of her life out as some local hermit in a little cottage near a river somewhere, just like Mama Socorro.* She is startled out of her daydreaming at the sound of a knock on the door downstairs. *Snap out of it, Dolores. You should go see what's so important about this dinner party tonight.*

She takes a final look at herself in the full-length mirror mounted on her wall and walks down the corridor leading to her father's study, admiring the family pictures posted along the walls. *So many faces that resemble hers.* She stops at Mama Magdalena's picture. The warm chestnut eyes stare back at her as if they were real. She shakes her head to collect herself, then walks the rest of the way to her father's study. She knocks at the heavy wooden door and waits for him to answer before entering. "Father, it's Lolita, you summoned me," she calls out playfully.

Her father answers, "Yes, my sweet and headstrong daughter, please enter."

She turns the polished copper knob and walks in. Her father is standing by the library wall, facing a row of large ornate leather-bound books. He runs his finger along the spines of a few of them and then turns. She walks up to him and gives him a hug and a kiss on the cheek.

He returns the embrace, giving her a tight squeeze and a kiss on her forehead, then steps back. His swarthy brown hair is graying at the edges. His soft hazel eyes seem more concerned than usual and the dark circles under them are more pronounced. He takes her small, delicate hands in his and sighs.

She looks up at him with her own golden orbs that have always made him see things her way, and asks, "What's wrong, father?"

He looks down at his only child. He strokes her obsidian hair with a gentle tawny hand she has only known love from. He breathes in deeply. "Lolita, tonight's dinner party was meant for you to meet a suitor. The Aquino family arrived in El Duelo a fortnight ago. They have expressed their desire for a union between our families and seeing as you have had no suitors after your altercation with Hector, their eldest son has requested to meet you."

She lets go of his hands and walks to the center of the room. Trying to keep her composure and control her tone, she spits out, "Father, I have worked at the bank for nearly a year now. I have no interest in meeting any suitors as I have no interest in having a husband. I'm frankly disappointed in you. Are you going to start pressuring me to choose a man to marry, like everyone else in this God-forsaken town? Do you think I don't hear them murmuring about me every time I pass? I hear them. They say I will end up a lonely old hag like Mami Magdalena and Mama Socorro. Do you think that too? Honestly, I would not mind ending up like her. It would be better than ending up like you, fearing what everyone will say so much that you would sacrifice your only daughter for the sake of your reputation!" She wipes away the tears streaking her face, annoyed that they are coming out despite her efforts to hold them in.

He stands firm. "Dolores, your grandmother was a widow and Socorro is an outcast that lives in fear. You are a young vibrant woman. Tradition is not just about reputation. It is God's will and command. A union would also preserve your livelihood as well as that of future generations. Maybe I have given you too much freedom. What about our legacy? Do you not plan to have children? Would you just let our family's lineage die alongside us? There are no other heirs in this family but you to carry on our name."

His words feel like daggers being plunged into her chest. She crumbles onto the floor weeping.

He kneels beside her and takes her face in his hand. "Come now child, I know you must be lonely too. You will always be free. I have been your shield against the wrath of the clergy and the church. I will always defend you, but this is not too much to ask. A marriage would also end all this talk concerning your wild ways. Ever since you rejected Hector, Father Humberto has had his eye on you. He has expressed concern over your lack of interest in suitors and your trips to the mountains. He says you are a bad example to the other girls in town, and that your defiance is a danger to the church and to us all. I'm begging you, Lolita. Please, listen to an old man who loves you more than anything in this world. Please don't fight me on this." He pulls an embroidered handkerchief from his pocket and places it in her hand.

She raises it to her face, wiping away angry tears and wiping her nose. She takes a deep breath and exhales loudly. Eyes downcast, she replies, "Father, I will meet the Aquinos, but I do not promise my hand and I refuse you to do so in my name. I lost faith in your precious God years ago, in case you hadn't noticed."

He gasps and pulls away from her. "Lolita, you can't be serious. You cannot say such things. Do you want to be labeled a heretic? This has gone on far enough. I forbid you to speak this way again. I will not let you ruin yourself right before my eyes! Have you gone mad?"

She stands from the floor, chuckling as he stares up at her in horror. "Oh, Father, according to this town, I have been mad for quite some time now. Do not worry, I will meet the Aquino brothers and be on my best behavior. Does that please you?"

Frowning at her defiance, he roars back, "Don't take that tone with me, young lady. I am simply trying to protect you."

She scoffs, "Oh, I know, Father. All I must do is sell my body and soul, like some fancy wench. I thought I was different, like you used to tell me, but I guess I am just a woman. That is clear now."

Stunned, he stammers back, "That—that is not what I said, Lolita."

She snaps back, "Sure, it isn't. I wish I were born a man too. I'll see you at dinner, *my lord*." She turns her back on him and walks out of the study without saying goodbye, leaving him kneeling on the mosaic tiled floor.

He grabs his head with both hands and tugs at his graying hair in desperation, whispering, "Lolita, I'm sorry."

Lolita runs down the staircase, wiping the remaining tears off her face and licking her salty lips. *This is such nonsense. A wife. A mother. This town can go straight to their so-called hell. What good is all our money if it can't even buy my freedom? I'm a damned bird in a gilded cage.*

Her mother stops her at the door with a slight tap on her shoulder. "Lolita, I can see you are upset. At least tell me where you are headed so I don't worry?"

"I just need to clear my head, Mother. I am going for a ride with Obsidiana. Everything is fine." She gives her a peck on the cheek and starts turning towards the door but pauses when she hears chatter coming from the kitchen. She turns back towards her mother. "Is there someone here?" she inquires.

"Well, I meant to tell you before I noticed your brooding. The Aquino brothers came for a quick visit before our formal dinner." Just as she finishes her sentence, two tall young men walk out from the corridor and appear before her eyes. One is slightly shorter and slimmer than the other with honey skin like her own, deep brown eyes and a shoulder length mane of thick chestnut hair. His broad smile is honest and genuine.

Lolita can't help but smile back. She looks over to the taller, broader brother. He is lighter skinned with pale green eyes and silky ebony hair as dark as her own. He stares back at her like an elegant cat eyeing a mouse it plans to devour. He reaches out to greet her with a powerful yet graceful hand. She gives hers as dictated by custom. He takes her dainty hand in his and brushes his lips ever so gently across her knuckles. The other brother follows suit. She maintains a defiant stance, but she is sure the rush of heat she felt beneath her cheekbones is betraying her.

The younger brother speaks first, "Lady Dolores, my name is Alvaro Aquino. It is a pleasure to meet you."

The older brother interjects, "Yes, a pure pleasure. Augustin Aquino, at your service. We look forward to dining with you tonight, Lady Lolita."

Amused, she replies, "Well, you two are certainly charming. But I must go now. I have some personal errands to run. I will see you both at dinner."

The younger one cuts in again. "May we join you, Lady Dolores? I'd love a ride about town."

"I'm not going into town."

Her mother stops her. "Lolita please, mind your manners."

She giggles and rolls her eyes. "Oh, sure, Mother, my apologies. I must be going now. I shall see you all at dinner." She turns and walks off towards the stables, muttering frustrations under her breath. She walks up to Obsidiana, a stately deep black mare with a silvery white mane the color of moonlight. She is Lolita's pride and joy. Obsidiana was the only gift from her father that cheered her up after the incident with Hector. She straps the saddle onto her gently, mounts her, and rides off into the midday fog, reveling in the dampness of the wind coating her face. She would ride towards the mountains at the far edge of town to meet her Mama Socorro, an old widow that was her Mama Magdalena's best friend. *Maybe she can help me decide what to do about the Aquino brothers.*

She rides hard and fast, leaning into the steady speed of Obsidiana's ample strides, feeling free again, if just for the moment. Lolita slows her down as they near Socorro's cottage, a small Adobe structure covered in creeping rose and thorny cat's claw vines. It is nestled at the foot of a long stretch of mountain ranges, named Sangre de Dios for the way the sunrise rims the snowy peaks in red at dawn. The headstream of the Santa Blanca originates here. Lolita stares ahead along with Obsidiana losing herself in the majestic beauty of the light rain dampening the mystic peaks, visible now through the clearing fog.

Socorro comes from behind the cottage and calls out to her, "Dolores, *mi niña*, come. We have much to discuss."

Lolita snaps out of her trance, unmounts Obsidiana and runs to her arms. Wrapped in her embrace, she allows herself to sob. "Mama Socorro, everything is going wrong. Father is forcing me to marry. He says the townspeople are starting to think I am a danger. It's like the whole town hates me ever since I rejected Hector. Tell me what to do."

Socorro replies, "Come inside. These are not things we can speak of out in the open. Are you sure no one followed you? I sense a presence around you that I have not before."

Lolita lets go of her and looks back at the direction she came from, suddenly overcome with guilt at her recklessness. "I'm sorry, Mama Socorro. I was not paying attention. I was so upset after my talk with father, but no, I don't think anyone followed me." Lolita whistles to Obsidiana and removes her saddle.

Obsidiana snorts and trots up to the troughs of oats and water Mama Socorro always puts out for her. Socorro strokes her back as she passes, then chants a short obscuring spell covering the cottage in a thick layer of fog again and leads Lolita inside.

Inside, the earth covered walls are smooth and tan, with built-in shelves displaying a vast collection of river rocks, crystals, and succulents, many of which Lolita herself had given to Mother Socorro over the years. Each one of them holds a memory she relives in short bursts as she passes by them. Socorro looks at her with increasing worry, then beckons her to sit on a wicker chair near the window. She sits and lets the sound of the weeping willows filtering the breeze calm her nerves. Socorro walks over to the kitchen and back to her with a ceramic mud cup filled with tea. She hands it to her, saying, "Anise for protection and sage for clarity. You are going to need it. The Aquino brothers will be the least of your concerns. Still, you are not safe. The winds howl of your doom, child. They carry whispers of gossip and of bigotry. In my dream walks, I encountered a large crowd led by a wounded swain with titian hair. He intends to see you slain at their hands. You must run far away from here before the corn moon rises."

Hector, thinks Lolita, gasping. "No, it can't be Mama Socorro. He wouldn't."

Socorro snaps, "Listen to me Dolores, and listen well. He will. This is not a fate that can be changed so readily. I have revealed too much already and must pay penance for my transgressions. I will go into the mountains at dusk and let my spirits guide me where they may. I love you with all my soul, Lolita. You have been my only companion after your grandmother Magdalena passed and you have been my child too over all these years. That is why I defy destiny and betray her blessings to warn you of this. If you are in El Duelo when the harvest moon rises, you will face a ghastly undeserved end. It is what your father is worried about. You must take this time to bid your parents farewell and prepare for a journey across vast oceans. I may meet back up with you when you least expect it, but even when we are apart, I am always with you."

Lolita knows not to ask questions. Mama Socorro has never been wrong about anything. She bows her head in deference and replies, "I understand." She sits and sips her tea in silence as Socorro prepares a wreath from fresh willow branches and little bundles of herbs.

She packs it into an ornate leather satchel and hands it to Lolita. "This was passed down to me by my mother and her mother before her. Keep it with you always. I have taught you almost everything I know about the herbs. I wish we had more time. Use them wisely. The wreath is for your Obsidiana."

Lolita stands, but her knees buckle, and she crumples into Socorro's breasts. Weeping, she confesses, "I'm so angry, Mama Socorro." Despite her efforts to maintain her composure, she is livid. Endless questions run through her mind as she holds on to Socorro, wishing she could melt into her and disappear. *I know Hector is hurt, but to go this far, to betray our confidence! Why should I have to run away like some common thief? Hector will have to answer to me for his impudence and confess his lies to Father Humberto. I will not let Hector run me from El Duelo and torment my parents with lies.*

Socorro strokes her ebony hair and wipes her tears away. Sensing her inner turmoil, she takes Lolita's hands in hers and stares into her eyes. "You are stronger than you know. I believe in you and I am here for you, no matter what you decide. Now, you must go, my dear. The Aquino brothers wait for you and keeping up appearances will keep you safe, at least for now. I'll meet you in your dreams by the weeping willows..."

Lolita kisses her cheek, and then looking into Socorro's sable eyes, she finishes with a whisper, "...and the moonlit stream."

With a newfound resolve, Lolita crosses the satchel over her body and walks out into the encroaching dusk, not looking back, as Socorro packs a bag for her own voyage. Lolita lets hair down and tosses her riding hat into the nearby riverbank. *From this day forth, I ride unfettered by this town's demands, come what may.* She whistles to Obsidiana, who comes bounding from the shade of the willows. Sensing her rage, Obsidiana snorts and stomps her front hoof. Placing a hand on her snout, Lolita calms her. "I'm okay, Obsidiana. Let's go." She climbs onto her back, saddle free, and they ride facing the sunset, toward El Duelo. As she rides, her raven hair blows wild in the wind, the gusts pressing her chemisette against her supple, bouncing breasts. As she approaches the hacienda, she sees Augustin staring at her from near the stables.

He walks up to them when she arrives, still gawking. "Good evening, Lady Dolores," he says, offering her a hand.

She takes it, dismounts Obsidiana, and answers, "Good evening, Augustin," with a sly smile.

Stunned by the outline of her frame beneath the delicate chemisette, he runs a hand through his coiffed ebony strands, smiles, and follows her into the stables. He watches with unbridled delight as she makes a bed for Obsidiana out of thick wool mats and fills a trough with fresh oats for her. He doesn't offer to help, and he is certain she doesn't want any. She is completely oblivious of his presence and her own dire need to get dressed for dinner. Still, that smile she gave him shows a wild side he intends to explore, if she will permit. He continues to stare at her longingly until she pauses. Lolita looks up at him, reveling in his piercing gaze. It causes her to blush. Despite his arrogance, Augustin's spirit captivates and thrills her. She cannot deny it.

She walks up to him and presses her small, narrow torso against his broad chest, her hardened nipples grazing the lapels of his dinner coat. She smiles. "Well, well, Augustin Aquino. Did you really come to dinner to ask my father for my hand in marriage?"

He replies, "Only if that is what you desire, Señorita Dolores, but I have no interest in forcing you, as you may have assumed. There are plenty of damsels in El Duelo to entertain."

She pulls away chuckling, "Yes there are. I'm sure they would love your company. So, tell me, what is it you think I desire?"

He smirks. "After speaking with your father, I think you are obsessed with an idea of being free that is impossible. I wish it wasn't true. You know, I too must follow rules that can often be unfair, but I'd rather not speak of our responsibilities now. I also think you desire me, Lolita, and I've wanted to undress you from the moment I saw you. I'm not sure it's a coincidence that I found you in such a state of disarray." He gazes at her longingly, waiting for her to respond.

She stares back at him, speechless for the moment, then grins. Her cheeks flushed, her smile wide and eager, she replies, "Well, what are you waiting for?"

Augustin pulls her slender frame closer. "May I kiss you, lovely Lady Dolores?"

She answers him by pulling him into a deep kiss full of yearning and release, as she lets all the rage coursing through her veins flow from her body into his. Lolita rips off his riding coat and vest as his lips move down her neck and his hands creep up her blouse. She runs her hands over his robust muscular frame, indulging in the ecstasy of his touch, her thighs quivering with anticipation. She throws her head back and moans as he pulls her trousers down and roams her skin with his tongue. They lose themselves in a fit of blossoming passion, giving their bodies to one another recklessly, forgetting about the dinner party completely.

Afterwards, they lie on the stable floor covered in sweat with the hay sticking to their skin. Lolita sits up, "We should go inside."

Augustin pulls her back to his embrace. "I could stay here with you forever, if the horses didn't stare so much."

Lolita bursts into laughter. She stands and pulls him back to his feet. "Let's go before they think I murdered you."

He chuckles. "Well, that's one way to put it." They dress and walk out of the stable and into the hacienda, giggling.

As they hear footsteps coming toward them, Lolita gives him a peck on the cheek and runs up the stairs to her room. He calls out, "Oh, come on, that's not fair!" as her mother gasps at Augustin's appearance.

The next morning, she faces her father brooding in his study again. This time she does not knock. She bursts in and declares excitedly, "Father, we need to speak. I have plans to leave El Duelo, and I came to ask for your blessing." She notices his dreadfully somber countenance. "Father, what is wrong? I would not expect you to be so taken aback by my news."

He shakes his head. "No, that's not it, my sweet Lolita. A messenger arrived earlier with a letter concerning you from Father Humberto. It is almost too much agony to bear to reveal its contents to you."

Lolita reaches out to him, taking his hands in hers. "Father, everything will be fine. Let me make you some tea to calm your nerves."

He shakes his head again. "No, Lolita, you don't understand. Hector swears you rejected him, only because you lie with demons when you bathe in the river."

Lolita scoffs. "That's absurd. Hector is a fool, and I will deal with him shortly."

His face remains stern. "That may be true, Lolita, but he is a fool that knows many of your secrets. He knows the path to Mama Socorro's cottage. He knows of your way with herbs. He is succeeding in turning the church against you. They sent a messenger with a warning. They have called an inquisitor to investigate. I promised a considerable donation to the church to buy us time, in the hopes your marriage to Augustin would end this nightmare, but I am not sure it will be enough. I have prepared a carriage with provisions for a fortnight's journey. If you can make it to San Cecilia, you may be safe. There are passenger ships that can take you to new lands there. You can be truly free as you have always dreamed, but we must act swiftly. If Father Humberto thinks you are fleeing, he will surely send mercenaries to find you."

Lolita listens in horror at her father's fear-laden reasoning. She takes a deep breath. "Father, I will not let Hector's vanity destroy our family. It is true. I have dreamed of leaving El Duelo for a long time, but not on these terms. I am going back to Mama Socorro's cottage tonight for some supplies and I will face Hector in the morning. He may know my secrets, but I also know his, and I will see if he was ever truly a friend to me."

His eyes fill with worry. "Lolita, it is not safe."

She stands defiant. "I know, but you raised me to be brave and honorable, and that is the only way I can be." She lowers her gaze as quiet tears run down her face. "I'm sorry, father." She walks up to him, cups his face in her hands and kisses his bristly cheek.

He pulls her into a deep embrace, holding on to her like a babe. "Lolita, it is I who has failed you. I should have left this God forsaken town ages ago."

She shushes him. "Hush, you have been the best father a girl like me could have. We will get through this together."

He strokes her ebony hair. "*Ay, mi Lolita*, I hope you're right."

She rides with Obsidiana back to Mama Socorro's cottage under the cover of darkness and the scant light of a thin crescent moon. She prepares a bed for Obsidiana, chants the obscurity spell, and heads to the river to relax. Lolita lays in a silk gown under her favorite willow tree on the banks of the Santa Blanca, reminiscing of better days, when she notices an alabaster stallion circling the fog clouded perimeter in confusion. Recognizing the horse as Augustin's, she whistles to it. They make their way through the dense brume towards her. The visibility is so poor, he does not notice her until she touches his thigh.

He dismounts and wraps her up in his brawny arms possessively. "Lolita, I called for you at the hacienda and your mother told me you came here. I was hoping we would have a chance to speak. Your father is in such low spirits, he would not even see me. Your mother told me how to find you here. I thought I was lost until you whistled."

She buries her face into his chest, breathing in his aroma of greenwood, sweat, and worry. "*Ay Augustín, no me entierres en la desesperación, mi amor, ayúdame a olvidar todas mis penas*. Let us not speak of serious things tonight. Come, let me show you Mama Socorro's cottage."

He bows his head in acceptance and follows her. He looks around, admiring the charming Adobe home as Lolita tells him of Mama Socorro.

She recalls how her father had finally let her go with her Mama Magdalena to the mountains. She had badgered him for weeks before he gave in to her demands. She tells him of the mountain's treasure troves of mysterious herbs, the unknown ones that Mama Socorro named, and the experiments they conducted, even on themselves at times, to figure out their uses.

He chuckles at her excitement. "So, you're telling me you are a sorceress, is that it? Is that how you bound me to your heart? Is there some tonic I could use to break that spell?"

Lolita cackles, "Oh, I didn't need a spell to conquer you, Augustin, my breasts were more than capable. Don't you recall?" She jumps into his lap, straddling his muscular girth with her smooth athletic legs, the silk gown gathering at their hips. As she plants soft hope-laced kisses from his cheekbones to his jaw, he groans with pleasure. She reaches her hands up to the sky, as he lifts the gown above her head and throws it to the floor. She moans with delight as his mouth assaults her neck and breasts with hungry animalistic need. "*Oh, Augustin, quiéreme hasta que se me olviden todos mis anhelos locos*, she moans. "Love me until I forget all my demented longings."

The lavender aroma emanating from her skin drives him wilder than an animated sire. Lolita claws at his clothes, exposing more and more flesh as she tears into the linen garments, desperate for his body to be as naked as her own. As he locks lips with her, tongues wrestling, she indulges in the idea of ripping through his skin, muscles, and bone, all the way down to his soul. She throws her head back and giggles at the barbarity of her thoughts. He gathers her back into a violent kiss, biting her lips as she pushes him away to stand. She takes his hands, pulls him to his feet. He doesn't resist as she leads him to the bed and thrusts him onto it. He chuckles as she pulls his trousers off, crawls up to his frame, and straddles him again taking in his anatomy as he stares up at her in adoration of the wild lust her hips display. The night slips into day as passion replaces apprehension, and Lolita allows herself to forget her plan to deal with Hector and her father's concerns regarding the inquisitor.

It is midday on a rainy Sunday when they wake tangled in each other's arms and soft linen sheets, warmed with the heat of their embrace. When Lolita opens her eyes and sees the light of day, all her worries come back into focus. She urges Augustin to get up and get dressed. "Augustin, wake up, please, we have to talk."

He startles awake. "What's wrong, Lolita?"

With a pained expression on her face, she replies, "I'm being investigated by the church. I had a friend named Hector that I grew up with. He was like a brother to me. A few years ago, he planned to propose to me in front of our families and friends, but I rejected him. I pushed him away from me in front of everyone. He never spoke to me again. My father says he has convinced the priest of our church, Father Humberto, that I practice magic and lie with demons. The church has requested an inquisitor."

Augustin listens in dismay, "An inquisitor! Lolita, we have to get you out of here. Why didn't you tell me this last night?"

Lolita sighs, "*Ay Augustin*, I don't know, maybe I just wanted to stop worrying for a minute. My father has prepared a carriage to take me to San Cecilia to find a voyager ship, but I refuse to do that without trying to clear this up first. I am going to town to confront Hector and Father Humberto myself. I've done nothing wrong. I should not have to flee in this way, leaving my parent's heartbroken and dishonored."

He stares at her in disapproval. "No, Lolita, that is not safe. Your father is right. If Father Humberto is convinced you are a heretic, he will not let you leave."

Lolita glares at him, rage piercing through her honey eyes like rays of fire. "And what of my family, Augustin? What will happen to them once the church knows they have helped me flee? What of your family? No, I am not a coward, and I will not sacrifice them to save my own skin. Nothing you can say will convince me of that."

Augustin pulls at his hair in frustration. "Fine, Lolita, so what is your plan? Get captured and thrown into the dungeons? You are being reckless!"

Lolita scoffs, "Ha, reckless? As if there were any good choices in this situation. Augustin, I do not need a lecture from you. I have my father for that."

He growls back, "Fine. I won't say anything more. I'll just watch you walk into a den of wolves and await your orders. Tell me, what would your grace have me do?"

She cups his face with her hands. "Augustin, my sweet knight, do not be cross with me. The whole world is already against me. I'm just trying my best. I can't let them destroy my family because of me. Go find Alvaro and come to the Hacienda tonight. Maybe we can all find a way out of this together."

He sighs. "Promise me you won't go see Hector. Wounded lovers never listen to reason and neither does the church."

She stares up at him longingly, resisting the urge to wrap her legs around him again. "I promise." Lolita fills her satchel as they dress in their riding clothes hastily, then walk outside to prepare the horses.

Augustin takes her hands in his, placing gentle kisses on each knuckle. "My whole heart is in your hands, Lady Dolores de Moya."

Lolita blushes. "And mine in yours; I will see you tonight Augustin."

He nods, releasing her hands. Then mounts his stallion and rides away, still wrapped in the scent of her earthy lavender-laced sweat.

Lolita whistles for Obsidiana and rides towards her father's hacienda, feeling hopeful. As she nears the hacienda, all hope vanishes as she sees two large carriages with the mark of the church at the gates. *It's too late, they have come for me.* She rides faster, eager to reach her parents and save them from being accused of aiding in her escape. She stops a few yards away from the hacienda, dismounts, crosses the satchel over her body and wraps the willow wreath over Obsidiana's nape. Then she presses her face to her snout. "Go back to Mama Socorro's cottage, follow the mountain streams to the head of the Santa Blanca and then go in the opposite direction. Don't come back for me. That is an order, Obsidiana." She smacks her on the hind quarters and watches her take off.

Lolita walks towards her home with her head held high, prepared to face her fate. Her father runs up to her as she crumbles into his arms, weeping. "I'm sorry, Father. I'm too late."

He strokes her hair and looks down at her with melancholy eyes. "Hush, you have nothing to be sorry for." Then he looks up at and pleads with the priest and inquisitor standing at their door. "Father Humberto, your grace, please, I beg mercy for my daughter. She is betrothed to Augustin Aquino. All this talk of magic and demons is madness. Hector lies because she rejected him as a suitor. Lolita may be a free-spirited girl, but she is not a heretic."

The priest looks back at him with disgust and says, "We shall be the judge of that."

The inquisitor addresses Lolita directly. "Come to me, child. If you are free of sin, you have nothing to fear."

Lolita puts one hand on her father's cheek and places a gentle kiss on the other. "Father, it will be alright. I know I can pass their tests."

Silent tears stream down his face and he shakes his head in objection. "Lolita, no."

She removes her satchel and presses it to her father's chest. "Keep it safe and give it to Augustin when you see him." She walks up to the inquisitor and looks into his eyes. "I will take any test you wish, and let you be the judge of my deeds. All I ask is that my family be left alone."

The priest scoffs. "Well, there may be a proper lady in you after all, Señorita Dolores."

The inquisitor nods. "Very well then."

The priest orders the guards, "Take the girl to the San Cristobal. She will await the inquisitor there."

Her father falls to his knees wailing as Lolita follows the guards into a carriage. The priest and the inquisitor climb back into their own, looking back on him in derision as they leave him to his sorrows.

When they arrive at the San Cristobal cells, the inquisitor addresses her again. "Come, child, you are not built for these prisons. If you confess your wrongs and tell me the whereabouts of the old woman you call Mama Socorro, you will not spend one night here."

Lolita squints her eyes at him in defiance. "I have nothing to confess, and I don't know where Socorro is. I did not know the church was investigating poor old ladies."

He glares back at her. "They told me you were stubborn. Perhaps some time in the cells will loosen your tongue and your loyalties." He signals the guards and turns away from her. They lead Lolita down a dank, rancid staircase leading to a corridor lined with rusted iron gates. Silent, sunken eyes glare at her through the bars as she passes. The guards snigger at the dread building on her soft features as she breathes in the stench. At the end of the corridor, another guard waits by a heavy wooden door, unlocking it as she approaches. The guard with eyes full of regret greets her. "Your room, your grace."

She replies, "Thank you, kind sir. It's nice to see not all of you have lost your manners with a lady."

The other guards chuckle dismissively, walking back towards the entrance. Lolita enters the obscure stone cell and stands facing the door as the guard lowers his gaze and closes it in her face.

Lolita spends countless days in almost complete solitude. Her father's donations are enough to keep her fed with crude, often spoiled meals she tries to hold down in hopes of surviving. Still, most days she wretches the entire contents of her stomach moments after finishing her meal. Without being able to see the light of day or the phases of the moon, she has no idea how much time has passed. The currents of the river can be heard through the cell's walls on those lonely nights. She holds onto her sanity by remembering its gentle waves enveloping her bones, trying to drown out the incessant wailing of other prisoners being tortured for confessions. She wonders if her father's influence will be enough to prevent the holy men from torturing her. She paces the length of the room from corner to corner, her frustration growing by the minute, when she notices her swollen womb in spite of her increasingly emaciated frame. She becomes desperate and cries out in delirious anguish, "Let me out of here! I have not stood trial! I demand the inquisitor charge me formally! Burn me at the stake if you like but let me out! *Let me out*!" She screams like this until her throat is sore and she collapses from exhaustion.

In her unconscious state, she dreams of Mama Socorro's cottage. It is overrun by Hector and his throng of zealots as she approaches. They are ransacking the home, pocketing some of the tonics, and throwing most of her belongings into a roaring heap of fire beneath her favorite willow tree, searing its weeping branches. She yells out for Socorro and is swept by the wind towards the riverbank as Socorro's spirit appears.

"Lolita, we are out of time. You are with child. Two to be exact, one boy and one girl, that will carry on our spirits. They will be born of the Santa Blanca when your human body perishes, but you must get to the river, or they will die alongside you. I can say no more. Go back now and do not lose yourself to despair. You will join me soon in the spirit realm and know the freedom this world could never give you."

Lolita wakes in the arms of her cell guard. He is wiping her face with a warm washcloth. "Please wake, Senorita Dolores."

She stares up at him, then down at her blood covered gown, and whispers, "Take me to the river, I beg you. Don't let me die here with my children."

He startles. "Senorita, you know I can't do that. They would hang me."

Her languid eyes plead for mercy. "Please, only for a moment, I cannot bear these walls any longer. Please, dear shackled spirit, grant this woeful girl a dying wish. I know your heart is not as hard as it seems. I can see that in your eyes."

He sighs as tears stream from his dark remorseful gaze. Then he stands, holding her fragile, skeletal frame in his brawny arms and carries her out of the dungeons into the moonlit darkness.

Lolita stares up at the harvest moon and smiles, just as Augustin appears from out of the shadows, pointing a dagger at the guard. He whispers, "Let her go, before I decapitate you."

Alvaro appears behind the guard as well, quietly brandishing a sword.

The guard remains stoic-faced. "I have seen you both standing vigil for her every night outside these gates and have not revealed you. I am on your side. Put your weapons away and I will hand her to you. She is too weak to stand. I am risking my life to help her in these final moments in repentance of my stone-hearted ways. I have been the guardian of souls perishing in those tombs for far too long. She asked me to lay her to rest at the river. Please forgive me for guarding her. I will surely burn in the pyres of Hell. I know that now."

Augustin sheathes his dagger as angry tears roll down his face. He glares and reaches his hands out as the guard places Lolita gently in his arms and walks away.

She looks up at him. "Take me to the river, Augustin."

He shakes his head. "No, I can save you Lolita. I'm taking you home. I have secured a voyager for us. I won't let you die here."

She brings a hand up to his face as her breaths become increasingly shallow. "No, my love, I am already dying. You must take me to the Santa Blanca to bear our children or they will die with me."

Augustin stares at her bewildered. He looks down and notices her small swollen womb and the scarlet blood staining her gown for the first time. "Lolita, what have they done to you?"

She squeezes his hand. "Please, we have no time. I can feel my spirit slipping away. Promise me you will take our children far away from this forsaken place. Two children will be born of the river when I pass, a boy and a girl, Neilos and Anahita. You must take me now."

He looks up to the sky in desperation, presses her to his chest and carries her to the river. Alvaro stands guard at the riverbank as Augustin walks into the water with her.

Lolita wraps her arms around his neck, "Kiss me one last time, Augustin, and promise you won't forget me."

He lowers his head, touches his lip to hers, and whispers, "Forget you, Dolores? My heart will lie in this watery grave with you forevermore. Only when you haunt me, will it stir with love again." They press their lips together as Lolita's body goes limp. Augustin cries out in anguish as he unwraps her from his grip and lets her slip into the Santa Blanca.

The skies darken and rumble over the river, eclipsing the moon in storm clouds. The water surrounding Augustin stirs and bubbles as the light of the moon illuminates two tiny bodies that appear on the surface of the water. Augustin gasps, gathers them to his chest, and looks around him as he hears Lolita's voice, "*Mis Hijos.*"

He stands looking up at the moon. "Lolita."

Alvaro runs into the water to retrieve them. "Augustin, we have to go. We cannot be discovered here."

Augustin recovers from his spellbound state and nods to Alvaro. They walk back to the riverbank and whistle for their horses, just as a carriage approaches. Alvaro draws his sword as Augustin clutches the babes defensively. The carriage stops, and Lolita's mother and father rush out. Alvaro lowers his sword. "Pardon me, Sebastian, Senora Lupita."

Sebastian replies, "Brave Alvaro, thank you for guarding my daughter. You have succeeded where I have failed. I am forever indebted to you. The guard from the dungeons informed us of the situation. He told us to find you near the riverbank." Guadalupe looks back and forth at them, "Where is Lolita?"

Augustin walks up to them and places one babe in each of their arms. "Neilos, and Anahita. She named them before she passed. She was dying and vanished into the river as they appeared. She told me to take them far from here. We must go. I have prepared passage on a voyager and have a travel carriage prepared. I shall take them to a new land, as Lolita wished to do." Tears stream down their face as they caress the cooing babes and nod in acceptance. They take the babes into the carriage as Augustin and Alvaro mount their own steeds. They ride towards Hacienda Aquino guarding the carriage.

When they arrive, Alvaro goes in search of a doctor and a wetnurse they will need for the trip to San Cecilia, as Augustin recounts the events of the birth to Lolita's parents and his own. Guadalupe weeps. Sebastian seethes. He stands. "Augustin, I was an imbecile to believe my wealth could shield Lolita from the worst of the church, but they will pay for this injustice. I promise you. El Duelo will burn to the ground before the fortnight for taking her from me in such a ghastly fashion. Go now, you must travel swiftly." Augustin embraces him as Alvaro enters the room.

"The carriages are prepared. We have to go now."

Augustin sighs. "Let's go."

Sebastian turns to face Guadalupe. "Go, my love, be with our grandchildren. They need you." He pulls her into a deep kiss and then releases her.

She cups his face with her hands and sighs, "*Mi Sebastian*, I'm not leaving you. If El Duelo burns with you in it, I will lie by your side in the flames." She takes his hand in hers as they turn to Alvaro and Augustin. "Go now children, a new world awaits beyond the sea."

Alvaro and Augustin bow their heads in deference, then turn towards the door. Their parents climb into a carriage with the doctor, wetnurse, and Lolita's babes. Augustin and Alvaro mount their steeds and they take off for San Cecilia under the cover of fog, guided by the scant light of the corn moon behind the clouds. The fog is so dense that El Duelo disappears behind them moments after they pass the Sangre de Dios Mountains. An ebony mare with no rider gallops towards them as the carriage halts.

Augustin smiles. "Obsidiana."

The mare whinnies and snorts as she joins the steeds.

Augustin sighs, "Lolita," as a gust of wind carrying the scent of lavender and earth assaults his senses. He closes his eyes and hears her voice again.

"*Augustin, mis hijos.*"

He looks over to the carriage carrying the twins and notices the wild laughter of their babes emanating from it. He breathes in deeply, reveling in the sweet aroma surrounding him once more. He waits for it to pass before resuming the journey.

Alvaro smiles. "She is with us still. She always will be."

"shh"
"not now"
"maybe later"
so, sealed my lips
and I waited
and waited
and now,
I have a ghost story
to tell

Marie Casey

X

Red Eyes

Liz M. Kamp

Miles roams the vacant corridors that form a labyrinth of twists and turns in the time-worn infirmary. The floor, laden with stone and filth, is damp with morning dew that seeps in through the cracks. The old structure moans with age and shudders in the breeze. Miles creeps past each door, peeking into the gloomy rooms and offices beyond. Nurses flutter silently from patient to patient, somber and strained. Every one of them wears a furrowed brow and a sweat-stained cap. Their frocks, splattered with blood and grime, billow in the breeze from the open windows. Miles shivers with the ominous presence of despair. He glances nervously over his shoulder, expecting the shadows to swallow him whole. When nothing drags him into the darkness, he sighs in relief and continues on.

He stands on his toes to peer out the tallest window at the naked trees that loom over the path below. They remind him of lanky skeletons, their twisted branches and clawed fingertips reaching toward the heavens. The hospital grounds are as gray as the skies, with a sea of amber grass scarcely visible in the distance. A brown leaf taps silently on the stony path below. All else is still.

Miles enters a great room, lined with beds on either side. Most beds are occupied with the sick and dying. Some are vacant, awaiting their next victims. Gray light creeps through a window but is too weak to illuminate more than a few square feet of the rotting wood floor. Dread saturates the dismal atmosphere.

Moans and cries supply the dark ambiance. Miles pretends it's music and listens for the melody. The song starts on one end, when a nurse disturbs the occupant in the furthest bed. As she makes her rounds, the cries echo one another, and the tune rises to a crescendo. Some voices are higher, and some are lower. Miles listens for the tenor and alto notes, and bobs his head in unison. Some days the music is cheerful and some days it is full of sorrow.

When the doctor enters, Miles hides in the corner or under a bed to see if he will notice. Miles is an excellent hide 'n' seek player. From his hiding place, he watches the doctor play games with different patients. The games compose more music, but it's always gloomy and never joyous. When he's finished, Miles follows the doctor back to his office, ruffles the curtains, and rattles the pill containers. The doctor stopped taking notice after a while and has learned to ignore him. Miles tries the same thing in the great room with all the patients, but they're too sick and miserable to notice him.

He ends his nights traipsing the halls in isolation. Most nights, he hides near the lamplight, away from anything that might seize him in the darkness. The cycle repeats every day, unwavering.

One morning, while the nurse makes her rounds, a strange new sound from the other side of the hall catches Miles's attention. He exits the orchestra of screams and searches for the source. Miles finds the normally vacant private bedroom on the opposite side of the hall occupied for the first time ever, as far as he can remember.

A young boy, nearly the same age as Miles, lies in the rickety bed. He sobs with tightly closed eyes, tears streaking his cheeks and soaking the soiled pillow. The boy's blond locks are drenched, and his skin is pale. Nearly as pale as his own, but not quite as see-through. More of a grayish white, like the overcast sky or the stone walls in the corridor.

Two grown-ups sit by the boy's side. They look like they want to cry with him. The man puts an arm around the woman and strokes his long mustache with the opposite hand. He is rather short and rotund, which reminds Miles of a walrus. The woman lays her head on the bed near the boy's limp hand and kisses his fingertips.

Miles supposes they are the boy's mother and father. He remembers a time when his own parents visited him here. They sat next to his bedside, too. Miles's mother actually did cry. A lot. He recalls the whole bed convulsing with her sobs. And then one day, his father carried her away, still weeping. He never saw them again. He thinks years might have passed since then.

Miles blinks and returns his attention to the boy. He is certain the boy's gaze lands directly on him. Miles freezes. No one has looked at him since the day his mother and father left him. He whips around to see if a nurse entered the room behind him. No. It is only Miles in the room, interrupting an intimate moment with this family. He turns back to the boy, who is now staring intently out the window at the skeleton trees in the distance.

Miles wonders what brought the boy here. He hasn't seen another child inside these walls before. Children don't usually get sick enough to stay here. He hopes the doctor can save him, but he also knows better. The doctor can't actually save anyone. It is up to Red Eyes who lives and who dies here.

Miles spends every night hiding from Red Eyes. He's the dark shadow man that lurks the infirmary at night. Miles's talented hide 'n' seek skills have kept him from the grasp of Red Eyes, but just barely. The cloaked figure is as tall as the ceiling, with red glowing eyes that peer from the darkness under his hood. Miles hides from him deep under the beds, far from the lamplight. He thrusts himself against the damp walls to evade the cold clutches of Red Eyes. One time, a blackened hand with pointed fingers lunged underneath the bed and grasped at him. Miles smelled the rotting flesh and dirt as he inched his way along the stone wall. Red Eyes persisted until Miles reached the other side and sprinted out of the room. He doesn't know how, but he's pretty sure he is the only human who has ever escaped his clutches. Red Eyes steals the shadows from people, and they disappear forever.

Miles is on the constant lookout for the scary cloaked figure and dives into the nearest hiding place when he sees him. He never wants to be carried away by that thing. He never wants to leave the comfort of this hospital he now calls home.

Miles returns to the boy's room later that night. He watches the boy's mother and father kiss him on his damp forehead and leave him behind. He observes the nurse while she gives the boy his medicine. She hands him a glass of juice to take the pills with, then she pokes him in the arm with a needle. The boy cries out in pain. Miles doesn't think it was very nice of her to trick him like that.

Miles learns that the boy's name is Henry. Miles likes Henry and wishes they could be friends. He hasn't made friends with anyone since his mother and father left him. He has become quite lonely over the years. Red Eyes is the only one that has seen him, but he terrifies Miles. Miles avoids him at night, hiding anywhere he can when he comes near.

Henry's mother and father return the next day and pretend to smile when they see him. Miles can tell their smiles are not real because they don't stretch to their eyes. Only their lips curl up. But Henry takes comfort in their pretend smiles and smiles back. His smile is real. Miles can tell because his teeth show and his eyes wrinkle. Miles likes Henry's smile.

He visits Henry's room every night. He watches Henry whisper to himself before bedtime and wishes he can hear what he says. Miles longs to share in his secrets. He looks after Henry while he sleeps and makes sure his blankets go up and down with each breath. Miles knows that if the blankets stop moving, Red Eyes will be close by, ready to take him away. He watches Henry's eyes flutter beneath his lashes and wonders what he dreams about. Miles misses dreaming his own dreams. He used to go to faraway fairy lands filled with magic and laughter. He hopes that's where Henry is now.

As soon as day breaks, Miles withdraws from Henry's room so he can have privacy with his family. But he reappears every night to watch over his dreams.

One night, Henry is so deep in slumber that his eyes don't move under his lids at all. Miles tiptoes right up to his bed to watch for the blankets to move up and down. He almost cries in relief when Henry's shoulder rises slowly under the linen.

A whoosh of wind captures his attention, and he whirls around. Red Eyes.

The cloaked figure stands in the doorway, barely visible from the hallway beyond. His scarlet eyes glow in the darkness. Miles feels the hairs on his neck stand up. His hands tremor as he stares at the thing he fears most. The figure gazes right through Miles and on to Henry. Miles freezes. Poor Henry is going to be the next victim. He won't let that happen.

"Get out!" he cries. He charges toward Red Eyes, cowering slightly at the size of the figure. "Get out of here! You can't have him!"

Red Eyes doesn't move. Miles can't read his expression. He can only see blackness when he looks under the hood. A shadowed face and glowing eyes. The cloak billows slightly in the breeze, but the figure remains unmoving.

"He's my friend and I won't let you take him!" Miles shouts again. He worries that all the patients will wake up from the racket, but no one stirs.

Red Eyes hovers in the doorway for several long seconds. Miles quivers as he stands his ground. For a moment, they stare at each other. And then, without a sound, Red Eyes turns and vanishes into the darkness.

Miles whips back around to make sure he didn't take Henry with him. Henry still lies motionless on the bed, but Miles knows better. He knows that sometimes Red Eyes takes people but leaves their body behind. Miles sneaks up to Henry's bedside again and watches for movement. After several long seconds, Henry snorts and rolls over onto his side.

Miles lets out a sigh of relief and reverts to the corner. He doesn't leave Henry's side all night. And he returns every single night to protect him. He won't let Red Eyes take him if he can help it.

Miles continues to roam the halls during the day and watches the nurses direct the orchestra of wailing and groaning. He likes to see how the melody changes with each day. Nowadays it's full of sorrow more than it's cheerful. Miles worries that Red Eyes is winning.

When the sun falls behind the trees, he returns to Henry's room. He needs to ensure Henry's safety. Miles watches as Henry sleeps peacefully every night. Until the night that he doesn't. Instead, Henry sits up in bed and stares directly at Miles.

Miles turns to see if there's someone behind him. There isn't.

"I'm looking at you, silly." Henry blinks and combs his hand through his hair.

"Me?" Miles says. "You can see me?"

"Of course, I can," Henry replies. "I've always seen you."

Henry explains to Miles that he watches him every night—just as much as Miles watches Henry. Henry tells Miles that he is bored lying in bed every night and is grateful for his company.

"So now what?" says Miles.

"Now, we play." Henry flips the covers off his lap and hops off the bed.

It's as if he was never sick. Henry's grinning face is full of energy, and he bounces on the balls of his feet. Miles beams at him from across the room. He can't wait to show him everything.

The boys run out of the room and down the corridor. They take turns being "it" in a game of hide 'n' seek. Miles is a million times better than Henry because he can fit in places like inside the back of the piano and in a drawer in the doctor's desk. Henry can only hide under beds and behind doors.

They play all through the night, exploring the vacant corridors and dashing to the shadowy corners when the night nurse gets up to use the bathroom. Henry returns to his bed before sunrise. He is exhausted, but he says he doesn't mind. He sleeps all day anyway.

Miles and Henry frolic in the empty halls every night. They spawn mischief and wreak havoc under the moonlight. They laugh and play and tease one another throughout the labyrinth of the hospital. Once dawn arrives, they go back to silence and await the next adventure.

Miles warns Henry about Red Eyes. He tells Henry he thinks he might be in danger. He tells him that Red Eyes is an evil shadow man that will take him away. Henry waves this off and insists they keep playing. He's not afraid of no shadow man. The only scary figure he's afraid of is the nurse that might catch him out of bed. She has mean eyes and a scowl that makes his hair stand up. He's done a pretty good job of staying out of sight when she nears, so thankfully, he hasn't been caught yet.

Miles groans in frustration at Henry's dismissal of Red Eyes. He enjoys playing with Henry, so maybe they can avoid the terrifying figure together.

They crawl into the great room full of sick adults and compare each and every snore. Mr. Fairbanks has a loud snort, while Miss Daphne nearly whistles. They giggle at one another as they crawl from bed to bed, betting on who will wake up from their snores first. Miles wins when he guesses Mr. Watson, but he knows it wasn't a fair game. Miles has seen Mr. Watson snort himself awake many times. He is as noisy in his sleep as he is during his waking hours.

Mr. Watson sits up in bed and stares directly at Miles and Henry. They freeze in their tracks, but Mr. Watson shakes his head and plops back on the pillow, snoring once again. The boys laugh harder than ever.

A gust of wind whips the door open wide, and they choke back their amusement. Red Eyes swoops in and soars high above the beds. The lanterns flicker, then the whole room plunges into darkness. Miles can see Henry's smoky breath wisp in front of him. Red Eyes floats to the ceiling and scans the room. His bright eyes glow next to the tops of the windows. Henry makes a move to continue on, but Miles silently shushes him. Henry backs up under the closest bed.

The cloaked figure flits through the darkness and hovers over Mr. Watson's bed. He bobs in place, staring down at the old man. Miles watches in horror, while Henry watches Miles with a curiosity.

Miles's jaw drops as Red Eyes reaches deep into Mr. Watson's chest and yanks his shadow out like a strand of yarn. Mr. Watson doesn't dispute, and soon Red Eyes disappears into the night with Mr. Watson's consciousness. Miles peers up at his bed and watches the limp and lifeless body lie still.

Miles doesn't leave Henry's side for the remainder of the night. The boys creep back into Henry's bedroom, and Miles protects his best friend from a mirthless fate. Once the sun rises and Henry's mother and father are back by his side, Miles makes his way across the hall to the great room. The gray sunlight creeps onto the beds and glowing dust bunnies flutter near the windows.

The room is quite peculiar today. Miles doesn't like it at all. There is no music. No one cries, no one even whimpers. Everyone lies in silence, too afraid to make a noise. Miles can see a few people shiver under their bedding.

He directs his gaze to Mr. Watson's bed. The mattress is empty, the linen stripped from it. A filthy, bare cot takes the place of Mr. Watson's once noisy dwelling. He is gone. Forever.

Miles mopes back to Henry's room, head drooped toward the floor. Determined to keep his friend safe, he vows to stay by his side, even during the daylight while Henry's family visits. When he appears in Henry's room, he finds the boy's mother weeping into her hands. His father embraces the trembling woman and gazes somberly at their son.

Miles races to Henry's side in a panic. He scans for any sign of movement. Henry lies motionless. No twitch of a muscle. No whisper of a breath. Miles whirls around in circles, searching for Red Eyes. Not a single shadow of evil lingers. He whips back around to Henry and hovers not an inch from his face. He sees every individual freckle and each wispy white lash. Henry doesn't move. His mother sobs in his father's arms. Miles turns his gaze to the top of Henry's shoulder and waits. After an eternity, he watches the mound in the bed raise ever so slightly before dropping again. Henry still breathes. He is safe. For now.

Miles drops back onto the floor next to Henry's bed and buries his head in his knees. He stays there, unmoving, until Henry's mother and father finally bid their son farewell and the nurse injects Henry with medicine. There are no pills for him to take with juice this time.

After the nurse retreats from his room, Henry lifts his sweaty head off his pillow ever so slightly.

"Thanks for staying," he manages to say.

"Of course."

"I can't come with you on an adventure tonight." Henry's gray face turns a nasty shade of green. He retches into a bucket near his bed.

"I know," Miles says.

"I'm sorry," says Henry.

"Me too," says Miles.

Henry tells Miles to go on without him, but Miles refuses. Red Eyes could return at any minute. He has to be ready.

The boys remain idle and in silence for the rest of the night, Henry too weak to say anything and Miles too fearful.

When the night is at its darkest, Miles climbs onto the bed next to Henry and lies in his shadows. He finds comfort in being close to his friend.

Henry doesn't get better throughout the following days. Miles worries for his friend, but slowly grows bored in the tiny room with Henry asleep all day and all night. After several days of stillness between the boys, Miles wanders out of the room. He decides it's safe to leave him during the daylight hours, because Henry's mother and father are there to protect him from anything evil.

Miles returns to his solo adventures, spying on the nurses and listening to the crescendo of screams across the hall. It's not the same without Henry anymore. Miles ignores this. He plays tricks on the doctor once again, billowing his curtains and tickling the hairs on the back of his neck. The doctor ignores his movements, as always, and Miles no longer finds joy in a game he once loved. He only misses Henry now.

He returns to Henry's room at night and shares all his stories with him. He tells him about the doctor rejecting his trickery and describes the exact melody the patients across the hall chanted in the morning. Henry listens in awe, too weak to respond, but Miles knows he cares.

One night, Henry's strength returns enough to fulfill his side of a conversation. He still can't get out of bed, but he speaks in full sentences. Miles considers this a good sign. He is convinced Henry will be playing hide 'n' seek before they know it. But first, they must ensure their safety.

Together in Henry's room, the boys formulate a plan to banish Red Eyes forever. They are tired of being frightened, and they want the hospital to themselves. The boys determine if they can bait him into a closet, they can lock him in and he won't ever be able to leave. Then they will take turns guarding him, and he'll be stuck in the tiny chamber forever.

The boys decide Miles will act as bait, since he's already dead. This would lure Red Eyes away from Henry so he can stay alive. They both know the shadow man has his gleaming eyes on Henry right now. Miles has to keep him safe.

Miles focuses on putting the plan into action. He doesn't know how he will lure Red Eyes, but he knows *where* he will lure him. Inside the doctor's office, behind the desk with all the drawers, is a locked closet. Miles will wait for Red Eyes there. Once Red Eyes is inside the closet, Henry will latch it since he has the ability to do so without much effort. The problem is the effort it will take him to get out of bed.

Miles has faith that Henry will pull through, and nearly skips through the corridors during the day. It is the brightest day he has seen in weeks. The golden sunlight sparkles through the windows, casting glittering beams across a normally dismal gray pathway.

Miles waits patiently for Henry's mother and father to leave. They linger an extra long time by his side today. They are cheered by his increased strength as they sit in the grimy chairs, holding onto their last strands of hope. Miles knows that after tonight, they will have all the hope in the world. Once they finally leave, Miles waits for the nurse to give Henry his medicine. She pokes and prods him and even passes several pills for him to swallow with juice. His health is almost back to normal. Far later than planned, Henry is finally alone in his room.

Once the time feels right, Miles pokes his head through Henry's doorway and winks at him. Henry winks back.

Miles navigates the maze of corridors to the doctor's office. He creeps into the corner of the dark closet and sits on the damp stone, elbows on his knees and chin resting in his palms. He waits in total blackness. The wind roars outside, and the walls shiver in response. An owl hoots, and Miles makes out the cry of a bunny that just became dinner. Any minute now, Red Eyes will come after him. Red Eyes has been on his trail ever since his mother and father left him. Red Eyes hates that Miles still haunts these halls, dancing just outside of his grasp.

After what feels like an eternity, Miles begins to worry. Maybe they need to tweak their plan. Maybe Henry is still too unwell for the task.

The door creaks open as Miles slowly creeps out of the closet. He turns his head in all directions, keeping an eye out for any movement in the shadows. His eyes dart to every corner and doorway. There is no sign of Red Eyes in the room. He sighs, relieved, then shivers in realization. Henry.

With terror rising in his gut, Miles bolts across the room and through the door. He rounds a corner to the long corridor with the great room on the right. Henry's room is on the far end. A yellow glow slices into the murky hall. It's coming from Henry's doorway on the left. Miles welcomes the slight comfort, knowing Red Eyes is afraid of the light. Almost as much as Miles used to be afraid of the dark.

Miles inches toward Henry's room, the yellow glow widening as he nears. He toes over the threshold and observes the room. He gasps at the sight of Henry and his surroundings. He's never seen anything like it before.

The doctor stoops over Henry's bed with his fingers laced and palms on Henry's chest. He watches as the doctor thumps on Henry's torso, hands thrusting up and down. Miles worries about poor Henry's little ribcage. It's going to shatter. Red Eyes will be able to snag his shadow without any trouble at all. The doctor, red in the face, pants and groans while sweat drips off his nose into a puddle on the floor. The scowling nurse crouches nearby. She is no longer scowling, but instead gaping. She has a pile of needles on the table next to her, but she just stares at the doctor, unmoving.

Henry is no longer pale or even the green color he turns when sick. He is gray and lifeless. His eyes are open, staring vacantly into the heavens. He doesn't look at Miles. He has no wink to give him.

Miles is shaking. All the hairs on his arms stand up. He doesn't know what to do. Is the doctor hurting Henry? He has never seen the doctor try to hurt anyone before. Something isn't right. He whips around and dashes out the door.

At the other end of the corridor, Red Eyes flits through the moonlight. He's carrying a thread of shadow. It's Henry's shadow!

"Stop!" Miles screams. He feels a sharp pain where his heart once was.

Red Eye halts, threatening to vanish into the night. He turns his head toward Miles and stares.

"You give him back." Miles is surprised by how calm his voice sounds. His eyes blur as they fill with tears, and he swallows the stone in his throat.

"You give him back," he repeats. "Right now."

Red Eyes remains motionless and silent. He shows no sign of understanding. Miles stands his ground, steadying his shaking hands.

"I said give him back." The tears spill over onto his cheeks. He refrains from wiping them away.

With a whoosh, Red Eyes evaporates and takes the last bit of Miles's hope with him.

Miles loses track of time. He hides in the doctor's closet and buries his face in his palms. He doesn't leave. He doesn't go to listen to the crying melody during the day. He doesn't spook anyone. He doesn't go looking for Red Eyes. He doesn't do anything. He doesn't even know when it's daytime or when it's nighttime. He doesn't care.

Henry's mother and father never come back. Miles doesn't watch them bring Henry's lifeless body away. He stays in the closet, scared and sad. He stares at the dirt and tries unsuccessfully to kick it. He thinks he can maybe get it to move if he tries hard enough, but he doesn't want to try any harder.

His frustrated grunts are interrupted when the door swings open and a pale face blinks at him from behind the moldy wood.

"Henry?" Miles is too scared to believe it's actually him.

"Yeah," says the pale boy. "Who'd you think it was?"

"I thought," says Miles in a whimpered tone. "I thought Red Eyes took you away."

"And yet," says Henry. "Here I am."

"So…so you didn't die?"

"Don't think so." Henry chuckles.

The boys sit in silence for several long seconds, neither knowing what to say to one another. Miles wants to tell Henry how scared he was of Red Eyes and how sad he was when Henry left him. Henry smiles in a way that Miles knows he doesn't have to say anything.

"Well." Henry straightens and creaks the door open wide. "Let's play a game of hide 'n' seek, shall we?"

Miles lights up at the thought of this. "You're sure you're up for it?"

"Of course, I am."

And the boys skip down the hall, hand in hand. They take turns being "it," and neither of them notice that Henry is as good as Miles. He even manages to hide in the drainpipe of the nurses' shower. Once Miles finds him (after hours of searching), they laugh and laugh and roll on the floor together.

"Wait a minute." Miles sits up. "You shouldn't be able to fit in there."

"So, you're the only one who can be good at this game?"

"No," Miles says. He faces Henry.

The pale boys stare at one another. Miles snags Henry's hand and holds it up to the moonlight. The lunar glow streaks onto the floor, uninterrupted.

"Henry," says Miles. "You're see-through. Like me."

"Cool." Henry holds his own hands in front of him and gazes at them, examining every inch.

"Henry," Miles says again. "I think you're dead."

Red Eyes never bothered Miles or Henry again. Neither of them knew why he brought Henry back to Miles. Neither of them knew why he let Miles stay on in the first place.

What the boys did know, however, is that they had each other. They spent years and years frolicking the corridors of that hospital, spreading mischief and mayhem. They spooked whatever nurse or doctor that crossed their path. They played pretend orchestra when it came time to administer medicine in the great room. And they battled for the best hide 'n' seek player there ever was.

The boys watched as people left the old building with Red Eyes, both nurses and patients. They watched the stone structure crumble to pieces, bit by bit over the years. They watched as the rooms became more and more bare, until they were completely vacant. They watched as the rodents and spiders no longer took solace in the decaying framework.

And when the hospital was nothing more than a pile of dust, the boys carried their adventures to the wild lands around them. With no boundaries, they were free to enjoy all the pleasure and amusement of each other's company for eternity.

Burgundy dahlias turn grey, a wilting bouquet.
Tiny demonic fairies flutter their wings, so black.
Back to back they lead ahead and follow behind; my bridesmaids.
A large dark shadow takes up my space, in the graveyard's moonlight.
The devil's come to collect, the vow I'd made.
For all the riches of the world, I had to become his bride, dressed in blood red.
His ally in this...the needy greed of my own gluttony itself.

Fizzy Twizler

XI

The Vigilante Witch of East End

Tara Jazdzewski

Thudding footsteps echoed in an empty alleyway.

Gray fog swirled, its long tendrils reaching for auburn hair. Slowly, with a glint of silver and red, a blade flicked up to cruel lips. A sickly sweet smile crawled across her face as she turned towards the shadows and spoke to an unseen companion. "Come here, my sweet," she purred at the darkness. "Let us hunt together."

The shadow stirred and the dark figure moved alongside her. She prowled like a large cat circling its prey, tapping the jagged edge of the blade against her thigh like a death knell.

In the distance, Katherine heard the sound of struggling, a hand muffling an attempted scream. Looking at her companion, she nodded and moved in the direction of the noise. Turning the corner, she stopped, taking in the scene before her. A tall, wide man with tanned features and big hands had cornered an underfed, pale slip of a girl, one hand tangled in her hair while his other roved her body. She whimpered, no longer trying to cry out for help, shrinking into herself as she tried to avoid the hand seeking out her most vulnerable places.

In a flash, Katherine moved from the shadows and pulled the man around to face her, the trembling sobbing girl sliding down the wall behind him. Her blade made quick work of the man, stabbing first his side, then his thigh. He roared, trying to grasp Katherine's hand, but she whirled away from his grasp and her foot shot out to kick his injured leg. Her opponent tried to grab her hair, but Katherine felt the movement of his arm and turned away. She grabbed his wrist while elbowing him in the stomach and lightening fast, her blade found his neck. With a squelch and gurgle, he tumbled to the ground.

Katherine bent down gracefully and wiped her blade on his grubby shirt. Flicking her hair back, she turned to look at the young girl huddled up against the wall. The child's eyes were wide, terror etched across her face. Katherine attempted to soothe her as she helped her ease up off the ground. She tried to guide the girl toward one of the inns, but the moment she saw a chance to escape, the girl darted away like a terrified rabbit.

Katherine tsk'd to herself and turned toward the shadow, releasing her companion with a slight nod of her head. It rushed to consume the slain man. Rough crunching sounds echoed behind her as she moved down the cobblestones, giving the gas lamps a wide berth.

In the dim glow of early morning gray, the biting damp was indicative of a chilled October morning. A sharp hiss escaped Katherine's lips. Hours of roaming, but just the one kill, she thought. Has all the East End filth gone elsewhere for their villainy this night?

Reaching above her shoulder, she patted the large head that towered over her, fingers slipping over onyx, silken, solidified shadow. The beast stayed, its patience never tested as its mistress's was. The pat loosened the faint smell of graveyard dirt into the air and it wafted past Katherine's face with the shift of the wind.

"Is there anything worse than a bad hunt?" she mused. "I really cannot think of an earthly thing I hate more than a long night out with nothing to show for it. London usually has much more to show for herself."

There had been rumors among the working ladies, whispered about in pubs, and murmured about in passing, that a man walked the streets who reminded some of the "man" called Jack. Katherine had finally gotten more information when she found a girl, not more than sixteen, who had come across a gruesome scene. Plying the girl with food and drink, Katherine was able to coax the story from her, and her renewed hunt began.

Time worked differently in the In Between. Her time there had changed her, shaped her, fed her. Katherine became vengeful and angry. It took little for her to jump at the opportunity to return to London, stepping through the dark portal conjured with the intent of letting her loose upon the great city. Jack had hoped the bloodlust would overwhelm her, wanting her to become a she-demon that would terrorize the barely-recovered East End mere years after his mighty reign. What he had not anticipated was that while Katherine absorbed the penchant for murder, a deep love of feeding, and enjoyment of bloodlust, she still retained her humanity. Rather than an out of control demoness, she became a vengeful witch on the hunt for undesirables, particularly those who reminded her of Jack. No one in the In Between had been tipped off yet and she continued about her business without anyone being any the wiser. It worked well for her, and she kept the kill count high enough to maintain her strength and stamina. East End made for an easy hunting ground. Jack had reigned supreme there due to its extreme poverty and an overabundance of undesirables.

Giving her head a slight shake, Katherine brought herself back to the task at hand. Pacing for a moment, she released the shades of humanity that had settled around her, and dropped the blood splattered handkerchief she had used after stabbing the man earlier. It fluttered to the ground and she stared at it, cream and crimson fading to a dirty brown of coagulated blood. Katherine's eyes slid out of focus as she contemplated the colors blurring together and she lost herself for several moments.

Warm sulfuric breath hit her cheek and pulled her out of her thoughts, and her hand reached up to the large head hovering above her shoulder. Snapped out of her ruminations, cold malice resettled over Katherine's now gray eyes, her remanence of humanity gone. Suddenly impatient, she wrapped her arm around the hound's massive neck and allowed herself to be pulled within the shadows. The duo made their way through the East End, returning to High Street with supernatural speed. Not much had changed in the few intervening years and Katherine stifled a shudder before sliding her callous armor back on. Shrugging into the calculating pupil of Jack, the walls rapidly slid into place and a sneer set on her hardened face.

The fetid smell of the slums choked the air. Urine and feces mixed with blood and spirits and other ungodly smells a proper lady would not care to place. The sky appeared hidden behind a barely perceptible haze. Katherine trudged through the filth, searching for one of her irregulars or a ladybird with enough knowledge to move her hunt along. She had trouble holding back her frustration when she realized she was being thwarted by some man: reviled, lecherous and debaucherous, tainting the cesspool of the East End with his villainy.

Stepping into the gas-light, Katherine strode toward two bawdy women chatting uproariously outside a derelict pub. One woman smelled strongly of drink, her bloodshot eyes narrowing at Katherine's lithe frame.

Her companion turned, and her face lit up with recognition. The woman reassuringly patted her friend's arm, murmuring quietly in her ear before meeting Katherine in the middle of the street.

"Saints alive! Katherine, is that you?"

Katherine's face transformed into a mask of genteel domesticity. "Dru," she purred.

Drusilla was tall and had an air of refinement not typically seen among the women of the night. The tight corset caused her voluptuous curves to heave with emotion. Katherine knew it was going to take some finessing to steer the woman the right direction.

"We heard something had happened to you! No one has seen you around in years. Just disappeared from your bed, they said."

Katherine leaned in conspiratorially. "Dru, not here. There are things I cannot say, cannot share about the king's service." She winked.

Slightly confused but comprehending, Drusilla nodded and obediently followed Katherine away from the busy pub. Katherine knew she would have to work around her true desires carefully; Drusilla was a few years older than her and had been in her mother's service for a while, helping treat the women seen as undesirable by London's Ton. In fact, Drusilla was not a working lady of the night by any stretch of the imagination. Highly controversial though it may be, Drusilla worked parallel with the ladybirds; several days a week, she dressed up and walked the streets with them, attending to their ails and helping them seek other care or assistance from local charities and missions.

Slipping into a dark alleyway, Katherine turned to look over her old friend. A pang of nostalgia hit her before she shook it off and adjusted the walls around her heart. "I need your help finding someone." Katherine gave her sweetest, most human smile.

"Where have you been? We heard you were lost during the fight against Jack. I don't believe you were in the service of King and Country." Drusilla looked at her nervously.

Katherine could feel her heart crack the longer she was in Drusilla's company, the closest person to her mother she had been around in many years.

"I cannot tell you where I have been." Katherine's voice broke slightly, the flood of memories from her time in the In Between washing over her. "I am in search of a man who is using White Chapel as a hunting ground, following in Jack's footsteps. I am going to stop him and end this reign of terror on the East End once and for all."

"What is it that you need?" Drusilla drew herself up to her full height, the anxiety that had played across her face wiped away by steely determination.

Katherine eyed the older woman. "We need to find a ladybird who has had contact with the man, or knows of someone who has."

Drusilla pondered for a moment before inspiration hit, and led Katherine in the direction of an old warehouse the coven occasionally used for larger meetings. Katherine sidestepped the filth and grime on the streets as Drusilla slowed in front of a row of dilapidated houses in an overcrowded rook. This was a part of East End Katherine was not familiar with, and the hovels here were the worst she had ever seen. Pulling out a handkerchief, she held it delicately to her nose, wishing she had sprayed it with scent. The fact that she was here without a properly thought out plan was not lost on her, but she needed results. The bloodlust warred with her scant humanity and Katherine desperately wanted to get another kill in before the sun broke through the gray London sky.

"What are we doing here?" Katherine looked around skeptically.

"One of these houses, in the back, holds a den of sin." Drusilla shuddered involuntarily. "Men from all over London gather here. Part opium den, part gambling house, and part brothel. We are here to see a man."

Bracing herself, Drusilla knocked a pattern on the door of a particularly dingy looking hovel. A squat man swung the door open, glowering at the two women in front of him.

"What," he barked.

"We are here to see Edgar."

The man arched his eyebrow at them, but moved his hulking frame to allow them to enter. "In the back, farthest door on the left. Be careful of roaming hands," he laughed as Katherine surveyed the room.

Typical houses in rooks were built backwards instead of vertically, with the poorest denizens shoved in, several families to a room, at the furthest reaches. This house, however, had none of that. Although the first room looked similar to what Katherine expected. It was lit by hundreds of candles, no gas or electricity to be found. Tables were scattered throughout the room and scantily clad women wove their way between them. Some served spirits, and some were attached to a specific man for the night. Moving further into the dark rooms, it became apparent that none of London's poorer members lived here. Picking up her skirts to walk more rapidly, Katherine followed Drusilla through the dank rooms.

Katherine blanched at the sight of drunk men groping women with lipstick smeared all over their mouths. This was a part of London she had never seen before she heard of Jack. Deep down, her class and upbringing held, and she shuddered at the sights around her. Katherine tried to take it all in: women sitting precariously on the laps of men, men drinking and laughing raucously together, a roulette wheel spinning, poker cards, and cheap cigars.

Suddenly, a man leered into her face. "Like what you see, sweetheart?" He stank of gin and cigar smoke, his clothes disheveled and shirt partially open. His scruffy beard scratched her face and he leaned into a whisper in her ear, "I can show you a real good time, savvy?"

Katherine's eyes were wide. All of her power and otherworldly knowledge seemed to seep out of her as soon as she crossed the threshold. She was no longer a murderous witch who spent untold years in the In Between as Jack the Ripper's pupil, but an upper class young woman of nineteen, inexperienced in the ways of London's seedy underbelly.

A hand shot out and pulled the older man away from her. A handsome young man of twenty pulled the man back, offering her a rakish smile. "Come now, Argus, leave these beauties alone. No one wants to put up with rancor." He steered the man named Argus away, throwing a wink over his shoulder at Katherine before disappearing at a card table.

Katherine hadn't realized how heavily she had been breathing until the men had left. She felt like a caged animal, backed into the corner like prey. She promised herself not to let that happen again and mentally shook herself as they continued on.

The second room was full of haze. Large hookahs littered the floor around puffs, pillows, and low cots. Men and women dangled precariously around them, their heads rolling lazily and arms falling limp as smoking pieces clattered to the floor. Katherine tried to hold her breath as they passed through the maze of human bodies.

Finally, the women made it to a long dark hallway. No lamps or candles lit the way; the noises coming from behind the doorways on either side were enough to make Katherine blush, but she set her jaw and continued forward. The last door on the left was the most sturdy piece of construction they had seen within the whole building. Drusilla raised a small fist and pounded on the door.

"What," snarled a voice behind the door. "You know damn well I do not like to be disturbed back here."

A woman's giggle could be heard over the animalistic noises permeating the hallway. Drusilla raised her fist and pounded at the door harder and longer.

"All right, all right. Hold your knickers." The voice drew closer to the door before it was unceremoniously flung open and a tall skinny man with half done up trousers and bruises down his neck and bare chest blinked blearily at Drusilla.

"Dru?" His loud voice dropped to a low rumble. "Why the hell are you here? Who's that?" He caught sight of Katherine out of his peripheral vision. "I'll be damned, she's one hell of a looker. Bring me a special treat to make it up to me, Drusilla?"

Dru pushed the man back in the room, "Hello, Edgar. I am here for a bit of information." She looked past the scrawny man to the pale woman hastily pulling a sheet around her naked frame. "You. Out. Now."

The girl whimpered and backed up against the wall, covering her body more, unwilling to enter the hallway without her clothing. Drusilla reached down and gathered up the young woman's things before shoving them in her arms and dragging her out of the bed.

"I said, *out*."

The young woman scrambled out of the room.

"Now why'd you have to go and do a thing like that, Drusilla? You know I am more than happy to share." He eyed Katherine hungerily, her class and rank apparent even in the dark, dank building.

Drusilla slapped Edgar's cheek so hard it immediately reddened and welted.

"I am not here for your games, Edgar. I am here for information. I know you know everything that happens in your establishment and everything that happens in the East End. Give me the information we seek so we can be on our way and you can get back to your whores and your opium."

Edgar's hand went to his cheek while she talked. His eyes shone like coal.

"You bitch," he stumbled towards Drusilla but before he could reach out and choke her, Katherine stepped forward and captured his arm in one thin hand.

"I don't think so." Her voice was smooth and melodic, and Edgar turned towards her with wonderment. The fire in his eyes had been replaced with compliance. She steered him toward the side of the bed, still rumpled and damp from his romp with the young whore.

Her fingers traced the side of his face, smoothing his hair back from his eyes. Drusilla stood back, watching her friend's daughter with apprehension. Katherine gripped Edgar by either side of the head and traced symbols with her fingers, low words muttered beneath her breath. Slowly, white gold light poured from her fingertips and she slid her fingers away from his head. Dru's breath caught as she stared at Edgar's face, encased with gold light with what looked like two deep prongs embedded into his temple.

"Tell me about the man who is stalking the streets of the East End." Katherine's voice was cool and calculating.

Edgar stared blankly at her, his mouth opening and closing like a fish.

Katherine concentrated her energy around the man's head. "Tell me about the man who is stalking the girls in the East End."

Edgar's words came in gasps and stutters. "Men."

"Men?" Katherine turned to Drusilla. "Do you think he means there is more than one man who is harming the ladybirds?"

Edgar nodded vigorously. "Men. More than one. There's a group of them. Headed up by Sir Henry Loyle. They came together while Jack was running the streets and decided that they wanted in on the action. At one point, I heard there were thirty of them. They like to knock around whores. But Henry's inner circle are the ones who go too far. They torture. I've lost a fair few girls to them. But we cannot do anything about it. Henry is the nephew of a lord. One important to Parliament. No one can touch him. He enjoys all the depraved acts and debauchery to his fill. Ain't nothing or no one that can stop him."

Katherine withdrew the light from Edgar's head and he turned to retch on the floor next to his bed. She grabbed Drusilla's arm, and the women made their way back through the hovel. Edgar heaved and gasped behind them, unable to call out to stop them.

Back in the early morning air, Katherine took several deep, appreciative gasps. She gagged shortly after, wishing the air here was sweeter. The refuse and filth still surrounded them, not much of an improvement over the opium-filled air.

Studying Katherine, Drusilla appraised the situation. "Nice bit of magic work back there," she said dryly.

"At least we got the information we were looking for, and faster than you beating the man to get it."

Drusilla inclined her head in acquiescence.

"Sir Henry...why does that name sound so familiar?"

Drusilla searched her memory. “Sir Henry is nephew of the Duke of Kennsington and Lord Melbourne's second cousin.”

“Do you have the whole peerage memorized?” Katherine laughed.

“Only the more salacious ones,” Dru mused.

“Lord Melbourne, Lord Melbourne. . . oh for all that is good and holy!” Katherine gasped. "Lord Melbourne was a friend of Father’s!"

“That is going to make things complicated,” Dru stated plainly. “Come on, I know another place like Edgar’s establishment.”

In the shadows behind them, a low growl rumbled. Bright green eyes shone several feet off the cobblestones, and wisps of smoke swirled and disappeared into the black mass.

Anger rose warm and deep within Katherine’s heart. She had longed to kill, to punish this man who hurt the women of the East End, the women her mother took care of. But to find out it was not just one man, but a whole gang of men whose sole purpose was to engage in depraved acts and bring back the fear the city thought it had left behind? The thought enraged Katherine to her core. Her sacrifice meant so little. Men could be so twisted and evil. She wanted to make them pay for their sins. It wouldn't be enough to punish them, to kill them. She wanted to subjugate them, make them serve her, to prolong their suffering. Her eyes flashed metallic as she fed her anger.

Turning a corner, the women stopped dead in their tracks. Ahead walked a man, his dark cane clacking along the cobblestones, a tall top hat perched hauntly upon his head. Katherine shook her head in disbelief. This was just too much; she was reliving her time with the coven searching for Jack. They followed him stealthily at a distance. No man would be out at this hour dressed like that, unless he was going to meet with Sir Henry's gang.

The man didn't realize he was being followed as he weaved his way through the streets. The hair at the back of Katherine’s neck rose as they rounded the final corner. The air was thick with fear and the intensity of predators on the hunt. The man they had been following ripped his top hat off his head and tossed it, and the cane, to the side of the lane.

“Starting without me, gents?” His deep baritone boomed through the early morning air.

“Cutting it a bit close, aren't you?” One of the men jibbed back to him. “Damn near time for these beggars to wake and start their pathetic existence for another day.” He spit derisively.

The men chuckled and turned back to their prey. Huddled in the center of the circle of men, several women shook in fear, hair falling from their pins. Several had their bodices ripped.

Katherine and Drusilla separated, and approached the outside of the group from two different angles. The men remained oblivious to their approach until Drusilla had a stiletto in the neck of the nearest man.

“What the hell?" The attention of the gang shifted from the huddling mass to the two women holding knives.

“You stupid bitch,” the man at Katherine's knife cursed. He leaned forward so the blade bit into his neck. "You fools are outnumbered and outwitted. Do you know who we are?"

“I'm not sure I give a damn.”

The men roared with laughter at Katherine's retort. They looked at each other, eyes shining with mirth.

“That one there's a real looker, ain't she?”

“That other one ain't half bad for her age. We could have some fun with these two, lads! Come on!”

Several men advanced toward Drusilla. With a flick of the wrist, she sliced the man’s throat in front of her. He let out a strangled gurgle and she released him to the dirty streets.

“Bloody hell!” one of the men sputtered, eyes wide.

Two men rushed at Drusilla. She stepped around the dead man, unsheathing a second blade from under her skirt.

The man under Katherine's blade squirmed. His elbow shot back to catch her in the softness of her belly. Katherine doubled over, the air knocked out of her. The man turned to strike her head on, his fist curled up and cocked back.

Katherine rushed forward, aiming her shoulder at her opponent's sternum. Her right hand reached around and her blade met his kidney. As he stumbled forward, Katherine’s heel caught his Achilles tendon. With a groan, her opponent dropped to his knees and Katherine's leg came up to meet his face. A sickening crunch rang out as his nose broke.

“Impressive.” The voice rang out, cold and clear.

Panting, Katherine looked up to see Sir Henry standing with Drusilla caught between two of his henchmen. He gave her a wicked grin before sinking his blade deep into Drusilla’s chest.

“No!” Katherine screamed as she watched Drusilla’s limp body tumble to the ground. It was as if time itself had slowed. The bloom of crimson spread from her corset to her cream colored linen shirt Henry observed her reaction with a maniacal glint in his eye and a sneer on his lips. Katherine blinked back tears and let out an anguished, animalistic roar from deep in her belly. The air around them stirred into a frenzy as Katherine's Hellhounds bayed their anticipation, ready to jump into the fray to serve their mistress. Blue electricity cracked around them.

"Run!" one of the women screamed. They grabbed each other's hands and retreated, their captors transfixed by the scene before them.

Katherine rose slowly in the air, her auburn hair a cloud of fiery fury, blue electrical arcs skittering away from her body, her eyes glinting silver in the gas light. With a twitch of her finger, she released her Hellhounds. Once loose, their nails clattered, causing sparks among the cobblestones. The air was thick with the scent of sulfur and the baying of a thousand wolves.

Panicked, the men looked around, unable to see the dogs surrounding them. One man's breeches stained as he pissed himself, the trickle pooling at his boots. He looked left and right wildly before he was lifted off the ground and tossed into the air like a rag doll. His screams faded with a crunch, followed by the metallic scent of copper. Six men scattered down the various streets, yet Katherine did not perceive their departure. Her silver eyes bore into Henry's while he stood frozen, transfixed by her terrifying beauty. She descended, moving with otherworldly grace. Watching him, Katherine was pleased to notice that Henry's pants looked taunt as he stared at her; she had the effect on him she was hoping for. His eyes drooped as Katherine leaned into him, one hand resting on his forearm, breath whispering against his ear. She raked a nail along Henry's neck, creating a thin line that beaded up with blood.

Strangled cries rang out in the night as her beasts ate their fill of the fleeing men.

Katherine returned her focus to Henry. Staring deep into his eyes, she placed her hands on his shoulders. "Come with me."

Henry's jaw went slack, his eyes vacant.

As Katherine strode down the street, she listened to the dogs playing with their food. Henry trailed behind her, his face devoid of emotion.

The Hellhounds had the last man surrounded. He looked to be in his early thirties, black hair once slicked back, now disheveled and falling into his face. Green eyes shining in terror, he spotted Henry and called out, pleading. "Boss! Help me! Boss!"

Henry stood behind Katherine, impassive.

"Boss, what the hell are you doing? Help me! This bitch is crazy. Lady, call off your goddamn dogs!"

The Hounds parted as Katherine approached their captive.

Henry stood outside the ring, staring blankly as the flash of Katherine's blade caught in the moonlight.

Smoldering rags that had caught a spark from the Hellhounds' race through the streets took hold of the refuse around them, and flames fingered their way up the derelict building used as a dumping ground. As the fire grew around them, Katherine's blade wove in and out of the man's body. She kept to muscle, refusing to allow him to succumb to the pain.

"The men in this city need to understand," Katherine said, her voice dripping with poison, "that they do not get free run of the East End. No matter what class. This abuse upon women will not be tolerated anymore." She released the man and turned as he crumpled to the ground, unconscious.

She reached up and patted the large head that hovered over her shoulder, smearing blood across its leathery skin.

Energy now spent, Katherine slowly slinked away into the shadows, Henry stumbling behind her. As the flames licked the sky, the rook now fully inflamed, the Hellhounds melted into the dark corners of the far reaches of the street.

Author Biographies

Kristin Cleaveland writes horror and dark fiction and is inspired by the beautiful grotesquerie of motherhood and the female experience. Her debut short story, "Lilith, My Daughter," appeared in the Winter 2021 issue of Black Telephone Magazine from CLASH Books. Her microfiction stories "The Dreamer" and "In a Blink" were included in Hundred Word Horror: Beneath and Hundred Word Horror: Cosmos, published in 2021 by Ghost Orchid Press. Kristin has a master's degree in English and has worked as a writer, editor, proofreader, and educator.

Judith Crow was born in Orkney, grew up in Lincolnshire and now lives in the far north of Scotland. Her work draws inspiration from folklore, experience, and the natural world. *The Backwater*, Judith's debut book, was a finalist in the Wishing Shelf Book Awards 2019. Judith followed this with *Dance with Me* in 2020 and her next novel, *Honour's Rest*, will be published in October 2021. When she isn't writing, Judith is a teacher at a lovely little primary school. She sometimes finds that writing gets usurped by crafting, music, and being a generally doting spaniel owner.

Carla Eliot is a UK writer living in Cheshire with her young son and little dog. She enjoys writing moody fictional stories, often encompassing an underlying message, and frequently dives into the paranormal. Carla featured in three of the *Blood Rites Horror* anthologies with her stories, 'My White Star', 'Windows to Your Soul', and 'In the Beginning'. When Carla isn't writing, she's reading, enjoying nature, or watching films.

A.L. Garcia lives in Massachusetts with her loving husband and two spirited children. She spends her days reveling in the chaos of her babes, writing, reading, and balancing other obligations, as many mothers do. She began writing poetry as a youth as a way of coping with abusive family dynamics. She joined the writing community in August of 2020, after independently publishing a personal narrative detailing the abuse she endured as a child. Her poetry is featured in Quill & Crow's *Crow Calls Volumes* and in her personal bilingual collection, *Broken Heart Mosaics.* She is a veteran of the U.S. Army and studied Sociology and Social Science at Towson University.

TARA JAZDZEWSKI is not only a writer of Gothic fantasy, but she is the founder of Jazz House Publications, a company of diverse voices who wish to change the publishing industry at the grassroots level. This is her second publication.

REBECCA JONES-HOWE lives in Kamloops, British Columbia. Her work has appeared in PANK, Dark Moon Digest, and in The New Black anthology of neo-noir fiction. Her first collection, *Vile Men,* was published in 2015. She frequently blogs about writer life and scathingly reviews V.C. Andrews novels on her website, rebeccajoneshowe.com.

LIZ "LIZARD" M. KAMP has been obsessed with all things dark and creepy since long before she lost her baby teeth. When she's not penning her latest work of fiction, she's wrangling her zoo of animals and enjoying the great outdoors with her husband. This is her first of many published horror stories.

CATHERINE MCCARTHY is a spinner of dark tales from Wales, U.K. Previously published works include *Hope Cottage, Door and Other Twisted Tales,* and *Mists and Megaliths.* Her Gothic novella, *Immortelle,* will be published by Off Limits Press in July 2021. Her short stories and flash fiction can be found in various places online and in anthologies including those by The BFS, Flame Tree Press, Curiosities, and Kandisha Press. When she is not writing, she may be found walking the Welsh coast path or in ancient graveyards reading Machen or Poe.

OLIVIA CLAIRE LOUISE NEWMAN is a writer, poet, and traveler. Between attempting to tame her rambunctious rescue dog, Arrow, and training for adventures, she is writing her first novel and indulging in Romantic literature. After being inspired by Mary Shelley's haunted summer of

1816, she fell head-first into her literary endeavors and has not come up for air since.

Alexandra "Lexi" Rose is a USAF veteran who writes LGBTQ+ contemporary and fantasy stories. Originally from Michigan, she traveled around the world and now resides in the United States Great Lakes region where she works in public relations, spends time with her partner, and writes stories. "Lucia and Tatiana" is Lexi's third published short story.

Helen Whistberry is an indie author and artist who began writing after retiring from a long career working in libraries. She has published six books in her *Small Towns, Real Women* series celebrating strong women overcoming adversity; two in her *Jim Malhaven Mysteries* series, light noir novels with a cozy mystery feel and touch of the paranormal; as well as contributing short stories to numerous anthologies. Her whimsical artwork often explores nature, and she loves to read and review books by fellow indie authors.

ALSO FEATURING POETRY BY

Sophie Brookes
Danielle Edwards
Melanie Whitlock
JayLynn Watkins
Ayshen Irfan
Sheena Shah
K.R. Wieland
Ginger Lee
Erin Quill
A.L. Garcia
Marie Casey
Fizzy Twizler

Quill & Crow Publishing House's
The Dark Poet Society

Discover more Gothic literature at
www.quillandcrowpublishinghouse.com

Printed in Great Britain
by Amazon

87488274R00130